C000135811

Arthur's Seed

Cuddfan, Myrddin's Legacy

David Cubbage

David Cubbage 6·6·21

Arthur's Seed

Cuddfan, Myrddin's Legacy

David Cubbage

ISBN: 978-1-8382129-1-9

Published by David Cubbage Publishing in conjunction with Writersworld, this book is produced entirely in the UK, is available to order from most book shops in the United Kingdom, and is globally available via UK-based Internet book retailers.

Cover design by Jag Lall in collaboration with the author
Cover photo images from Shutterstock and Pixabay

Copy editor: Sue Croft

WRITERSWORLD
2 Bear Close, Woodstock,
Oxfordshire
OX20 1JX
United Kingdom

www.writersworld.co.uk

The text pages of this book are produced via an independent certification process that ensures the trees from which the paper is produced comes from well managed sources that exclude the risk of using illegally logged timber while leaving options to use post-consumer recycled paper as well.

Dedication/Acknowledgements

I believe my journey as a writer began on the day I was born. The passions, the emotions and the experiences I shared with friends during my childhood are reflected in my story, as are my later life experiences.

To acknowledge all of you who helped guide me along the path that led me here today would take up more than one page; you are many, and all of you have helped me one way or another throughout these ten years when *Arthur's Seed* was but a short story, and made it possible for me to bring it out of the shadows and into the light.

This dedication is to all of you for the unending support and encouragement that helped to bring my story to fruition, and I make no apologies for the length of this list.

Tony Pickstock, a friend and colleague who was the first person to read *Arthur's Seed* and wrote the beautiful poem that describes my story, for his unceasing support and enthusiasm for me as a writer.

Jean Hughes who, like Tony has stood by my side throughout with wise words of encouragement to get my work published.

Rick Rowe-Davies who, as a script writer assigned to write a screenplay of the book, suggested to me that George, one of my main characters, should be deaf. His off the cuff remark spurned me on to turn an ordinary little boy into an extraordinary hero.

David Roper of Wyrmwick Creations, a friend and colleague with whom I have worked on many occasions producing armour for films. As a favour to me he designed and produced the beautiful Dragon Helmet used to illustrate the cover.

Jackie Arnold, who encouraged me to publish my story and introduced me to Denise Black, a well-known actress who told me I had a special gift and not to give up on a writing career.

My sister Anita and brother-in-law Roger Curtis who have seen me through difficult times and continually urged me to 'get it published'.

My daughter Emma, her husband Glyn Jones, and my granddaughters Isabelle and Sophie, who brought love and fun back into my life and allowed me to rewrite certain passages with feelings I had long denied myself.

And last but not least, the three people who have guided me through the path of self-publishing: Graham Cook of Writersworld, whose expertise in this field surpass all my expectations; Sue Croft, my copy editor, who has tirelessly polished and honed my manuscript into shape beyond my wildest dreams; and Jag Lall, my cover designer, who has brought out the hundreds of ideas scrambled inside my head and produced a cover that, I'm sure, will stand out from the crowd.

Contents

Arthur's Seed

Poem by Tony Pickstock

Planted for your imagination; for who said he was asleep?
For all the stories you were told; this the truth will now unfold.
The magic, the mystery that you now read, is the secret of Arthur's Seed.

When the two worlds are so far apart; the secret lies within his heart.
You will enter within this legend's soul, on a maiden's voyage on yacht Nicole.
Across the sea and up the streams, to the island made from dreams.

His vision was his inner sight, that one day they would reunite.
His dream to share this forgotten land; and one day to hold her hand.
This is what made him strong; to bring her back where she belonged.
Golden sand and silver water; the return of Arthur's daughter.

1

Sole Survivor

Treat the sea with respect, and she will unlock the gates to heaven.
But treat her with contempt, and you will open the gates to hell.

The inhabitants who live along the beautiful rugged coastline of North Wales are used to the odd summer storms that are spawned far out in the Mid-Atlantic, finally unleashing their power around the west coast of Ireland, and into the Irish Sea. Most are forecast in advance by weather stations, but during one evening in the late summer of 2014, a violent storm appeared from nowhere, as if created by the devil himself. All emergency services were put on alert as winds exceeded storm force ten, igniting the sea into a state of frenzy. Any vessel caught unawares on the open seas in a storm of such magnitude, would surely be destined to a watery grave.

The silhouette of a yellow helicopter swooped low over the surface of the raging seas of Caernarfon Bay. Its pilot held the controls in a firm grip as he steered a straight course through the buffeting gale-force winds and lashing rain. But this was no ordinary aircraft. It was an RAF Westland Sea King air sea rescue helicopter, and well equipped to deal with the adverse weather conditions. Its crew of four had been scrambled at 22:00 hours from their base in Anglesey, by the coastguard station, after picking up a distress signal from a personal location beacon.

The down-draught from the rotating blades quelled the surface of the waves into a rippling frenzy, framed by a ring of dancing spindrift, as the aircraft hovered perilously close above the violent crests of the waves. The door slid open, and Winchman Flight Sergeant Duncan 'Woody' Forest peered out into the raging sea below. A shaft of light, shining from beneath the aircraft's belly, cut through the blackness to reveal a body being battered by the remorseless swell. The force of the rain peppered his face with hundreds of red-hot needles, making it difficult to judge the condition of the victim from where he was standing. But alive or dead, his mission was to pluck the body from the sea as quickly and as safely as possible. Only when the casualty was secured aboard, could he assess the situation and decide on their next move.

Winch-operator, Sergeant David 'Dutch' Holland secured him to the hook of the winch, and Woody stepped out into space. Once free of the aircraft he was lowered steadily towards his target. The force of the wind spun him round like a child's spinning top as the pilot feathered the Sea King's controls to hold their position in the ever-increasing gusts. He flinched as his body plunged into the icy waters and made a quick grab for the victim's lifejacket to stop it from drifting. On drawing it close to his chest, he could now see it was the body of a young girl and that she was seriously injured. The tiny flashing beam of light from her location beacon illuminated her ashen face and streaming hair, and although she wasn't conscious, mercifully she was still breathing. Now time was of the essence; physical injuries aside, the effects of hypothermia make cold water a killer. It was vital to get her into the warmth of the aircraft as soon as possible.

Without any more thought for himself, he placed the strop connected to his harness around her body and signalled Dutch to lift them. On breaking free of the surface, the merciless waves made a last-ditch attempt to grab them back into their heartless clutches. During their slow ascent towards the helicopter Woody checked for any signs of wreckage or other bodies and was surprised not to see anything. On reaching the doorway, Dutch grabbed Woody's harness and pulled him and the young woman into the safe confines of the aircraft. He slid the door shut, and except for the muffled noise of the engines, the cabin fell reassuringly silent.

While they lifted her onto the onboard stretcher, the pilot gained height before turning his mighty bird around, setting a course for the hospital at Bangor on the mainland. The co-pilot immediately radioed the hospital to tell them to stand by to receive their casualty, her condition, and their ETA. He then updated the coastguard with the news of their successful rescue.

In the light of the cabin, Woody could now examine his patient more closely for other injuries. As he carefully deflated her bloodstained lifejacket and removed it, he noticed the name handwritten on a waterproof label: Izzy Moorefield Yacht *Nicole*. He recognised the name of the yacht as the one reported missing two weeks previously. He remembered, because they had been involved in the search when she had failed to return to her home port of Deganwy Marina. The yacht, skippered by James Moorefield, together with his wife and their three children, had disappeared without trace.

As he gently wiped away the blood that had started to leak from a wound on her head, he couldn't help noticing her strange clothing. He would have expected her to be wearing yachting waterproofs, especially in a storm of this magnitude, but she appeared to be dressed in some sort of fancy-dress costume – even her shoes were unusual.

Peering down at this poor young girl clinging on to life, he couldn't help wondering why, after all this time, she had suddenly reappeared without any sign of wreckage or other bodies. From the time they had lifted off from their base on Anglesey to the time they had plucked her from the sea, was, by his calculation, no more than twenty minutes. According to the news reports, the last any one had seen or heard from them was a month ago when a local fisherman had met the parents in the small harbour town of Menai Bridge after leaving Deganwy Marina to begin their two-week sailing holiday.

So, what had happened to them during the past four weeks, and why had this poor young woman been the only survivor?

2

Four Weeks Earlier

Alison Moorefield drove the family estate car into a parking space at the entrance to Deganwy Marina in North Wales. Her husband James immediately got out and collected a trolley from beside the gate to transport his family's luggage down to their yacht. Izzy quickly followed her father out and released Bella, an Irish Setter, from her incarceration in the rear of the car. She took her for a short walk around the boatyard to stretch her legs and do the normal things dogs do after being cooped up for their two-hour drive from their home in Manchester.

James opened the lid of the roof box, peered inside, and surprised by the volume of food his wife had brought just for a two-week break, commented, "I think we'll need more than one trolley for this lot." Not that *he* knew much about shopping. He was a barrister and far too busy with his work to concern himself with that sort of thing, so left his wife, a GP, to take care of all the household duties, much to the disapproval of his more emancipated daughter. He grunted and began loading its contents into the trolley. "Come on, you lot, I need a hand here," he shouted through the car's open window.

Daniel, a typical 20-year-old university student with long hair pulled into a ponytail, took the hint and reluctantly finished his text to one of his many girlfriends. He put his phone away and got out to help his father, leaving George in the back seat playing on his games console, slaughtering dragons. He looked back at his younger brother and frowned. "Come on, lazybones, that means you too," he said.

But George couldn't hear him; as usual, his hearing aid was switched off. Frustrated by his younger brother's antics, Daniel grabbed him by the scruff of his collar and tried to pull him out of the car, but George jerked his neck free and with a grin, slid back into his seat.

"Leave him alone, Daniel!" cried Alison as she got out of the car. "I'm sure we can manage the rest between us. Let him be."

"You shouldn't mollycoddle him, Alison," James retorted. "He may be deaf to the world, but he's still a member of this family and I insist that he shares in the workload when required." He knelt on the seat in front of George, snatched his console from his hands, stuffed it into a kitbag and thrust it onto his lap. "Now take this down to *Nicole* like a good chap and turn your hearing aid back on. If you don't, I will confiscate your games for the duration of the holiday, and you won't like that!"

Since suffering from meningitis at the age of seven, George had become deaf, and as a result, locked himself away in his own fantasy world of dungeons and dragons. But he could lip-read when he wanted to, so reluctantly he did as his father ordered and turned his hearing aid on again.

"Now that's better, isn't it!" James remarked sarcastically.

Alison pushed crossly past her husband as he returned to finish loading the trolley, and gently helped her son from the car. "Come on, Georgie darling, let's get another trolley to help your grumpy old father take all our stuff down to *Nicole*." As a doctor, Alison had always felt guilty at not being able to diagnose her son's illness early enough to prevent the onset of his deafness. As a result, she spoiled him.

Izzy and Bella were eagerly waiting at the gate to the marina basin to let them in. Alison, holding on to George's hand, locked the car and joined her husband and Daniel to help them push the two laden trolleys towards the gate. Taking a fob from her pocket, Izzy placed it in front of a small sensor, and as if by magic, the gate slowly opened. As soon as there was enough space for Bella, she squeezed through the narrow gap, dragging Izzy with her down the ramp. As the rest of the family followed, still arguing over George's behaviour, the gate shut behind them.

On their way towards *Nicole's* berth at the far side of the marina, they passed dozens of boats of all different types and sizes, bobbing up and down in the gentle swell. As they reached the final corner and *Nicole* came into sight, *Misty*, a fifteen-metre fibreglass cabin cruiser entered the marina with a full crew of four bronzed young men dressed in shorts and T-shirts emblazoned with 'Misty Crew'. With lines and fenders in hand, they were readying themselves for the co-ordinated ritual of securing the boat to its berth, navy fashion. On the helm was Commander Jeremy Hawkins, retired RN, who acknowledged them with an affectionate salute as his vessel glided gently past. You could hear wolf whistles from the crew for Izzy over the babble of the engines. Not that she took any notice – she wasn't interested in boys, and unlike her elder brother, didn't approve of fuel-guzzling power boats either. Using the power of the wind to drive a sailing vessel through the sea suited her principles of a greener lifestyle.

The procession halted at the end of the pontoon and Bella jumped aboard, followed by Izzy. After unlocking the hatch and sliding it open, she disappeared below deck. James climbed aboard and Daniel handed him the contents from each of the trolleys, one by one. Alison, meanwhile, took a neatly folded ensign from one of the cockpit lockers and set it on the flagpole at the stern of the yacht. "We are now officially in residence," she said with a smile.

Izzy knew they would all appreciate a brew and bacon butties when they had finished unloading the bags and cases. A sailing tradition on most yachts, she had gone into the galley, put bacon under the grill and filled 'Old Whistler', her nickname for the kettle, to make tea and coffee. As the unmistakable aroma of grilled bacon drifted up to the deck from the galley below, Bella darted down the steps and sat with her tail energetically sweeping the floor, waiting patiently for a rasher to fall off the pan in her direction.

Alison looked down into the galley and smiled at her daughter. "Well done, Izzy," she said, clearing the clutter from the cockpit table. "We'll take it up here, it's such a glorious evening. I do hope this weather lasts."

Izzy passed the tray of drinks up to her mum and then handed a large plate of bacon butties to George, who eagerly took the thickest one he could find and sank his teeth in with delight. "Yum," he said, grease oozing down his chin.

With a wink at Bella, Izzy gave her a couple of pieces of bacon she had held back for her, which she devoured in seconds and then looked eagerly up for more.

James looked across the cockpit at his family as everyone tucked in, and said, "What a great way to start our holiday!" He picked up his cup from the tray and raised it into the air. "To us," he said, as the others copied his sentiments in return. Little did they know that the following weeks would see the future of the family put in jeopardy and their lives changed forever!

3

The Holiday Begins

It was nine o'clock in the morning when the Moorefields slipped *Nicole's* mooring ropes and chugged gracefully out into the Conwy Estuary. The weather was perfect for sailing and ahead of them was a glorious blue sky punctuated by a few fluffy cumulus clouds on the horizon. Bella barked in excitement, wagging her tail furiously as she ran up and down the side of the deck like a beast possessed.

While Izzy steered *Nicole* into the buoyed channel, Alison, James, and Daniel got into their various positions ready to hoist the sails in sequence. Izzy shouted, "Going about!", warning members of the crew of the manoeuvres she was about to carry out. She turned the bow into the wind in one swift action, allowing the sails to be effortlessly raised in unison. Once hoisted, the sails flapped, begging for life, so Izzy obliged and spun the wheel hard over so as to position *Nicole* to take full possession of the wind. She cut the engine and they flew out into Conwy Bay. All she could hear above the creaking noise of the rigging was the sound of rushing water as the yacht's streamlined hull sliced a path through the waves. They were finally off.

Within ninety minutes or so they were rounding Puffin, a small island jutting up out of the sea, separated from Anglesey by a stretch of water known as Puffin Sound. As Izzy steered around the north side of the island, they could see and hear the thousands of squawking seabirds that populated the cliff face, and the seals basking in the glorious morning sunshine on the rocks below. There was an extremely pungent smell of guano in the air.

"I hate the smell of bird poo!" George shouted, squeezing his nose tightly with his fingers in the hope of reducing the effect of the caustic stench.

"Excellent fertiliser, though," Izzy remarked knowingly.

"Lots of fortunes made from bird poo," added Daniel.

The cries of the seagulls were deafening, and so was Bella's continual barking at every bird that dared to come within spitting distance of the boat. There was a feeding frenzy going on all around them. All manner of gulls dropped out of the sky with folded wings, piercing headfirst through the swell only to resurface some metres away with a small silvery fish in their beaks.

Izzy, trying to avoid the aerial bombardment, steered *Nicole* towards the middle point between the black and white-striped lighthouse on her starboard side, and the big, red-painted Perch Rock Beacon on the port side. Puffin Sound could be treacherous for the uninitiated; rocks projected out into the sea from both sides. The gap showed up before them as a seething mass where the two currents met to do battle, and as the lighthouse bell eerily rang out its chime to warn of the dangers, Izzy lined up *Nicole's* bow to penetrate the turbulent surge. The boat began to react to the waves, standing almost motionless for a split second, then lurching forward after James loosened the main sheets to allow the sails to take full advantage of the wind.

After rounding the north point of the island, Izzy steered *Nicole* in the direction of the green can that marked the starboard entrance of the channel into the Menai Strait. Once past Anglesey's ancient Beaumaris Castle and pier, the channel was easy to follow to Menai Bridge, the small town named after one of the two bridges that connected Anglesey to the mainland of Wales, and provided a chance for the crew to relax and enjoy the eye-catching scenery that formed the magnificent backdrop on both sides of the channel. As they passed the striking Victorian structure of Bangor Pier on their port side, the impressive Menai Bridge came into sight ahead. A few minutes later, the crew dropped all the sails and Izzy steered *Nicole*, now under power from the engine, towards the nearest available mooring buoy near Menai Bridge.

Izzy caught sight of a group of herons roosting in the treetops on a little island on her starboard side. They seemed to be following the boat with their gaze as they motored by. She thought how odd that Bella didn't bark; instead she just stared back at them with her head tilted to one side. George spied them out of the corner of his eye and said he thought they looked like dragons - typical of him.

Daniel leaned over the pulpit and hooked the white pickup buoy from a swinging mooring with a boathook. Pulling it up onto the deck it revealed the heavy chain, which he hauled up and slotted into the anchor winch. Izzy pulled the engine Stop lever, and the engine fell silent once again.

"Well done, Team Moorefield," James applauded with a broad smile.

"Did you see those herons as we came in, Mum?" Izzy asked.

"No, far too busy securing the sails with your father."

"They were huge, like dragons," George added with a massive grin.

"Are you off to kill them now, Georgie?" taunted James.

But George couldn't hear him. In his eagerness to get back to his games console, he had switched off his hearing aid and scrambled below deck once again.

"I'll put the kettle on. Tea for everyone?" Alison asked.

"Yes, please," they choroused.

James looked at his watch and shouted down towards the galley, "Can't be too long, meeting the old girl in an hour."

James had arranged to meet up with Aunt Gorawen at Menai Bridge. Gorawen wasn't really an aunt, just a very dear family friend and Izzy's godmother. Izzy adored her and spent most of her holidays, when not sailing, at her large old house on the island. Gorawen had agreed to look after Bella for the duration of their holiday. Otherwise, a dog's physical needs would require them to stop off and land at regular intervals along the way, thus interrupting the all-important part of their sailing holiday.

"The old girl wants my advice over some old legal papers," James sighed. "Still, it will give your mother a chance to do a little more shopping," he added sarcastically as he walked towards Izzy and gave her an affectionate pat on the head. He winked. "Seems it's someone's special day tomorrow." It was Izzy's sixteenth birthday the next day and she was excited at the thought of celebrating it on the yacht.

While Alison was down in the galley making the tea, James and Daniel lowered *Nicole's* tender into the water to prepare it for the short journey to Menai Bridge. After securing it to the stern of the yacht, James clambered down while Daniel retrieved the electric outboard motor from a locker and handed it to his father. James clamped it onto the transom, and after checking the battery was fully charged said, "Right, that's ready to go." Clambering back on board, he shouted, "Now where's that tea?"

With the family fully refreshed, Alison reappeared from below and made her way to the stern of *Nicole* with her shopping bags. Turning to face the children and looking straight at George, she said, "Look, we will be back in a couple of hours, so please behave."

George totally ignored her and persisted in tapping his thumbs on his games console. He had turned his hearing aid off yet again, and to add insult to his father's orders, was now wearing a homemade *Do not disturb* sign round his neck. James, frustrated by his son's defiance, stretched across and snatched the console from him in exasperation. George shrieked and looked up at his father in annoyance, trying to grab it back.

"You know what I told you. This is your final warning."

George reluctantly switched on his hearing aid and tutted loudly.

James, returning the console to him, said, "You know how important it is to be alert when you're on board any vessel at sea. How on earth do you expect to hear any warnings when it's switched off? It's for your own safety," he added, stabbing his finger against George's chest to drive home his point.

"Don't worry, Dad, I'll keep an eye on him," Izzy said reassuringly to her father.

"That's all very well, Izzy, but he's got to learn," James retorted, looking at his watch. "Now, we're going to be late, and you know Gorawen doesn't like to be kept waiting."

He climbed down into the tender and looked back up at his wife impatiently, pointing to the watch on his wrist. Alison glared at him for rushing her and clambered down in a huff to join her impatient husband.

Izzy lowered Bella, unceremoniously tucked into her life jacket complete with carrying handle, into her mother's waiting arms. "Be good for Aunty Gorawen, Bella," Izzy shouted. As if she knew what her mistress was telling her, she replied with a single yelp.

Daniel released the tender's rope and threw it to his mother, and as it was taken by the rushing current, James slipped the outboard into gear. Away they went, first doing a complete circle around *Nicole*, before steering towards the direction of St George's Pier at Menai Bridge.

"Any problems, I'll ring you on the mobile, so keep your phones switched on!" Alison shouted.

As the children watched their parents' progress from *Nicole*, suddenly, and without warning, Bella took an almighty leap out of the boat, and with an undignified splash started paddling as if her life depended on it, back towards the yacht. James glowered. There was no way he was going to attempt to retrieve her, and he certainly wasn't in the mood to share the boat with a smelly wet dog. Alison looked back towards her children, who were laughing, and shrugged her shoulders in despair. It seemed as if Bella would be joining them on their sailing holiday after all.

By the time Bella reached *Nicole*, their parents had disappeared from sight. George and Daniel ran for cover as she clambered up the boarding ladder. They knew what was coming, and sure enough, Bella shook her whole body from head to tail showering Izzy with a salty deluge. But she couldn't be angry with her – she hadn't really wanted her to go in the first place. Once she had removed Bella's wet life jacket, she shouted down to Dan for a towel. He resurfaced a few seconds later and with a big grin on his face, threw it to Izzy, who smothered Bella in it. After drying the worst from Bella's back, Izzy went below to change out of her wet clothes, but turned on her heels as Bella attempted to follow and yelled at her, "No! You're not dry yet, and you pong. Dad's not going to be best pleased with you when he gets back as it is, without you stinking the boat out!"

Bella knew she was in the doghouse and sheepishly disappeared, her tail between her legs, back to the cockpit. As she did so, she turned her glance towards the little island and the roosting herons. They were still there. She seemed to sense they were watching her and curled up in a ball on the deck. Burying her head between her front paws, she closed one eye, but kept the other kept firmly open … just in case.

Meanwhile, James and Alison had arrived at the pier. As they clambered out of the tender, Alex, a local fisherman, Romanian by birth, who had settled on the island twenty or so years ago, met them with a warm smile as he prepared to board his boat. Izzy had once rescued him in her dinghy when his old fishing boat had broken down, and ever since then the family had become firm friends.

"How nice to see you both again, I was just off to do some fishing," he said in his distinctive accent. "You have brought the nice weather, I hope?" He shook hands with James and gave Alison an affectionate kiss on her cheek.

"We hope so, Alex," she said. "We've just started our holiday."

"And the little ones?" he asked.

"Oh, they're not so little now," replied James looking at his watch. "Well, it's nice to see you again, Alex, but we must dash … we have to meet someone."

As they climbed the steps to the pier, they saw and heard Gorawen's battered old Land Rover draw up at the end of the car park. She got out and walked to greet them, giving each of them an affectionate hug. She was a short, rotund figure of a woman with piercing green eyes, and although her appearance was that of a seventy-year-old, she was very sprightly with a full head of beautiful red hair. "Where's Bella?" she asked.

"She jumped ship," replied Alison.

Gorawen looked shocked. "What!" she exclaimed with dismay.

"We had her with us," replied James, "but Alison lost her grip and she jumped overboard."

"She's Ok, though," Alison retorted, glaring at James for blaming her. "She swam back to *Nicole*."

"Oh well, never mind, we have more important matters to discuss," Gorawen replied as she went to the car and opened the rear door. "Get in, dears," she said, beckoning with a tilt of her head.

Taking two steps past the car Alison turned round and called, "I have to get some things for Izzy's party. I'll see you later."

"No, both of you," Gorawen ordered.

"But I thought you just wanted to see James," Alison replied.

"I need to talk to both of you, together."

"Why? What on earth has happened now?" sighed James, climbing into the back seat.

"I will tell you when we get back to the house," replied Gorawen. "Now get in the car, please, Alison." Alison knew it would be pointless arguing with her so reluctantly did as she was told, sitting down beside her bemused husband.

Gorawen started the engine and turned her head to check on her disgruntled passengers in the rear. "Now buckle up, dears," she said with a smile as the car jerked forward. "My driving is not what it used to be. We have to be prepared for unfortunate incidents on the roads these days."

Once clear of the narrow streets of the town, Gorawen headed towards the Beaumaris coastal road, which ran parallel with the Strait.

James tried to impress on Gorawen that time was critical for them to catch the tide to allow safe passage through the Swellies, a potentially dangerous stretch of water in the Menai Strait, before the evening.

"I hope we're not going to be too long. We told the children we would only be a couple of hours."

"We're going to be a bit longer than a couple of hours, my dears," Gorawen murmured quietly, more to herself than to them.

Alison looked at James and sighed disapprovingly, then taking out her mobile from her bag, rang Izzy's number. After several seconds without a reply, she said impatiently, "I'll try Dan's."

Before she could select his number, Gorawen said mockingly, "It's too late! It's already started!"

"What on earth do you mean, Gorawen? What's already started?" James frowned, beginning to feel apprehensive.

"I'll show you what I mean."

She pulled the car over to the side of the road, turned the engine off and got out. A very puzzled James and Alison followed her to the other side of the road. They gazed out through the gap in the trees over to the Strait, expecting to see *Nicole* on her mooring. To their horror, all they could see was a mysterious curtain of mist, obscuring her entirely from view.

"Oh my god, look at that!" cried James. In a panic, Alison immediately dialled Dan's phone number, expecting him to answer.

On *Nicole*, the three siblings were completely unaware of what was happening around them. The eerie mist, rising from the sea, had invaded every corner of the yacht both above and below deck. The children were slumped on the sofas in the saloon cabin as if sleeping. Even Bella appeared to be out for the count, coiled in a tight ball on the cockpit deck where her mistress had banished her earlier. More mystifying were the six herons. They had left the trees and were now perched on *Nicole's* rigging. The only sound on the yacht was the trill coming from Daniel's phone. But no one stirred.

James and Alison, unaware of what Gorawen was doing as she stood behind them, stood silently, looking across the Strait in disbelief. Gorawen's eyes were closed and she was quietly whispering to herself. The fog began to lift, and there was a look of relief on James and Alison's faces.

But by the time the mist had evaporated, their relief turned to dismay on discovering *Nicole* had disappeared completely. All that was left was the bright orange buoy she had been moored to just a few moments before.

By now, James and Alison were beside themselves with worry. Alison continued trying to contact the children on their mobiles. Gorawen looked at her coolly and said, "You won't get through, Alison – no phone can reach them where they're going."

James and Alison stopped in their tracks and spun round to face her. "What on earth do you mean?" James shouted roughly. "What's happened to *Nicole* – and the children?"

Alison broke down sobbing. Gorawen put her arms round her shoulders to comfort her, but Alison pushed her away. "I'm going to phone the coastguard!" she shouted.

With that, Gorawen snatched the phone from her hand and threw it onto the back seat of the Land Rover. Alison tried to retrieve it, but Gorawen grabbed her arm to stop her and said reassuringly, "Please believe me when I say the children are not in any danger." Alison pulled away and stood by her husband's side, grabbing his hand for support. They couldn't believe what they were hearing.

James, frustrated by Gorawen's apparent calmness and lack of consideration for their children's safety, thrust his face towards hers, shouting, "What the hell do you mean, you stupid woman, saying the children are not in any danger … of course they are!"

Gorawen let out a sustained sigh, then without warning lurched forward, and grasped their shoulders in a firm grip. They tried to pull away, but it was useless, and anyway they no longer knew who they were dealing with. She closed her eyes and chanted a few words in an odd language, then opened them and released her grip. James and Alison immediately stopped struggling, put into a deep trance by Gorawen's magic. Ordering them to get back in the vehicle, they obeyed without question and she shut the door behind them. Climbing into the driving seat she turned the key in the ignition. The engine started, and glancing at her charges in the rear-view mirror, she smiled, put the car into gear and moved off from the side of the road. She pushed a cassette tape into the player on the dashboard, and as the music played, began to hum merrily along with the tune.

As the final wisps of mist released their grasp on *Nicole* and evaporated into the warm air, the yacht glided gracefully out beneath a vivid blue sky and into the bright yellow sunshine. Beyond her bow lay the contours of land, a line of trees leading down from a hillside to a beach of white sand. In the distance, what seemed like a flock of massive birds flew over the shoreline until they finally disappeared beyond the hills. Behind *Nicole*, suspended from the sky, was a shimmering curtain, draped rainbowlike, onto the glistening surface of the sea.

4

Unknown Waters

Aboard *Nicole* Izzy, Dan, and George were still asleep on the saloon sofas below deck. Bella awoke first. Drowsily she staggered to her feet and began barking for all she was worth, waking Izzy and Dan from their enforced slumbers. Oblivious to the strange events that their parents had witnessed from the shore near Menai Bridge, Izzy went up on deck to see why she was barking. She knelt down and stroked Bella's back. "There now, what's all this noise for?" Bella stopped barking and wagged her tail, letting out a single yelp as though she was trying to tell her mistress something. Izzy slowly got to her feet and peered out over *Nicole's* bow.

Astonished to see that *Nicole* had broken away from her mooring and was now drifting aimlessly in open waters, she yelled at Daniel to join her on deck. As her brother, still half asleep, stepped up into the cockpit, he said, yawning, "What's all the fuss about, Izzy?"

"We've come adrift from our mooring, Dan, and I don't know where we are! I don't recognise any of these landmarks."

"What?" replied Dan. "How the hell did that happen?"

Realising the seriousness of their situation, he began to panic. "While I lower the anchor to stop us drifting anymore," he shouted, "can you get our present position from the chart plotter, Izzy, so at least we know where we've drifted to."

Izzy leaned over to the wheel binnacle where the chart plotter was mounted and switched it on. She waited a few seconds for it to power up, but the screen remained blank. "It's not powering up, Dan, there seems to be no power at all. Even the compass has gone mad, it's spinning like a frenzied wombat," she cried.

"What?" he replied incredulously as he released the anchor into the sea.

Izzy thought he hadn't heard her, so repeated herself a bit louder. "No power on the chart plotter, and the compass is spinning like a frenzied wombat!"

Dan rushed over from the bow to where his sister was standing. "Yes, I heard you the first time, Izzy," he said sarcastically.

"No need to get angry with me, Daniel Moorefield! We all need to stay calm, especially for George's sake. Think about what dad would do in a situation like this."

Pointing his finger in the air he exclaimed, "Of course, that's it, the batteries!" And he rushed below deck to check them. Returning a few minutes later he said, puzzled, "They all seem to be Ok as far as I can tell."

"What do you mean, as far as you can tell? I thought you were the engineer of this family."

"Whose losing their temper now? I don't have a meter with me to check the voltage, but all the connections are tight and none of the overloads have tripped, as far as I can see. But because none of the lights are working down there either, it's far too dark for me to check if everything is working correctly. So, in my honest opinion, dear sister, as the family's engineer … I honestly don't know why we've lost power."

Meanwhile, below deck in the saloon, George finally stirred from his sleep. He was still wearing his *Do not Disturb* sign around his neck. He stretched out his arms and yawned, then seeing he was alone, decided to continue playing his game on his console in peace. After several unsuccessful attempts to turn it on, he muttered to himself, "Oh drat, the batteries are flat … that's odd, they were new ones yesterday. I'll see if anyone's got any they can lend me." He strolled up onto the deck to join his brother and sister, who were still arguing. "Have either of you got any spare AAA batteries I can borrow – my games console's dead."

Dan turned towards his brother and shouted at him. "Don't bother us with trivial things like your bloody games console, George, we've got more important things to worry about up here." But George couldn't hear him, like everything else electrical on *Nicole*, his hearing aid wasn't working either, even though he had done as ordered and left it switched on.

Izzy kicked Dan's shin for being so cross with their little brother.

"Ouch!" he cried, rubbing his leg. "What did you do that for?"

Before Izzy had a chance to reply, he turned his attention towards George after noticing he was wearing his *Do Not Disturb* sign again. Losing his temper, he stretched out his arm towards his younger brother and ripped the sign from his neck with an angry jerk. George squealed, snatched it back and stuffed it down his t-shirt. Dan exploded and knelt in front of him, shouting in his ear, "And I suppose you've got your bloody hearing aid switched off too." George angrily shook his head.

Izzy had seen enough and pushed Dan over onto the deck with the flat of her foot. "Daniel Moorefield!" she yelled. "What would mum think of your behaviour to George? I know he can be frustrating at times but really, was there any need to screech at him like that?" She knelt down and put her arm round George to comfort him. "Now apologise to your brother!" she shouted at Dan.

George looked forlornly into his sister's eyes. "I haven't switched it off, it's not working, Izzy!" He pulled his hearing aid out from his t-shirt and gave it to her to confirm it was switched on. She nodded, and handed it to Dan, who on close inspection discovered George was telling the truth after all.

He looked at his little brother sorrowfully, regretting his thoughtless outburst. "Oh, George, I'm so sorry, perhaps the battery needs replacing."

George looked at Dan with a smirk. "It *is* a new battery. Mum put a new one in for me before we left home."

"That's strange," Dan replied. "Izzy can't get the chart plotter to work either. I wonder if the engine will start." He got to his feet, went over to the engine ignition switch and turned the key. The engine was completely dead.

Izzy got out her mobile phone from her pocket and looked down at the screen. "My phone's completely dead too – nothing. But I know it was fully charged this morning when we left the marina."

Dan tried his and shook his head in disbelief. "Nothing on mine either, not a sausage."

They looked at each other in total silence. Izzy grabbed both her brothers' hands, and biting her lip asked anxiously, "What are we to do? Mum and Dad must be out of their minds with worry by now!"

*

Gorawen turned off the main road and drove into a narrow lane. She slowed down and stopped in front of the pair of heavily rusted iron gates that secured the driveway to her house. Her driveway was in fact a narrow causeway that separated her house from the shore. She whispered a little verse to herself and they magically opened, allowing her to drive through. They closed behind her with a loud clunk. Gorawen had no need for modern technology to protect her privacy, not when she had the use of her own magical powers.

She glanced over her shoulder to check on James and Alison, still sleeping peacefully in the rear of the car. Although the tide was beginning to flood the causeway, she accelerated and drove across, spraying a wall of water either side. "Just made it in time," she muttered to herself. "Another ten minutes and the road will be completely impassable."

Gorawen pulled up outside her rambling old house, and as she switched off the engine two large dogs came bounding out from a side gate to meet her, barking and wagging their tails on seeing their mistress get out of the car. She knelt down to stroke them. "Hush, my loves," she cooed, "you will wake our guests." In an instant they were quiet, except for their heavy panting as they eagerly followed her back into the house, leaving James and Alison asleep on the back seat.

Ten minutes later, Gorawen re-appeared and opened the rear door of her car. She stretched inside, and gently gripping James and Alison's shoulders, chanted a brief verse. Her two sleepy passengers slowly opened their eyes and looked at each other in bewilderment.

"Now, before you say anything, let's go inside the house, and I will make us all a nice cup of tea while I tell you what has happened to the children … and we'll have no more shouting, please," she instructed.

Without saying a word and feeling a bit wobbly on their feet from their enforced nap, Alison and James followed her into the house like two scolded children. She led them into her large drawing room and directed them to take a seat. They did as they were told and sat down on an ancient threadbare sofa, gazing at each other in stunned silence while Gorawen went into the kitchen to make tea.

A few minutes later she returned to the drawing room carrying three mugs of tea on a large copper tray. "Now I know you must have lots of questions for me, my dears," she said as she put the tray on a side table, "but please believe me when I say the children are not in any danger."

James and Alison were still in a state of nothingness, and although their eyes were wide open, were not taking in a word of what was being said. Gorawen noticed Alison shivering, and bending down to feel her hand, said in a soft voice, "Why, you're freezing, my dear. I forget how draughty and cold this old house can get." She walked over to the window and stood for a moment peering out towards the sea. Judging from the amount of spray coming off the rocks below, she could tell it was high water. They were now completely shut off from the rest of the world.

The frayed edges of the shabby brocade curtains fluttered as the wind whistled its way through the gaps in the rotting wood of the window frame. With two determined tugs she closed the curtains, putting a barrier between them and the unwelcome draught. "Do you know," she said, hugging the tops of her arms, "I think it's cold enough for a fire."

She walked over to the ornate stone fireplace at the end of the room. On the mantelpiece were several framed photographs of Izzy playing with Bella as a puppy. In the centre was a photo of a young man in his mid-twenties. She gazed at it and winked, caressing the frame softly with her fingers, then knelt in front of the soot-stained blackened hearth, placed some kindling in the fire basket and added a few seasoned logs on top. She muttered a short verse and the contents of the fire basket burst into flame.

"That's better," she said, warming her hands in front of the blaze. Turning back to face her guests once more, she walked over and sat down opposite James and Alison in an old armchair. She stared into their glazed eyes and clicked her fingers with a loud snap. Like waking from a terrible nightmare, they sat bolt upright and turned to face each other without saying a single word.

Gorawen handed each of them a mug of tea from the tray. "Now drink this, it will help to warm you up." Unbeknown to Alison and James, she had added a little something to the tea while she was in the kitchen, in the hope of keeping them calm. "Now that I have your complete attention, my dears, I can begin." They both did as they were told and drank their tea in silence as Gorawen talked.

"When I brought Izzy to you as a new-born baby nearly sixteen years ago, and persuaded you to adopt her, I said to you at the time that one day she would have to be told her true identity. Well, that day has come."

The tea was beginning to work its magic, and although Alison wanted to erupt with anger at what Gorawen had done to them, she found she couldn't. Instead, the words came out as a calm if somewhat disordered statement. "But – but – I thought we would tell her ourselves when she was older." She looked nervously at her husband for support, and continued. "Tell her that we adopted her, I mean … she's far too young … she can't deal with the shock of discovering we are not her real parents!"

"Nonsense, my dear, you've always underestimated the child's maturity. *Now* is the right time. She is old enough and responsible enough to handle the truth. After all, she turns sixteen tomorrow and would be considered an adult in the world she was born into."

The tea seemed to have less effect on James than it did on Alison. Being a barrister, he knew the law and began to argue his point. "Surely that's up to us, Gorawen. It's most certainly not your decision to make. You may have arranged her adoption, but in the eyes of the law, we are her legal parents."

Beginning to feel more like herself, Alison suddenly found her anger.

"Why now, Gorawen? We were supposed to be on holiday, for God's sake! And why involve the boys? What in God's name have you done?"

Even though they had both witnessed the inexplicable events of the day at first hand, Gorawen knew they had no idea of the extent of her magical powers, other than the occasional experience of her herbal potions. They would be powerless to get the better of her, but out of desperation they were demanding immediate answers, ones she wasn't ready to give. Perhaps it was time for a second, more potent brew of her special tea, she thought.

Standing on the foredeck of *Nicole*, Izzy and Dan were also seeking answers to what was happening to them. They had no idea where they had drifted to, and they certainly couldn't understand why all the electrics on the yacht had failed. George was on his own, crouched on the floor of the cockpit with his legs tucked up close to his chest. He rocked backwards and forwards as if in a trance, muttering to himself and clutching his *Do Not Disturb* sign. He was still upset that he couldn't play his games and use them as a distraction from what was happening around him. He had no idea what his brother and sister were saying; as his father said, he really was deaf to the world. The irony of his situation was, for once, not his fault.

Suddenly Bella started barking and ran towards the bow-sprit. Izzy and Dan, startled by her outburst, looked up and turned their heads in the direction of Bella's gaze. From around a narrow headland jutting out into the sea, they could see two longboats with a dozen or more oarsmen in each, driving at good speed towards *Nicole*. Izzy cried out, "Thank goodness! Rescue."

Dan remarked drily, "At last. Now we might find out where we are."

Izzy ran over to George and gently grabbed hold of his hand to pull him to his feet. He was still cross, so tried to resist until she knelt in front of him so he could read her lips. "Georgie, look." She pointed to the boats in the distance. After realising what his sister was trying to show him, he looked at her, grinned, and jumped to his feet. The eager pair joined Dan on the bow of *Nicole*, and as the boats got ever closer, they could see each one had a red pennant flying from its stern. Izzy couldn't make out what the insignia was on the flags until George cried out, "Dragons!" Sure enough, as the boats drew nearer, they could see a golden dragon emblazoned on each pennant, glistening in the sunshine.

On the foredeck of the leading longboat was a figure dressed in strange scarlet clothes. As they drew close enough to make out the crew's faces, the man dressed in scarlet shouted out an order in a peculiar language. Although Dan didn't recognise it, Izzy knew it was Welsh, having been taught the language from an early age by Aunt Gorawen.

The longboats halted just a few metres away from *Nicole* on her starboard side. The oarsmen raised their blades into the air, releasing droplets of water onto the laps of the crews. The man dressed in scarlet, clearly their leader, stood up, removed his hat, bowed gracefully, and looked over towards Izzy and her brothers. With hackles raised, Bella bounded over to the guardrail and growled a warning that their unwelcome guests should keep away. An embarrassed Izzy grabbed hold of her collar for fear of her jumping into the boat and savaging its crew. Red faced, she apologised to the man and calmed Bella down. Bella's sudden sign of aggression didn't seem to bother the crew's leader at all. He just bowed again and said in English, "Please don't be alarmed, we mean you no harm. My name is Angwyn, I am an officer of the King's Navy."

"Can you tell us where we are, please, sir?" asked Dan.

"Why, you are in Cuddfan, sir," Angwyn replied. "Would you mind securing the lines we throw to you to your vessel, so that we may tow you into safer waters?"

Dan was undecided whether they could trust Angwyn or not. "Where the hell is Cuddfan?" he whispered to Izzy.

She shook her head and whispered back, "Cuddfan is Welsh for hideaway, but I've never heard of a *place* called Cuddfan." After a brief silence she added, "I think we should do as they say, Dan. What alternative do we have?"

"Why don't we just put the sails up and sail back to Menai Bridge?" Dan suggested. "We don't need an engine to get us back."

"Did you not notice the lack of wind, Dan?" Izzy replied with a smile. "And besides, I've never heard of Cuddfan before so I have no idea what course we should set. Without the GPS and a compass, where shall we head for?"

Dan sighed. His sister was right, as usual.

Poor George was confused; he kept looking up at Dan and then Izzy, trying to read their lips. Suddenly he tugged on Izzy's t-shirt to attract her attention. On realising how frustrating it must be for him not being able to hear any sound at all, she knelt down so they were face to face. "Sorry, Georgie, you don't know what's going on, do you? The situation is a bit delicate, so I will explain once our brainy brother decides what we're going to do next."

Angwyn could see there was some sort of disagreement going on between Izzy and her brother. Suspecting they were unwilling to trust him he said, "If it pleases you, my lady, I am mindful of your names." He paused for a moment then pulled out a picture from a soft leather pouch suspended from his waist belt, and studied it. He stared directly at each of them in turn and said, "Your name is Daniel, sir, you are the eldest. Your younger brother is George, and you, my lady, are Isabella." There was a pause. "Oh! I'm afraid I don't know your dog's name."

In stunned silence and disbelief, they turned and looked at each other. Izzy whispered to Dan, "How on earth does he know who we are?" She turned back to Angwyn and asked, "How do you know our names, sir?"

Angwyn hastily returned the picture to his pouch and said hesitantly, "I am not at liberty to say, my lady. I am simply following my captain's orders to tow you into the estuary, where he will pick you up later and take you ashore in the royal barge. Please do as I request. I assure you with my life, we mean you no harm."

"I don't think we have any choice, Dan," Izzy whispered.

"What say you, my lady?" Angwyn asked reverently.

"Why does he keep calling me 'my lady'? she muttered under her breath. 'I'm no one's lady."

Dan stepped forward, and summoning up the imperious tone of voice he had heard his father use in court, he said, "Sir, we will allow you to tow us into the estuary, but we will stay on board. Oh … and for your information, Angwyn, our vessel draws two metres, so please don't ground our yacht." He looked round at Izzy and with a childish grin said, "I think that told him who's in charge here." She chuckled, and thought how proud their dad would be to hear him asserting himself like that.

"Thank you, sir. Would you mind raising your anchor so we can get our boats into position to tow you?" asked Angwyn.

Dan replied, "I'm afraid we can't start the winch – we have no electrical power – so it will take me a bit longer than normal to raise the anchor manually." Angwyn stared at Daniel with a puzzled look.

As *Nicole*, now under tow from the longboats, approached the mouth of the estuary, Dan could see a fortified stone tower projecting skywards above the rocks. A flag with the same dragon insignia flew from the top of its pointed roof of black slate, flapping snake-like in the late afternoon breeze. In the shade of the overhanging roof was an observation platform, completely encircling the walls, from which two watchmen peered out. Within thirty minutes or so of travelling upriver, the oarsmen stopped rowing and Angwyn asked Daniel to release the lines and lower *Nicole's* anchor. Dan obliged, and as he and George watched them slowly disappear from sight, Izzy went below into the galley, announcing she was going to make a pot of tea. A few seconds later she popped her head up again. "Oh, the damned pump doesn't work either. No electrics again!"

"Don't worry, Izzy, we've got some bottled water, we can use that."

His sister couldn't contain her feelings any longer and tears began to roll down her face. "What's happening to us, Dan?"

"I really wish I knew, Izzy," he replied.

"I wish Mum and Dad were here right now," she gulped.

Dan changed the subject in the hope of lifting her spirits. "Come on, where's that tea you promised? Let's go and put Old Whistler on."

All three went below as Bella put her head on her paws and looked out over to the island. What could she sense that the others couldn't see?

Back at the house on Anglesey, Gorawen had finally given up trying to reason with James and Alison and had resorted to using her magic again to put them to bed for the night in a spare room. It had been a very tiring day for her. The magic she had used to arrange *Nicole's* journey to Cuddfan had drained her powers far too much for her to deal with the argumentative couple anymore. It would be another day tomorrow and a good night's rest might help to cool all their tempers.

5

Appointment with the Past

A ll seemed quiet on *Nicole* as the now ebbing tide slowly swung her bow around to face downstream. Izzy and her brothers were waiting patiently below deck when the barge they had been expecting approached her on her starboard side. The only sound that could be heard over the faint cries of the gulls feeding on the shoreline, were the blades of the twelve oarsmen as they dug them into the rippling surface of the estuary to thrust them forward. A tall man, standing on the foredeck of the barge, gave an order for the oarsmen to stop rowing. On hearing his voice, Bella lifted her head and peered out towards him. Strangely, she did not bark, but instead got to her feet, wagging her tail as if she recognised him. He shouted across to the yacht, "Ahoy, *Nicole!*"

On hearing his voice, Dan jumped to his feet and made his way topside to see what was happening. George was still asleep with his head on Izzy's lap, so she carefully eased her body sideways and gently placed his head on a cushion so as not to wake him. Getting to her feet, she followed her brother up on deck and stood by his side. She grabbed hold of his hand, and in a show of support Dan gently squeezed it. As they both looked out towards the man on the barge, he removed his hat and bowed towards them. "My name is Captain Owain of his most noble Majesty's Navy. I believe you are expecting me." Izzy and Dan looked at each other and nodded. "If it pleases you," he said courteously, "may we secure our vessel to your yacht so I may come aboard?"

Dan nodded and watched as the crew tied their ropes to *Nicole's* cleats, after which the captain stepped aboard. Izzy could not understand why Bella did not growl; she always growled at strangers. Even she herself felt put at ease by the captain's voice. But before anyone could speak, George appeared from below, and rubbing his eyes asked, "What's happening?" Dan stretched out his other hand to his brother, which George quickly grabbed. Then, noticing the captain standing on the deck, George asked him, "Are you coming to take us prisoners?"

"Of course not, Master George," replied the captain. "You are guests of our most noble majesty, the King."

Daniel, who was normally frosty towards outsiders, seemed unusually friendly towards the captain and replied warmly, "I'm afraid my brother is deaf, sir, but he can read your lips if you're face to face."

With that, the captain knelt down on one knee in front of George, looked into his eyes, and repeated his statement. George grinned, then unexpectedly put his arms round the captain's neck and gave him a hug before stepping back to stand beside his brother. The captain acknowledged George's embrace and smiled back at him. For the first time since entering this strange world, the three siblings shared a sense of calmness in the presence of Captain Owain.

"Before I take you ashore, would you mind if I place four of my men aboard your vessel to guard her for the duration of your stay? I assure you they will not venture into your private quarters."

Izzy looked at Dan with a grin and shrugged her shoulders. He nodded in agreement and said, "By all means, Captain, but they are welcome to use *Nicole's* galley if they wish."

"Thank you, Master Daniel, that is kind of you, but they will be relieved of duty when necessary by other guards. Besides, I would rather they remain alert on deck at all times."

"Very well, sir," replied Daniel. "We appreciate your concern for the safety of our yacht – she is very dear to us."

"Of course she is, Master Daniel, and we will take very good care of her for the duration of your stay with us in the Kingdom of Cuddfan." He turned towards the barge and gave an order to one of his crew members to alert the guards in the cabin to join him on *Nicole's* deck.

The four men-at-arms, resplendent in their light armour and each carrying a spear, appeared from inside the cabin and joined their captain on the deck. Once they were standing to attention, Captain Owain asked Izzy and her brothers to join him on the barge. Bella waited patiently until the captain turned towards her and beckoned with his head to jump aboard. Izzy was amazed at her behaviour; she was not normally known for her obedience to anyone, let alone a total stranger.

While the crew pushed the barge away from *Nicole*, Captain Owain invited them into the comfort of the cabin for the duration of their journey to the shore.

As the barge drew alongside the narrow wooden jetty that jutted out from the sandy shoreline, two men who had been waiting for their arrival took the lines and secured them to three stout bollards. Captain Owain then led his guests to where a horse-drawn coach was waiting on a track a few metres away. Standing patiently behind the coach were eight mounted men-at-arms in full armour. The coachman climbed down, opened the door and unfolded the steps from inside. Captain Owain beckoned them to enter and explained, "The coach will take you to the hunting lodge where you will be guests of Lord and Lady Gochwyban and accommodated overnight. Tomorrow, when the tide is right, I will re-join you and we will journey upriver together to the royal palace."

As they clambered in and took their seats, the captain grabbed Bella as she attempted to follow her mistress and held her back. She began to struggle, but before Izzy could protest, he bent down and whispered something in her ear. She immediately stopped and stepped back to stand by his side. Izzy was astounded.

"If it pleases you, my lady, I will take care of Bella for the night – you will be reunited tomorrow morning."

He was about to shut the door when Izzy looked at Bella and said, "Now you be good for Captain Owain." Bella replied with a single bark.

The captain smiled at her, then gently shutting the door gave an order to the coachman, who climbed back into his seat and took the reins. The captain, Bella by his side, stepped back and signalled to the coachman to move off. The heavy coach lurched forward and shook as the six black horses took the strain, then pulled away up the slope and turned into the forest. George knelt on the seat and gazed out of the rear window, where he could see the troop of cavalry following behind them. "Wow!" he said. "This is exciting, we've got a royal escort. We must be very important."

But Izzy wasn't listening. She was deep in thought and said to Dan, "You know, I'm sure they were speaking Welsh back there, a bit different to what Aunt Gorawen taught me, but similar all the same."

Her brother pondered for a moment and replied, "If you think of it, we can't have travelled that far from Menai Bridge time-wise, so it makes sense that we must still be in Wales."

"But that doesn't prove they are Welsh … I have a strange feeling we're a lot further away from Wales than you think. Besides, what's with the armour and strange clothes they're all wearing?"

It was dark when they finally arrived at the entrance to the hunting lodge. The sudden jolt of the coach coming to a stop, catapulted a sleeping George off his seat onto Daniel's lap. A little dazed from being woken up, he got to his feet and sat back in his seat next to Izzy. They could hear muffled voices from outside and waited nervously to see who they were going to meet next. A woman's voice was heard over the confusion outside. Dan pulled back the curtain to see who was there and appeared to like what he saw. The door to the coach opened, and as the coachman unfolded the steps and stood back, a young woman dressed in an elaborately embroidered blue gown, edged with fur, appeared in front of the open door. She curtsied gracefully and looking at Izzy said, "Good evening, my lady. On behalf of my parents I welcome you and your brothers to the hunting lodge." Stepping aside, she bowed her head and beckoned them with a sweep of her hand to step out of the coach.

In his eagerness to greet the lovely young woman before anyone else, Daniel tried to push past his sister, but Izzy put her arm up to stop him.

"Excuse me, dear brother, I believe the young lady was addressing me," she said, indicating her chest.

Dan was a little annoyed at being pushed back and glowered at her. Izzy stood in the doorway of the coach for a moment, still barring her brother from passing, and looked down at the young woman. She still couldn't understand why everyone kept addressing her as 'my lady'. But then she thought to herself *What the hell, if it winds Daniel up, why not encourage it!* She stepped down and gently took the young woman's hand.

"Captain Owain told us we are to stay here overnight. If that's the case, may I know your name, or is that a secret too?"

The young woman blushed, looked at Izzy, curtsied, and replied, "Apologies, my lady, I am Lady Angharad."

"Well, Angharad, my full name is Isabella, but please don't call me that – my friends call me Izzy. I gave the last bit of my name to my dog – Bella.

And talking of dogs –", she grinned, "these two mongrels are my brothers, Daniel and George. But I think you already knew that, didn't you?"

Izzy had broken the ice, so she looped a puzzled Angharad's arm in hers and together they climbed the steps to the entrance of the lodge like two old schoolfriends. She glanced back at her brothers and said, "Come on, boys, keep up!" Daniel and George, shocked by Izzy's odd behaviour, looked at each other and jumped quickly out of the coach for fear of getting left behind.

Their footsteps echoed as they made their way through a long marble corridor to a pair of heavily carved oak doors, guarded by two men-at-arms with crossed spears. They stood to attention, and bowing their heads as their mistress approached, pushed open the doors, allowing Angharad to lead her guests into the sumptuous room beyond. The walls were panelled in oak and lined with elaborate tapestries depicting ancient hunting scenes. The fragrant smell of wood-smoke filled the air as it rose gently from the massive log fire in the centre of the room and meandered upwards through a large bronze funnel-shaped chimney, suspended from the ceiling. They stood silently in awe at the scale of their surroundings.

"This is the Great Hall," Angharad informed them.

"Wow!" exclaimed Dan. "This would make a great place for a party!"

"My family's feasts are renowned throughout the kingdom, second only to the palace," replied Angharad proudly. "Please, if you would make yourselves comfortable over there ..." she pointed to the cushioned chairs around the blackened hearth ... "I will inform my parents of your arrival." She turned and disappeared through a doorway next to a large wooden screen that formed part of the wall.

"Well, this is better!" cried Dan as he dropped unceremoniously into one of the chairs.

"I know why you've changed your tune," Izzy chuckled. "Could it be our hostess?" she said mischievously as she warmed her hands by the fire.

"Oh ... of course not, I'm just being polite," Dan stuttered.

As Izzy looked around the room, she noticed the elaborate carving on the screen next to the doorway through which Angharad had disappeared earlier. She was admiring its craftsmanship when she had the odd feeling someone was watching her. Curiosity getting the better of her, she walked slowly towards it.

Noticing what Izzy was up to, Dan called out, "I think you ought to come back, Izzy, we don't want to upset our hosts." But she couldn't help being drawn to the screen, and with her eyes firmly focused on the finely carved fretwork, she gestured behind her back for him to be quiet. Stopping one step away, she cautiously stretched out her hand to touch the screen. Dan had seen enough. He rushed over to her side and grabbed her arm. "For goodness sake, Izzy," he whispered, "come back to your seat." But she sensed movement on the other side, and determined to find out who it was, pushed him away and slid her slender fingers through a narrow gap in the fretwork. She was now close enough to see a shadowy figure on the other side peering back at her through the darkness. She saw a pair of piercing green eyes looking back at her, and without any warning something grabbed hold of her fingers. A tingling sensation shot through her arm and into her chest. An uncontrollable feeling of longing reached into her soul and flooded her mind with an emotion she had never felt before. There seemed no escape as wave after wave of yearning spread through her body.

In that instant, a male voice from behind the screen shouted, "No!" and the grip on her fingers was suddenly relaxed. She pulled her hand away in shock. Her legs turned to jelly and she dropped trembling to her knees.

Dan helped Izzy to her feet and whispered angrily into her ear, "There, I told you to come back to your seat, didn't I, now look at you!" But Izzy wasn't concerned about what her brother was saying, she was still trying to make out what had happened on the other side of the screen. She could hear a man shouting angrily and a woman sobbing in the dark. Then all fell silent. Seconds later a flustered Angharad reappeared, and trying to divert Izzy's attention away from the screen, cried nervously, "I am so sorry, Izzy, please accept my family's apologies."

But Izzy was having none of it and yelled, "Who the hell was that, Angharad?"

Before she could reply, a portly gentleman burst through the doorway, followed by a small round middle-aged woman. "A thousand apologies to you, my lady, it was only a servant girl who wanted to see you close up. She got above herself, that's all, so I've sent her back to her quarters with a severe scolding."

Izzy whispered quietly into her brother's ear, "That was no ordinary servant girl!" But for the sake of Dan's evident embarrassment in front of their hosts, she decided for the time being to play down her emotional encounter.

Trying to avert everyone's attention away from the incident, the man announced, "What a terrible host I am. I have not introduced myself to you – I am Lord Gochwyban, my lady, and this is my wife Edwina. We are Angharad's parents." They bowed graciously. "Now I'm sure you would like to take some refreshment after your long journey."

He led them back to the hearth and gestured for them to be seated. Dan waited for Angharad to take her seat so he could sit beside her. She was flattered that she held a fascination for him, and was not going to discourage any attention he bestowed upon her.

Lord Gochwyban stood awkwardly in front of his guests. The incident at the screen had obviously unsettled him. Addressing Izzy, he said, "I know you have lots of questions you would like to ask me and my family, my lady, but we have strict instructions from his majesty not to answer them. We are honoured to receive you and your brothers into our humble household. Your rooms have been made ready for your short stay here, and tomorrow, Captain Owain will escort you to the royal palace where I'm sure the answers you seek will be forthcoming."

Izzy could see her hosts felt stressed about answering any questions. She wasn't stupid, and considering the day they had experienced, she decided to let it go with a smile and said calmly, "Thank you, Lord Gochwyban. I hope, as you say, our questions will be answered when we get to the palace tomorrow. I'm sure one more day being kept in the dark won't matter."

He wasn't sure what to make of Izzy's comment, but decided it was time for him and his wife to depart. "Thank you, my lady, for your understanding. Sadly, my wife and I must now attend to a pressing matter, but we will leave you in the capable hands of our daughter." He clapped his hands loudly and servants appeared carrying trays of food, followed by a young woman with a Welsh harp. She sat down in an alcove and drawing her fingers lightly across the strings, began to play. Lord Gochwyban bowed, and urging his wife towards the doorway, bade them goodnight.

As the music filled the hall and entered their consciousness, the tensions of the day seemed to drift away with the smoke from the fire. Daniel couldn't take his eyes of Angharad. All through the evening, while they ate and drank, he seemed spellbound by her charm and natural beauty. It was all too much for George, who fell asleep amongst the large cushions in the chair. The trauma of the day also proved too much for Izzy, so finally she gave in to her body's natural desire for sleep, leaving her brother in an intense conversation with Angharad.

Izzy was awakened by Dan shaking her shoulder. "Come on, sleepyhead, time for bed. Angharad is going to show us to our rooms." He pulled her gently from the chair and then scooped up George in his strong arms and followed Angharad through the archway and up a flight of stairs. She opened the door to a candle-lit room with two large beds in the centre.

"Mother thought that you and George might like to share, master Daniel."

"Thank you, Angharad," replied Dan. "He will be frightened if he wakes up alone in the night in a strange place." He lowered George gently onto the bed, removed his shoes and pulled the sheets over his sleeping body.

Angharad pointed towards a door. "The water closet is through there." Dan looked puzzled.

"Toilet," Izzy remarked knowingly with a smile.

"Ah, yes – of course" he replied, not wanting to appear stupid. "Thank you so much for your kindness. I'm sure I speak for all of us, Angharad, when I say you have made us feel most welcome in your beautiful home."

He glanced at Izzy for her approval. She smiled and nodded in agreement and added, "Yes, thank you, Angharad," and looking at her brother with a smirk, wished him goodnight.

Angharad led Izzy out of the room and into the hallway, closely followed by Dan who peered round the side of the door, giving him a chance to take one more peek at her. He really wanted to kiss her goodnight, but nerves failed him. Instead he gently closed the door and floated over to the bed in a self-induced trance. He grabbed a pillow and danced quietly around the room while pressing it to his chest saying *I'm in love!* to himself several times over.

Angharad showed Izzy into her room. Now that they were on their own, Izzy saw a chance to get some answers, but Angharad was one step ahead of her, and unwilling to divulge what she knew, simply wished her goodnight, and left her alone with her thoughts.

As the sun rose over the hunting lodge to welcome in the dawn, Dan was awoken from his night's sleep by George, who was jumping all over the bed. Dan cried out in desperation, "Georgie, can't a guy get some sleep?" George picked up a pillow and pulled it into his chest, mimicking his brother's little dance the night before. He jumped over onto Dan's bed but bounced back off, landing on the floor in a heap. Dan rolled over to the edge of the bed and stared George in the face, yelling, "Ha! serve you right for making fun of me!"

The door burst open and Izzy walked into the room carrying a large willow basket filled with clothes. She was dressed in a long flowing gown, similar in style to the one Angharad had worn the night before. Surprised to see his sister in what appeared to be a dress, Dan shouted, "Oh my God, Izzy, you're wearing a frock!"

"I wouldn't say anything if I were you. Wait till you see what *you* have to wear," she said, placing the basket on the bed.

"Why? I'm not wearing anything they give me," he replied as he searched desperately around the room for his clothes.

"Too late, they have already taken them. Apparently, we must blend in 'for security reasons'. I have a lovely little number for you, Dan. It's either that or go naked."

George got the gist and looking somewhat worried, delved into the basket, scattering its contents unceremoniously on the bed. "What's in here for me?" he asked.

"Right, sort yourselves out, and I'll see you in the hall in twenty minutes for breakfast," Izzy replied as she walked towards the door, only to turn at the last minute. "And George," looking straight at him, "make sure you wash!"

George grabbed a pillow from the bed and threw it at his sister, but she was far too quick for him and shut the door behind her before it could make contact.

When Dan and George finally made it into the Great Hall, Izzy and Angharad had already finished breakfast. The boys were still in a jocular mood, pointing at each other's new outfits and laughing. Angharad stood up from her chair, looking at Dan, who was trying to pull his hose up to his waist. "My, how handsome you look, Daniel," she said affectionately.

"Really?" replied Dan. "Maybe I could get used to wearing this clobber after all."

"Come on, you two, I said twenty minutes," snapped Izzy.

"Oh! Someone got out of the wrong side of the bed this morning," replied Dan with a smirk.

Before she could reply, George produced a folded piece of cardboard from inside his doublet, handed it to her with a kiss and said, "Happy birthday, Izzy."

"Yeah, happy birthday, sis," added Dan.

Izzy was taken completely by surprise and looked down at her brother's precious *Do Not Disturb* sign. On the back was a hand-drawn picture of *Nicole* sailing with dragons in the sky. It was evident to her that it was Georgie's handiwork. She read the message out loud. *Happy 16th Birthday, Izzy, lots of love, Dan, George, Mum and Dad, kiss kiss kiss.* On the bottom was a sketch of a paw print with 'Bella' written across it.

This sudden show of thoughtfulness from her brothers brought a tear to her eye. Usually they would rely on their mum to remind them of any birthdays – except their own of course. It was a birthday card she would cherish for the rest of her life, especially as they had had to scribble it on Georgie's treasured homemade sign.

Seeing his sister's eyes welling up, Dan remarked, "Got something in your eye, have you, Izzy?"

"No, I was just touched you remembered my birthday."

A familiar bark broke their exchange as Bella bounded into the hall, skidding on the slippery floor and jumping straight into her mistress's lap. "Bella!" she cried, giving her a hug. "You're far too big to sit on my lap!"

A voice from behind uttered a command and Bella immediately jumped off Izzy's lap onto the floor, almost standing to attention. Izzy looked round in astonishment and recognised the face of Captain Owain.

"I have taken the liberty of educating Bella into our ways, my lady. I hope you don't mind."

"Mind? of course not. How wonderful. You will have to tell me your secret," she replied.

"As you please, my lady," he said, bowing as if it were a command. "The tide is now in our favour, so if you are ready, we should continue our journey to the palace."

George hastily grabbed a piece of bread and a slice of ham from the table as they all rose from their seats and followed the captain through the door out into the sweet-smelling herb garden. Dan was in conversation with Angharad and stuck to her side as they strolled onto the lawn.

On hearing the sound of galloping hoofs coming from behind, they all slowed down and turned round to see a lone cloaked rider hurtle past and stop in front of them, cutting off the pathway to the river. It was clear that the rider was a woman, but the hooded cloak threw a shadow over her face, hiding her features. The horse circled round them, stamping its hoofs in the rough ground, sending clouds of dust into the air. Captain Owain stepped between Izzy and the rider to protect her, but then bowed his head and withdrew. He had obviously recognised the rider's identity.

The woman lent forward in her saddle and gazed down at Izzy, who instantly experienced the same sensations she had felt the evening before when she discovered the figure behind the screen. After a few seconds, the rider turned her horse and galloped off on a narrow track leading into the forest. Frustrated, Izzy couldn't contain her temper any longer and screamed at the Captain, "What the hell was all that about?" Before he could reply, twenty men-at-arms on horseback, dressed in full armour, came thundering by and disappeared into the darkness of the forest.

"Wow!" cried George excitedly.

"That was awesome," Dan commented to Angharad, who looked shaken.

Izzy repeated her question. "Well, Captain? Judging from your reaction, you obviously know who that was! So, who is she?"

"I'm afraid I am unable to reveal the identity of the rider you refer to, my lady."

Izzy finally snapped. "I am not your bloody lady! When on earth is someone going to tell me what is happening to us?" She looked down at Bella and yelled at the captain, "And you can give me back my dog!"

But before she could snatch her away from him, Dan grabbed her by the arm. "Calm down, sis, I'm sure we'll get a full explanation when we get to the palace."

"Calm down? Calm down? Where has the real Daniel Moorefield gone? What have you done to my moaning brother, Angharad?"

Captain Owain stepped up behind Izzy, and Dan watched in dismay as he placed his hand on her shoulder and whispered, "Please forgive me, my lady." Immediately she slumped motionless into his arms. He assured Dan and George that Izzy would be fine, but they must make haste to catch the tide. The boys, still shocked by their sister's ill-mannered outburst, politely agreed and followed him as he carried her towards the pontoon where the barge was waiting to take them to the royal palace. He stepped aboard, opened the door to the cabin and laid Izzy gently onto a day bed. Bella followed and sat down by her mistress's side. Gently closing the door behind him, he asked the boys with some urgency to join him on the deck. George, not wanting to disobey the captain's order for fear of being put to sleep too, jumped aboard and looked back at Dan. "Come on, lover-boy, we're all waiting for you!"

As Dan reluctantly pulled himself away from Angharad and joined his brother, he shouted across to her, "Will I see you again?"

She looked back at him with a warm smile and replied, "If he wills it, then it will be so."

George put on a performance of being sick, complete with sound effects, at this display of adoration. Dan turned on his heels and attempted to clip his brother on the ear, but George was too quick for him and ducked.

The helmsman gave the order to cast off, and once the mooring lines were released the oarsmen used their blades to push the barge out into the middle of the river. As they began to row, Dan stood leaning on the corner of the cabin, looking longingly back at Angharad in the hope their parting would be brief. He peeked in on Izzy through the glass of the cabin door and then went to join his little brother on the foredeck. George was sitting cross-legged, staring into space. Dan sat down beside him and gently nudged his shoulder. George looked up at him as he asked, "Everything Ok with you, little man?"

George tried to smile, but Dan could see he wasn't his usual self and placed his arm around his shoulder. "Oh, I'm alright," George told him, "just a bit confused at what's happening to us."

"Yes, I know, we all are. But I'm sure, as the captain said, we will find out soon enough when we get to the palace, wherever that is."

"Are you sure we're not in any danger, Dan? Look what happened to Izzy when she tried to argue with the captain – he made her go all unconscious."

Before Dan could answer, the captain appeared from behind and knelt down in front of George so he could read his lips. "Oh no, master George, your sister is just sleeping. I promise you with my life, you are all very safe. No harm will come to you."

"You will have to excuse my brother's concerns for our safety, Captain," said Dan. "We are all still uneasy about what has happened to us in the last couple of days. And I do apologise on behalf of my sister for her earlier outburst, it's so unlike her to lose her temper so violently. But you must realise, we have been separated from our parents and thrust into your strange world called Cuddfan by some kind of freak accident. You all know our names, yet your clothes, your mannerisms, the way you talk – they're all quite different from our own and everyone here refuses to tell us why. We just want someone to tell us the truth."

The captain regarded them sympathetically. "I do understand your anguish, this must all be very strange for you. Please believe me when I say, master Daniel, I am as much in the dark as yourselves as to why, or even how you arrived in Cuddfan. The King has seen fit that he and he alone will explain to you why you are here. All I have been told by his majesty is to guard your presence here with my life. And there is no need to apologise for your sister's behaviour. I have two daughters of my own so I am used to a woman's scorn! As a man of the sea, I have discovered a woman shares the same nature as the mighty oceans – one minute she is calm and welcoming, the next instant she will fly into a furious rage for no apparent reason at all. As sailors, we trim our sails to get out of danger, and as men we must do the same. Treat a woman with respect and she will unlock the gates to heaven. But treat her with contempt, and she will unlock the gates to hell. Would you not agree, master Daniel?" Dan smiled and nodded in agreement. "You will find the truth you seek soon enough when we arrive at the palace."

He stood up and helped George to his feet, then addressing them both said, "We are nearing the Devil's Nostrils and the journey is going to get a little rough. May I suggest you both take shelter in the cockpit – I would hate to think of you falling overboard, these waters are treacherous and unpredictable."

George and Dan looked at each other and rather quickly did as the captain suggested. As they jumped down into the cockpit, they felt the barge lurch suddenly forward, almost throwing them off balance. They turned and looked dead ahead. The low riverbank was now beginning to steepen rapidly into a deep rocky gorge and the once calm river was becoming a raging torrent. The captain rushed over to assist the helmsman, who was struggling with the heavy wooden tiller to keep a steady course.

The oarsmen dug in the blades of their oars to slow their progress down. As the barge turned the bend in the river, they could hear the terrifying roar of rushing water. Five hundred metres ahead was a vertical cliff, towering up above them with nothing in between it and the river. Two massive stone towers, like sentinels, jutted out of the face of the cliff. A series of thick ropes and large pulleys ran down from the top of each tower to what appeared to be a drawbridge below.

As they approached, it was lowered across the gap, revealing the entrance to a tunnel beyond. Once settled on the bed of the river, Dan could see it was some kind of aqueduct. The flow of the river, now diverted across it, caused the water level to rise in the tank-like structure, dividing the river into three separate streams. On either side of the aqueduct, the river disappeared into a rocky ravine below, forming two individual waterfalls several metres across. Now it was up to the skill of the helmsmen and the captain to steer the barge safely into the narrow channel.

George peered over the side of the barge as they crossed the manmade conduit to see the raging torrent drop some fifty metres. They surely would have gone over the waterfall and been smashed to pieces if the helmsmen had misjudged their moment. The thought terrified him; he hated heights.

Daniel, far from being scared, was impressed by the sheer scale of this feat of engineering, realising that if the aqueduct had remained shut, any boat would be dragged over the edge of the waterfall by the tremendous power of the rushing water. What an ingenious security system, he thought.

The entrance to the tunnel was further secured by a large metal portcullis, which was open, allowing the barge to pass through. But once inside, it was swiftly shut, leaving the tunnel in semi-darkness. The sudden drop in temperature made the boys shiver, which was exacerbated by the droplets of cold water dripping on their heads from the tunnel roof above. The barge, still being driven forward by the force of the current, made good headway, and within a few minutes a patch of daylight appeared at the far end. The shadow on the bow of the barge gradually lightened and moved slowly towards them as they exited the darkness of the tunnel and entered into the daylight once again.

Nothing could have prepared the boys for the remarkable vision they were about to witness. In front of them stood a castle towering up above a craggy island situated in the middle of an emerald green lake, about a mile across. The whole was completely encircled by a continuous vertical wall of pinkish, blue, and yellow rock stretching skyward. The only form of light in this vast subterranean world was the sky above, softly framed by the vegetation growing around the side of what appeared to be the eye of a massive volcano. The sun shone down, illuminating this mysterious hidden world and reflecting like gold on the copper-clad roofs of the castle's six towers. The captain informed them that they were deep inside an ancient volcano where for centuries their ancestors had mined copper.

As the crew tethered the barge to a pontoon on the river bank, the captain went into the cabin to wake Izzy from her enforced slumbers. She was rather subdued, and after apologising profusely to him for her earlier outburst, re-joined the boys with Bella, to disembark.

The captain led them through the gates of the palace, accompanied by several men-at-arms who escorted them into a small circular courtyard before taking their leave. In the centre of the paved area was a huge oak tree, gnarled and craggy with age. Izzy couldn't help noticing the sweet scent of jasmine in the air, reminding her of Aunt Gorawen's garden. A table and three cushioned seats were neatly set out ready for the palace's guests, and refreshments had been laid. The captain beckoned them to sit and partake of the fare. On the ground were two pewter bowls, one filled with water and the other with meat, obviously for Bella. She needed no encouragement and helped herself.

The captain bowed his head towards them and said, "I will inform his Majesty of your arrival." He begged leave, and disappeared through an archway in one of the alcoves.

George couldn't contain himself any longer, so while stuffing himself with food, he described to Izzy in graphic detail their journey upriver to the waterfalls, narrowly defying death, and the mysterious tunnel that eventually led them here.

After a short time, the captain reappeared and came to Izzy saying, "If it pleases you, my lady, could you accompany me to his Majesty's chambers."

Dan immediately got to his feet and exclaimed crossly, "What! Surely he wants to see us together? Why would he want to see my sister alone? This concerns all of us."

The captain turned to Daniel and politely replied, "His Majesty has asked an audience with the Lady Isabella only."

To Dan's surprise, considering Izzy's demeanour a few hours ago, she turned to him and said, "Don't worry, Dan, I will speak for all of us … besides, I've got lots of questions of my own to ask his Majesty."

She rose from her seat, curtsied mischievously towards the boys, and followed the captain through the archway. Bella attempted to follow, but Izzy turned and glared at her. She lowered her head, and letting out a quiet squeal returned to join the boys, much to Dan's surprise.

Izzy was led through a series of corridors and up several flights of stairs until finally they arrived at a door where two guards in armour stood. The captain knocked on the door and a voice from within said "Enter." He opened the door for Izzy then closed it quietly behind her. Her breath was taken away by the beauty of the circular room. It was filled with furniture made from exotic woods and curved bookshelves lining the circular wall, housing thousands of books. She noticed two Irish Setters, just like Bella, lying peacefully asleep on the floor in front of a stone fireplace.

She stood nervously in the centre of the room for a moment; her earlier display of boldness in front of the boys had now deserted her. Standing with his back to her on a balcony overlooking the lake, was the King. He turned to face her, and reaching out both arms walked towards her. "Welcome to my home, Isabella. I am so sorry for all the mystery and intrigue, but it was vital for your safety."

Standing before her was a handsome, charismatic man, who appeared to be in his late thirties, early forties. She couldn't help noticing his beautiful head of flaming red hair, just like her own. He was dressed in a gown of red and gold brocade, and as he touched her shoulder, she was filled with a strange emotion. Here was a man she had never met before, yet strangely, felt she had known all her life. After all that had happened to her and her brothers during the past couple of days, with everyone continually evading their questions, why didn't she feel any anger towards him? She couldn't understand the calmness that seemed to engulf her body and mind.

He stood for a moment looking intently into her eyes, coughed nervously, and said, "Isabella, I am your father."

Izzy froze in a state of shock and stood in silence looking down at the floor, trying to take in what he had just told her. She raised her head and stared at him without saying a word, then began violently shaking her head.

"No, no, no … this is a bad dream … I will wake up in a moment … of course it is … it must be …"

"It is true, my darling Isabella … you are my daughter."

Izzy's voice began to rise. "It's not true … it can't be … no, you're mistaken … I'm Izzy Moorefield, I was born in Manchester."

He attempted to put his arms round her in the hope of calming her down, but she pushed him away with the flat of her hands. Without warning, she found her inner anger, and screaming hysterically hit out at his chest with clenched fists. He seemed shocked, almost puzzled by her reaction, but due to an innate reflex to defend himself, grabbed hold of her wrists. Izzy's whole body was trembling. Not being able to show her anger with her fists, she glared at him, her eyes wide open. Then he felt her body go limp, and as he released his grip on her wrists she dropped slowly to the floor. He knelt beside her on one knee and shook his head. He was completely baffled as to why she had reacted so violently and had no idea what to do next. His concentration was broken by a commotion going on outside the room, punctuated by the screams of a woman.

He looked up and glanced towards the door as it burst open. A young woman rushed in wearing a hooded cloak. It was the mysterious rider from the hunting lodge. She shouted at the King, "You oaf, Arthur! What did I tell you!" She pushed him angrily with her foot and knelt down close to Izzy's motionless body, caressing her face affectionately with her hand. "I knew we should have got my mother here to explain to the child, but no, you had to do it your way."

Arthur slowly got to his feet and gazed at her in bewilderment. She looked up at him with fury in her green eyes and said, "You have no idea of the power of a woman's emotions, have you!" Gazing down at Izzy tenderly, she brushed her hair from her face. "Especially one so young and sensitive as our beautiful daughter."

6

The Truth Behold

The small hooded figure of a woman walked through the dim oil-lit corridor of the palace. She stopped at a door where two men-at-arms were chatting to each other as they guarded the entrance. She stood silently in front of them for a moment, then lowered her hood. They immediately stopped chatting and stood to attention One of the guards bowed his head and opened the door, allowing her to pass unchallenged into the room. After taking a few steps inside, she turned back towards the guards and instructed them: "We are not to be disturbed. You are forbidden to allow anyone to pass, even the King. Do you understand?"

The guards both nodded in compliance for fear of the consequences of disobeying Lady Gorawen, and hurriedly closed the door behind her. To make quite sure no one could force their way into the room, she turned the large iron key in the heavy-duty lock and placed it deep inside the pocket of her cloak. She then removed her cloak and draped it gently at the bottom of the bed where Izzy lay fast asleep. After quietly whispering one of her special little verses, the oil lamps and the laid sticks and logs in the hearth ignited, bathing the room in a soft warm glow.

Deep in thought she gazed down at her sleeping granddaughter. This was going to be an awkward conversation between them. She really didn't know what to expect. The girl she had known and loved for the past sixteen years was a calm and considerate child most of the time, a little stubborn maybe, but in the end, always putting others' needs before her own.

Gorawen moved silently towards the window, opened it wide and walked out onto the balcony. She looked down to see the light coming from Arthur's room, directly below her. The orange glow from the oil lamps reflected onto the back of the figure leaning on the handrail. It was Arthur, no doubt feeling sincere regret at what damage he had done by being so hasty to reintroduce himself to his daughter before anyone else.

Now it was up to her to sort out his majesty's mess and reunite Izzy with her real mother and father in a more civilised way, as she had initially planned. Without further ado she closed the window, and stepping back into the room, pulled out two glass phials from a leather pouch hanging from the belt around her waist, and placed them on the table next to the bed. She emptied the pink liquid contents from one phial into a jug of water and gave it a stir with a small dagger, also taken from her waist belt. Grabbing the other phial from the table, she removed the cork stopper, sat on the bed beside Izzy, and wafted it from side to side under her nose.

Izzy slowly opened her eyes and without warning, sat bolt upright, almost knocking the phial from Gorawen's hand. She scrunched up her nose and closed her mouth in an attempt to evict the pungent vapour from her airways. Gorawen placed the cork back into the phial and said warmly, "Aah, there you are, Izzy."

Izzy, seeing her aunt sitting beside her on the bed, cried, "Oh, Aunt Gorawen ... it was a dream after all." Believing she was at home, she threw her arms around her neck and said, "Thank goodness ... what a terrible nightmare I've had." But slowly, looking round and not recognising her surroundings, reality began to creep in and she gradually released her grip from Gorawen's neck, slumping back onto the bed in the sudden realisation that the last few days had actually happened. "Where are we?" she asked. Shuffling her body up from the bed she rested her back against the headboard and stared coldly at her aunt for answers.

Gorawen seized the jug from the table and filled a glass with the elixir she had prepared. She handed it to her and said, "Before I answer any of your questions, Izzy, and I know you have many, please drink this – it will help you to relax while I tell you the truth."

"Help me to relax? After what the boys and I have been put through these past few days? Do you really think drinking your special brew is going to make it all better, like some sort of sticking plaster to hide my pain?"

Gorawen could understand why Izzy was so angry and upset, but if they were both going to get through this in one piece, it was vital for her to calm down, and drinking her specially prepared brew would do the trick. But Izzy pushed it away, spilling some of it over the bed linen.

"Anyway, what are you doing here?" Izzy asked sullenly. "And more important, how the hell did you get here?"

Gorawen was beginning to lose patience. After all, this confrontation was none of her doing, it was Arthur's rashness that had forced them into this situation. She could feel her irritation rising to the surface, so to Izzy's surprise she drank all of the elixir meant for her, and carefully refilled the glass. "You see, Izzy," she said calmly, taking another sip, "it's perfectly harmless. I promise to tell you the truth and try to answer all your questions, but only if you drink this for me. Then we can have a civilised conversation without any shouting."

Izzy gave in, snatched the glass from her aunt and drank it down in one gulp. Gorawen took the glass from her and placed it back on the table. Looking at her with a smile, she said, "There, that's better, isn't it?"

It would take a few minutes to take effect, so Gorawen got up and walked over to the fireplace to place another log into the flames. She turned to face Izzy who, she hoped, by this time would have become a bit more amenable, and returned to sit beside her on the bed. "Now, before I answer any of your questions, I have something vital to tell you which will hopefully explain why you and your brothers were brought here in such secrecy."

Izzy nodded and tried to apologise for her earlier behaviour, but Gorawen interrupted her in mid-sentence by placing her finger to Izzy's lips. The elixir was obviously working, so she began her prepared speech.

"On this day sixteen years ago, a baby was born, in this very room, on this very bed. I know, because I delivered her myself. That baby was you, Izzy my darling. Bronwyn, your real mother, is my daughter ... and yes, Izzy, that makes me your grandmother."

Izzy sat back in complete silence. Her mouth opened as though to speak, but the elixir was doing its job. So Gorawen continued. "I remember that day very well. I was so proud of my daughter for bringing such a precious gift into the world. My first and only grandchild. I gave you to your father, Arthur, to hold, and while cradling you in his arms he walked to that balcony over there to show you his kingdom. That kingdom was Cuddfan, the island you arrived on just a couple of days ago, an island created by the great Celtic sorcerer, Myrddin. It was hidden from the rest of the world hundreds of years ago and is hidden still."

Izzy appeared to be a little confused, so Gorawen asked, "Do you remember as a child I told you stories of King Arthur?" Izzy nodded. "And

I told you that after a bloody battle in which Arthur was mortally wounded, Myrddin his sorcerer took him away to an island where he and his loyal knights were cured of their wounds and left to sleep in a hidden cave until the time came when his people would have need of him again."

"Yes, I do remember the story," Izzy replied, "but surely that's a myth, a fairy-tale?"

"No, my darling, it's true – well, most of it – maybe not quite as Hollywood tells it, but all the same he was and is real. He is your true father, Arthur, the warrior king of the Celts. He wasn't asleep in a cave below ground waiting to be called upon to save his people, as many chroniclers of the past would have you believe. The same magic used to heal his wounds made him immortal, and with a little help from Myrddin and his powers, the kingdom of Cuddfan was created, or as we Celts know it, the Otherworld. Arthur has ruled over Cuddfan for centuries.

"Everything was well in the kingdom until twenty years ago when he married Bronwyn and made her his queen. It wasn't a popular choice and many in power fought against the marriage. There were many violent uprisings, which Arthur tried to suppress. Then when you were born, he feared you could be forcibly taken from him and put to death by those who had more traditional views of how the kingdom should be run. Now, it is the tradition in the Celtic culture for the firstborn of any nobleman to be fostered to another family for the first few years of their life. Arthur was convinced that if he fostered you to a family in the kingdom, he could not be sure they would be able to protect you.

"So, I suggested to him that I would find a family in the New World. That way you would be safe and I could keep an eye on you as you grew up. He agreed, though very reluctantly, and only if I promised to bring you back to Cuddfan on your sixteenth birthday. Sadly, Bronwyn was so hostile to the idea that when I finally smuggled you out of the kingdom a few days after you were born, she left the apartments she shared with Arthur and moved into rooms at the far side of the palace with her ladies-in-waiting.

"Now he had lost his wife as well as his daughter. He was heartbroken, and over the years became a lonely and bitter man. He locked himself away from his subjects in this dingy old palace, regretting the day he had made that fateful decision to entrust you to me. He surrounded himself with a loyal group of warriors who, in revenge for those who had forced their king's hand, hunted down those who rose against him until he felt safe in the knowledge no one would ever oppose him again.

"You see, my darling Izzy, your father believes it's now safe enough for you to return to the kingdom in which you were born, and stand by his side in the hope that together you can restore stability to the kingdom. That is why, one year ago, I eventually agreed with him to make plans to engineer your return on your sixteenth birthday, but only if he took Bronwyn into his confidence and involved her in his plans."

"However, I have since learnt that although your father discussed your return with her, he changed his mind at the last minute and she was forbidden to see you until the stupid man had spoken to you himself. But he didn't count on my daughter's resolve. She heard from someone close to his household the date you were to return, and where you would stay overnight before being taken to the palace for his meeting with you. So much for his secret master plan!

"Bronwyn knew Arthur would tighten up security for your arrival, but she wanted desperately to see you, even if it was just a glimpse, so she secretly arranged with her friend Angharad to be smuggled into the hunting lodge. They both knew that Angharad's father wouldn't allow the queen anywhere near the lodge on the day of your arrival as he is very loyal to the king. Between them they hatched a plan which would allow your mother to secretly see you and hear your voice from behind the screen in the Great Hall.

"Unfortunately, a stable boy noticed Bronwyn's prize stallion in the stable and remarked, quite innocently, to the Master of Hounds, that the queen must be staying at the lodge. Angharad's parents got to hear of it and knew the queen must be hiding somewhere near the Great Hall – even so, the plan would have worked if you hadn't been drawn to the screen. And when you pushed your fingers through the fretwork, she just couldn't resist touching them. Such was the bond between you both, even after sixteen years of separation. You reacted to her touch in a way no one could have foreseen. Of course, her distress quite gave the game away. Angharad's parents intervened and locked her in her room until you and your brothers had left the lodge. But she managed to escape after overpowering the servant who brought her breakfast, and rode into you on the path just as you were leaving. After returning to the palace, and discovering what your father had done to you with his crass behaviour, she immediately summoned me here to act as an intermediary and bring some form of normality back to Arthur's outlandish plan. And so here we both are."

Gorawen paused and looked at Izzy, trying to gauge her reaction to her story. But Izzy looked back at her with a cold stare and pulled her hands away. She had heard enough and said mockingly, "That's a heart-warming story, Aunt Gorawen, worthy of any fairy-tale. Or am I supposed to call you 'grandmother' now?"

"Alright, Izzy my dear, if it's just a fairy-tale, how on earth did you get here?" Gorawen asked.

Izzy buried her head in her cupped hands and screamed. After a short pause she raised her head and stared into Gorawen's eyes. "Ok, if it's true, why on earth didn't you tell me when I visited you at home? Over the year that you planned this so-called reunion, you must have had lots of chances to tell me. And why involve Dan and poor George?"

"Would you really have believed me if I had told you at home?" asked Gorawen. "You're having a hard time believing me now – and that's after you have witnessed the magic of this land at first hand."

Izzy's icy stare began to thaw and her shoulders drooped. Gorawen took her hand in hers once more. "Look, my darling, you have had a distressing few days in which your world has been turned upside down. I don't blame you for not believing me, but I had no alternative. I arranged for Daniel and George to accompany you in the hope they would give you their support when you most needed it – have you not all become closer in the last few days?"

"Well, yes, you could say that," agreed Izzy, "but poor George – the magic of this damned kingdom has deprived him of his only form of communication. And what is it about this wretched island that prevents anything electrical from working?"

"Ah well, you see, when Myrddin created Cuddfan, he foresaw that the invention of electrical and ultimately electronic devices would eventually cause the downfall of man. Right or wrong remains to be seen. But he created a kind of forcefield around the island that would stop any electrical device from working here, thus hoping to prevent the kingdom's discovery by the modern world."

"Ok. If I'm to accept my true parentage, what about my adopted parents, they must be so worried by now. Have you told them what's happened to us and where we are?" Izzy asked.

"Of course I have, my darling. While you and the boys were being transported to Cuddfan, I sat James and Alison down in my house and told them the truth. They had always been a bit unconvinced about your parentage when I took you to them as a baby. And before you ask, they have, after some persuasion from me, accepted that you will stay here and take up your rightful place with your father."

"What! Hang on a minute," exclaimed Izzy. "I don't mind getting to know my real parents, but I'm certainly not staying here for the rest of my life, no way! And what plans do you have for Dan and George? Are they destined to be trapped here in this kingdom for the rest of their lives too?"

"Oh, my dear Izzy," replied Gorawen tenderly, "please credit your loving grandmother with some compassion for your adopted family's welfare. After all, they brought you up as I asked."

"That's all well and good, but no one has considered me in all this. I happen to be very happy as Izzy Moorefield living in Manchester, thank you very much!"

"I know, Izzy. I hear what you're saying. But listen to me. You can return to Manchester any time you want! All you have to do is summon me here, just as your mother does, and I will transport you back to the New World at the drop of a hat. Then I can bring you home again when you're ready to return. Look, I have persuaded James and Alison to take a month's holiday. As a matter of fact, they are flying to Rome as we speak. By the time they return to North Wales, *Nicole* and the boys will be waiting for them in Menai Bridge, just as if nothing had happened."

Izzy pondered for a few seconds, got up from the bed and walked to the window. Peering out into the darkness of her new world, she looked upwards beyond the eye of the volcano through Myrddin's shimmering veil to a starlit sky beyond. Turning to face her grandmother, she asked bluntly, "Do you promise to return me, Dan, and George to our own world if I decide not to stay here permanently in Cuddfan?"

"Of course, my child. I will abide by your decision either way. Look, as James and Alison will be away for a month, why not give yourself that time to make up your mind? I have already squared it with them and they understand you need time to get to know your real parents, so why not treat it as a holiday? If in the end you decide not to stay, I will make sure you and the boys return home on *Nicole* – I promise!"

"Ok," Izzy replied slowly, "I will stay here with the boys for one month as you wish. But only one month, no more!"

Gorawen was overjoyed she had finally persuaded Izzy to stay, even if it was only for four weeks. She had done her part and now it was up to Arthur and Bronwyn. Walking over to her granddaughter she held out her arms and said affectionately, "Now come and give your grandmother a big hug."

They embraced, and as they did so, Izzy whispered into her ear, "If you break your promise to me, I will never, ever, forgive you." Gorawen nodded and kissed her on the cheek.

Pulling away from Izzy she said, "Now, I must release your real parents from their misery and tell them what we have agreed." She retrieved her cloak from the bed and placed it around her shoulders with a confident swoosh. She took the key from her pocket, and as she turned the latch she looked back at Izzy with a smile. "You rest now, my dear, and I will return here in one month to ask you for your decision. If you need to speak with me before that day, ask your mother, and she will summon me to your side."

Gorawen calmly opened the door, and hiding the smug grin on her face for achieving the impossible, left the room. As the door closed behind her, Izzy was left on her own to consider her past. And contemplate her future.

Arthur was in his chamber, nervously pacing up and down like an expectant father when Gorawen crept unnoticed into the room. Bronwyn was sitting quietly in a chair in the corner, watching her husband with folded arms and, if looks could kill, Cuddfan would now be without their king. Gorawen coughed loudly to attract their attention and announced, "I should give her an hour or two before you attempt to talk to her again, my dears. She has agreed to stay for one month to get to know you both, then she will decide on her own terms whether to settle here or not."

The frosty atmosphere in the room immediately warmed with Gorawen's news. Bronwyn got up from her chair and threw her arms around her mother. "Thank you, thank you, Mother. I knew *you* would sort this mess out," she said, while Arthur looked mortified.

"Now, now, Bronwyn dear," Gorawen replied, "you can be a mother again, but remember, you are also a queen, so if you want your daughter to remain in Cuddfan, you must forget your differences with Arthur and be seen by all as a loving couple once more. You must both come together in harmony for your daughter's sake. I have done my bit, so it's up to you both to persuade her to stay indefinitely. But be gentle with her – she is not a girl, or should I say a woman, to be trifled with. I fear she has inherited both her parent's traits, good and bad."

As she walked towards the door to leave, she brushed past her daughter and whispered in her ear, "Don't be too hard on Arthur, my sweet. I know he can be frustrating at times, but then," she sighed, "he is a man. And he does love you very much." With that, she opened the door and disappeared down the corridor.

Arthur rushed over to Bronwyn and putting his arms round her waist said warmly, "Can you ever forgive me for what I've done?"

Bronwyn took his hands and held them tenderly. "The only way to melt away the frost between us is for you to grant me my only wish, dear husband. Allow me to see Izzy on my own, just for a moment, and I won't ask anything else from you. After seeing her at the hunting lodge I just want to hold her in my arms and feel her in my heart again."

Looking deep into her eyes Arthur replied eagerly, "Yes, of course, my darling, if it means we can be together again as man and wife. Go, go now, and tell our daughter from me how sorry I am for being such a fool."

Since being told of her daughter's return a year ago, Bronwyn had dreamed of this moment. Now she couldn't wait a minute longer and ran with lightning steps into Izzy's room, taking her completely by surprise. They stood in silence. Words could not describe her feelings at that moment as with tears of joy she ran towards Izzy and finally embraced the daughter she had lost on the day she was born.

7

Family Reunion

The courtyard was bathed in the flickering glow from several large oil lamps strategically placed on the ground to give warmth as well as light. Daniel and George, unaware of the drama that had unfolded in the rooms above, were seated in the courtyard with the captain when Izzy returned. Bella noticed her first and ran to her mistress's side.

"Oh Bella," Izzy cried as she bent down to stroke her, "what tales I have to tell you all!"

The captain immediately rose from his seat, knowing they would require some privacy. He bowed gracefully and took his leave. George, eager to tell Izzy about their tour of the palace while she was away, hit her with a tirade of facts and figures before she had a chance to sit down. Dan interrupted him in full flow.

"Georgie, I'm sure Izzy's got a few things to tell us herself before you fill her in on our little adventures with the good captain!" He got up from his chair and gave his sister a big hug. "Are you alright, Izzy? You've been gone so long we were beginning to think they'd locked you up and thrown away the key."

"Oh, I'm fine now, thank you, Dan. But if you had asked me that an hour ago, my answer would have been very different. Come on, let's all sit down and I will tell you the real reason why we've been brought here."

As Izzy relayed her incredible story to her brothers, she couldn't help feeling a little guilty at accepting her predicament without first asking them if they were prepared to stay on the island for a while longer. She was also very fearful of losing their love when they discovered their sister wasn't really their sister. For her, nothing could change the way she felt about them and she desperately hoped it would be the same for them. After several minutes Izzy finished her story and anxiously waited for their reaction. She needn't have worried. As Dan pulled her up from her chair and hugged her, he told her that he would always love his kid sister and would remain there for as long as it took. "Besides," he said, "it's not many guys who can say their sister is the daughter of the legendary King Arthur."

George asked if she could make him one of the Knights of the Round Table so he could go on a quest to slay real dragons. He didn't want to go home just yet because it was the best holiday ever.

The captain returned and stood in front of Izzy. He bowed and announced, "Their most noble majesties have asked me to inform you, my lady, that they would be most honoured if you and your brothers would join them at supper later this evening in their royal apartments."

Izzy turned to her brothers and asked, "Well, boys, would you like to meet King Arthur and Queen Bronwyn?"

The boys nodded eagerly. Izzy turned to the captain and said, "I think that's a yes, Captain! Look, I can't keep addressing you as 'captain'. You must have a first name?"

"'Tis Owain, my lady," he replied.

"Ah yes, forgive me, Owain, I seem to recall you did tell us when we first met. I've been introduced to so many new people lately, it's difficult to remember everyone's names."

"Not at all, Majesty" he replied politely.

"Well, Owain," Izzy announced, "would you please inform their most noble majesties we will be delighted to join them for supper. But we would welcome a little time to freshen up before I introduce my brothers to my parents."

"Of course, Majesty. The servants have already prepared your rooms and have laid out fresh clothes for each of you, so I will now find someone to escort you to your apartments." He bowed and took his leave.

"Don't they talk strange!" Dan remarked. "Oh, My Most Noble Majesty!" he jested, trying to imitate the captain.

"They're just being polite, Daniel," Izzy replied. "After all, your sister is royalty, don't you know!"

Daniel bowed to Izzy with a sweep of his hand and George, not sure exactly what was going on, followed his brother's lead and bowed too. Then in fits of laughter they bowed to each other and giggled loudly. It made Izzy incredibly happy that her brothers had rediscovered their humorous side, especially George. Their comic antics reminded her how very much she would miss them if she decided to stay on Cuddfan.

Resplendent in their newly acquired court clothes, Izzy, the boys, and Bella, approached the door to the king's private chambers. Although Izzy hadn't seen her father since their distressing meeting earlier that day, she felt quite at ease. Her brothers on the other hand were quite nervous at the thought of meeting such a legendary figure and stood back behind their sister. Two men-at-arms stood to attention and opened the door to reveal the richly furnished room beyond.

Arthur and Bronwyn were seated at the head of a rectangular table in the centre of the room; it was set with all manner of mouth-watering food and delicacies. They rose from their chairs and rushed over to welcome their guests. Before Izzy could introduce her brothers, Bella ran towards the two setters lying beside the hearth where the flames of a log fire warmed the room. As soon as the two dogs caught sight of Bella, they stood wagging their tails vigorously. Bella instinctively began nuzzling her head beneath their chins, letting out soft whimpering noises.

On seeing the dogs' behaviour, Arthur laughed, and turning to Izzy said, "We are not the only ones to be reunited with our family today."

Izzy looked puzzled, then realising the significance of her father's statement, smiled at him and raised her eyebrows at the pleasant surprise that her much-loved Bella had been born in the same place as herself.

"Yes, Izzy, it was I who sent you Bella on your tenth birthday," he informed her with a boyish grin.

The dog's antics had broken the ice, putting everyone at ease, and as Izzy introduced her brothers, the mood lightened from a reserved formal dinner to a relaxed family gathering. Because of George's handicap, Arthur and Bronwyn had thoughtfully placed his chair on the opposite side of the table from everyone else so he could read their lips. Throughout the evening they chatted to the boys and kept them entertained as though they too were family.

Izzy's thoughts, however, turned to her life spent growing up in the Moorefield's crazy household and the joy of long summer days spent sailing with family and friends aboard *Nicole*. During that afternoon when Gorawen had told her the truth about her parentage, she had almost certainly decided that there was no way she would even consider abandoning her carefree life as the daughter of James and Alison

Moorefield and replacing it with being the daughter of a king and queen in a land she knew nothing about. Yet, since being in their presence for just a few hours, she could not ignore the fact of their apparent love for her, especially her mother's, and the courtesy they had shown towards Dan and George. She wondered what sort of life she would be expected to lead if she decided to stay. Turning to her father she said, "I know very little about your history, Father, or the history of this land. I have so many questions I wanted to ask you tonight, but time has passed so quickly I fear some may remain unanswered."

Arthur smiled at her, and rising from his chair walked over to a wooden chest sitting on a table in an alcove. He pulled out a key from a leather bag hanging from his waist and unlocked it. The lid sprang open, and reaching inside he pulled out a parcel wrapped in velvet cloth and tied in a single bow with a silk ribbon. He brought it back to the table and returned to his seat. "Izzy," he said, "before I show you what is in this parcel, I would like to apologise to all of you seated around my table this very special night. I am truly ashamed of my actions for the way you were brought here, against your will, from your world to Cuddfan. I pray you will all forgive me." He turned to his daughter who was sitting next to him and continued, "To deny your mother the right to see you, her only daughter, until I had spoken with you was indefensible and selfish of me. I will understand if you hate me for what I have done to you both.

"But please, I ask one thing of you – do not judge the people of our hidden kingdom on the actions of its foolish king." He placed the parcel on the table, stood up, and pushing his chair away got down on bended knee. Bowing his head, he said humbly, "Will you please forgive me, daughter of mine?"

Izzy stood up from her chair and knelt beside him. Throwing her arms around his neck she said, "Oh Father, I could never hate you! You have proved to me tonight that you are not only worthy of being called a king, you are truly a man any daughter would be proud to call father. Now please, get up from your knees and be seated beside me. A king should never kneel to his subjects, not even if one of them is his daughter."

As they both took up their seats again, Bronwyn gently grasped Arthur's hand in hers and squeezed it affectionately, then kissing his cheek whispered, "Now I remember why I fell in love with you."

Daniel was touched by his sister's words and now saw Izzy, his nagging kid sister, in a new light. *Maybe* he thought *just maybe, one day she will make a great queen.*

Arthur coughed nervously and said, "Izzy, you asked me a moment ago of my own history. I was born a Celtic prince before the dawn of the 6th century, and like you I was fostered to another family at an early age, as was the way of our ancestors. By the time I was the age of Daniel here, I had fought and won my first battle. Since the day of my final conflict in 542, the stories of my life have been mutated by various chroniclers throughout the centuries, until the truth is now but a shadow. On the day Bronwyn told me of your forthcoming birth, I decided to draft a true account of the history of my life and that of my people."

He picked up the parcel from the table, untied the ribbon and opened the cloth, revealing a richly tooled bound book of soft red leather. Written on the cover in gold lettering were the words *The True Account of King Arthur and his People*. Placing it into Izzy's open hands, he continued, "There are blank pages at the end of this book for you to add your story, and maybe one day you will be able to put our history right with the rest of the world."

With an expectant smile, Izzy opened the cover of the book to peer through its beautifully illustrated pages. She turned to him and kissed him on the cheek. "Thank you, Father, I will treasure it always."

Bronwyn, noticing that George had fallen asleep, announced quietly to her husband, "Look at poor George, we have tired him out with all our chatter."

Arthur replied, "Well, it has been an emotional day for all of us, so perhaps we should retire and look to our beds for a restful night's sleep, in the knowledge we will awake refreshed to greet another day."

Everyone agreed wholeheartedly, and after wishing each other a fond goodnight, Daniel picked up his little brother and carried him out into the corridor to walk to their room a few doors away.

Izzy, being the last to leave, turned around to give her parents a warm hug, then thanking them for being so kind to her brothers, headed towards her room, closely followed by a sleepy Bella. Granny Gorawen, as she now called her, had brought Bella's basket and her favourite blanket from her house on Anglesey. There were also a few scraps of meat left in a bowl for her, which she devoured in seconds. Sniffing her rug, she climbed into her basket and turned in ever-decreasing circles before curling up in a ball and closing her eyes.

Izzy's bedchamber looked very cosy and inviting. In the dim candlelight she noticed the framed photograph of the Moorefields taken on holiday the year before, placed on a table beside her bed. She guessed that Granny Gorawen had dropped it off to make her feel at home when she had popped in to bring Bella's basket and blanket. She was totally exhausted. After all, as her father had said, it had been a very emotional day. The servants had laid out a white linen nightdress and robe for her at the bottom of the bed, so she quickly swapped her heavy evening gown for the more comfortable nightdress. The book her father had given her, and the inviting glow of the firelight, tempted her to curl up by the hearth and read for a while. She fell into the large comfy armchair and opened the book at the first page.

The fire in the hearth soon became embers, and the candles used to augment the light from the flames melted and formed a decorative alliance with the candlestick. Izzy finally fell asleep and her book lay on the floor beside her chair, where it had gradually slipped from her grasp as tiredness defeated her consciousness.

Without warning, the darkness of the room was infiltrated by a flickering light as a man dressed in household colours and armour entered her bedchamber, carrying a lantern in one hand and a sword in the other. He walked towards Bella's basket, knelt beside her, and felt her body with the flat of his hand. He then rose to his feet and turned towards Izzy, looking down at her sleeping body for a few moments as if reflecting on his next move. His sword twitched uneasily in his trembling hand as he hesitated, then swiftly returning it to the scabbard hanging from his belt, he bent down and shook her shoulder. "Lady, please awake, you are in mortal danger!"

Startled awake by the shadowy figure standing over her, and confused by her unfamiliar surroundings, Izzy cried, "What … what's happening? Who are you?"

"I am the night watchman of the palace, my lady. The king's life has been threatened by intruders and I am to escort you to his chambers to join him and the queen."

Still bemused and rubbing her eyes to focus, she asked blearily,

"Where is everyone?"

"They are all safe, my lady, but we must make haste so that we can search every room until we know the palace is secure."

Izzy asked him to wait for a moment while she grabbed her robe from her bed, but she noticed the man was becoming agitated at her slowness to heed his bidding and she wondered why Bella had not been wakened by the disturbance. Without warning, two roughly dressed men entered the room, and as one forcibly grabbed Izzy from behind, the other hit her across the face with his fist, knocking her unconscious.

He turned and yelled at the night-watchman, "We ain't got all night to swap niceties with 'er majesty!"

The night-watchman went to draw his sword, but the other man grabbed his wrist before he could pull it out fully and glared icily at him. "You'd better decide which side you're on, my friend!"

He scowled and pushed his half-drawn sword back into its scabbard. The man struggling to support Izzy's limp body hastily whispered to his rough companion, "Come on, we ain't got much time … tie her up and let's get out of here."

After binding Izzy's hands behind her back and tying a gag around her mouth, he thrust a sack over the top half of her body and secured it with cord. Then heaving her over his associate's shoulder, he checked the corridor and whispered, "All clear."

The other associate pushed the night-watchman forward towards the door with an angry jerk saying, "Now it's time to do your job – lead us to the tunnel so we can re-join our friends. Any funny business and 'er majesty gets this." He thrust a dagger in his face to show he meant business. Shutting the door cautiously they made their escape, passing the slumped, blood-stained bodies of the two guards they had despatched earlier.

As Izzy slowly regained consciousness, she could hear the muffled voices of her kidnappers through the thick rough sack. Her thin nightgown and wrap, offering little protection from the damp and cold, suggested they must be below ground. Her captors stopped in front of a heavy iron door. The night watchman was thrust forward again to do his job. He pulled out a key and unlocked it. The hinges were so rusted with age he had to use his shoulder to force it open, which it did with an eerie squeal. He stood silently aside while his two rough accomplices pushed past him to join their friends. Izzy sensed a chill breeze on her bare legs as they carried her out into open ground. Without any warning. she was thrust upright and felt the cold dampness of soil beneath her bare feet. As the sack was unceremoniously wrenched from her head, she attempted to scream out, but her cries for help were muted by the foul-smelling cloth they had stuffed in her mouth.

Izzy looked around at her surroundings and could see about thirty men, all roughly dressed and wearing hooded cloaks. A few metres away in the trees stood a string of saddled horses and a covered wagon. A man stepped forward from the shadows and stood facing her. His stare was as cold and threatening as his voice. "So, you are Arthur's daughter. I too have been waiting for your return, Majesty, and so has my master."

He took her chin in his rough hand and gripped it tight. "Oh, he will be pleased to see your little face, my dear. Pity about your poor dog though. Shame we had to put the poor thing down." He looked round to his men for a gratifying response and joined with them in the laughter. But not for long. Izzy kicked him between his legs with all her might. In agony, he fell to his knees, grabbing his nether regions with both hands.

"That's for Bella," Izzy muttered belligerently through her gag.

After a few seconds of stunned silence from his men, he shouted at one of them angrily. "Put her majesty in the cart … and tie her bloody feet up this time!"

As one of his men stepped forward to tie her feet, he stood up, and still flinching with pain drew his knife from its sheath and pointed it at Izzy's throat. "When my master has finished with you," he snarled, "I will make you sorry you did that! Now get her majesty in the cart before I do something I will later regret!"

8

Kidnapped

George jumped out of bed and strolled out onto his balcony. His stomach was telling him it must be near breakfast, but not having a working watch he had no idea of the time. After dressing, he opened the door and took a couple of paces into the corridor to find some food, almost tripping over the bodies of the two guards outside Izzy's room in his hurry to find something to eat. George at first thought they had fallen asleep until he saw the pool of blood on the cold tiled floor. Panicked, he ran into Dan's room screaming, wrenching the bedclothes off the bed in the hope of waking him. It didn't do much good, so he shouted into his ear. Poor George had to dodge his brother's heavy hand as he retaliated for being woken up. Finally, George got his message across and Dan ran out of his room to see the evidence for himself.

Coldness invaded his body as he cautiously stepped over the blood-stained lifeless corpses of the guards in the corridor. His mind filled with dread at the thought of what he might find beyond the door to his sister's room. He signalled George to hang back and turned the latch. Slowly pushing open the door he peered nervously inside. On discovering the room was empty, he screamed at George, who was peering round the doorway, to fetch Arthur. He felt an enormous sense of relief to find that Izzy had not succumbed to the same fate as the guards, but his thoughts now turned to the likelihood she had been kidnapped, and as he noticed her bed hadn't been slept in, he guessed her assailants had struck in the early hours of the morning.

Arthur burst into the room, closely followed by two guards and George.

"I think they've taken Izzy, sir," cried Dan. He pointed to the basket where Bella lay. "And they've killed Bella!"

George, in tears at the thought of his sister in danger, knelt beside

Bella and stroked her body. "I think she's still breathing, Dan," he sobbed.

Arthur turned to his guards and ordered one of them to fetch his physician, then to sound the alarm and ready his knights. "Where on earth is the night-watchman?" he shouted.

"He's nowhere to be seen, Majesty," replied the guard.

"Then search the palace for him, I want him here!" he roared. "He will answer with his life if something has happened to my daughter."

Bronwyn, on hearing the alarm, ran into the room to join the others. She was horrified and pleaded with Arthur to hurry and find her.

"I will leave no stone unturned in our search. It seems our night-watchman may have been privy to this heinous crime against our family. He will pay heavily for his treachery."

As Bronwyn turned to comfort George, the king's physician came through the door carrying a large bag. He was a man in his mid-sixties with greying hair and a short neatly trimmed beard. Still dressed in his nightgown and breathless from the climb up the stairs, he bowed and said, "Please accept my apology for my state of undress, Majesty, but your guard woke me from my sleep and I had no time to array myself suitably."

Arthur put his arm around his shoulder and steering him towards the basket where Bella lay, applauded him for his sense of urgency. "No matter, John, you did right to hasten here. I think someone has poisoned our noble Bella, but life is still in her heart. Please do everything possible to bring her back to us." As the physician bent down to examine Bella, Arthur turned to Bronwyn, who by this time was seated with the boys on Izzy's bed. "Let us leave John to his work and return to my apartments. There you can help me get ready to lead my men to find these villains and return Izzy to our household."

There was a lot of commotion within the royal apartments as extra guards were being stationed at all the entrances. As Arthur entered his day-chamber, his squire was ready to arm him. Bronwyn announced that she would ready herself for the pursuit too, but Arthur asked her to withdraw and take care of George while they were away. Bronwyn, however, was not a woman to be argued with, and Arthur knew that his request would fall on stony ground. Dan was also minded to join the chase and told the king so. Arthur appreciated that this was a crime against all of Izzy's family and that Dan would not be content staying behind in the palace to wait for news, so he consented. Before the king's squire could complete the task of arming his master, Arthur grabbed a small ivory horn hanging from the wall above the hearth and rushed out onto the balcony. He took a deep breath and blew into it, emitting one long, high-pitched note that reverberated around the valley.

What happened a few minutes later would stay with George for the rest of his life. From the top of the mountainside, the silhouette of an enormous winged creature flew towards the balcony and the source of the ear-piercing sound of the horn. George's heart was beating so fast he could feel it throbbing beneath his chest, and eager for a better view, crept slowly forwards to stand by Arthur's side.

Daniel stood with his mouth wide open in disbelief at what he was witnessing. As the creature came out of the shadows and into the early morning light, its features and size became apparent. It was a dragon, blood-red in colour and just as George had imagined, except for its size. Each wing must have been at least fifteen metres in length. It hovered in front of the balcony and George could feel the wind created by the raw power of the creature's wings as it flapped hard to keep its heavily armoured body airborne.

George looked up at Arthur, who was gazing into the yellow eyes of the dragon and nodding as though having a conversation with him. The dragon let out a piercing cry that echoed across the surface of the still waters of the lake. His great wings ceased beating, and twisting his body to face the rocks below he dropped like a tossed stone, disappearing from view. George rushed to the edge of the balcony and grabbed the rail with his hands, then looked downwards just in time to see the mighty creature stretching out its wings to hover millimetres above the surface of the water. With a mighty thump of its wings it then ascended skywards and evaporated into the downy clouds above the eye of the volcano.

Arthur's knights were assembled in the courtyard below as he, Bronwyn, Dan, and George walked down the steps to join them. Three horses stood already saddled for them and a young squire appeared and helped George into a covered wagon that held provisions and arms. As they mounted, Arthur passed comment to Daniel, "I hope you ride well, sir? I'm afraid we cannot hold back even for you."

"Please don't worry about me, your Majesty – I've been riding since I was five years old."

Once out of the palace they were joined by a man on foot holding the reins of his horse. "I have picked up their tracks, Majesty … there are at least thirty riders and a light wagon and by my calculations they have a good ten-hour lead over us." The man remounted and Arthur gave the command to move off.

Being bound and tethered to an iron ring in the bottom of a dirty old wagon was not precisely what Izzy had expected she would be doing when she fell asleep the night before. But she was Arthur's daughter, and her steel, grit, and determination to overcome adversity were winning through. Her thoughts went out to Bronwyn, who by now must have discovered her missing. It was unthinkable that she'd been snatched away from her mother so soon after being reunited.

The wagon stopped and she could hear orders being shouted out. The canvas that was covering her was pulled aside and the palace watchman, still in uniform, appeared. Gently he pulled her up into a sitting position. "We are stopping to eat, my lady, and I have been told to bring you some food." He put a wooden bowl containing some sort of broth onto the bare boards of the wagon, took out a knife and carefully cut the cord that bound her hands together.

With her hands free, she untied the gag and let out a sigh of relief to breathe normally again. Without warning she slapped the man in the face with the flat of her hand. "That's for Bella!" she cried.

Recoiling from her furious assault, he put his hand over his reddening cheek where her hand had so violently made contact and replied, "I suppose I deserved that." She scowled at him, and if looks could kill, he would have been struck dead. "But you judge me wrong, lady … I was supposed to poison your dog with the potion given me by my associates. Instead I replaced it with a sleeping draught so it would look as if it had been poisoned."

"You mean she is still alive?"

"I would hope so. I often take it myself when I have finished my night duties at the palace to aid my sleep during the daylight hours."

Izzy felt her rage towards him lessen after this welcome news. So Bella wasn't dead. She thought it must mean he had some redeeming qualities but she couldn't understand what had turned him. "Why are you doing this to me? Do you hate your king so much you would turn traitor?"

Thrusting the bowl into her hands and giving her a spoon from his bag he pleaded, "Please eat while you can, lady, we will not be stopping again for a while."

Izzy took the spoon from him and tasted the broth. At least it was hot, she thought, but not hot enough to stop her from shivering. On seeing Izzy's discomfort, he removed his thick woollen riding cloak and placed it around her shoulders. "Thank you," she said gratefully, "at least you show a little compassion towards me, unlike your companions. You have obviously nothing in common with these men."

"Please keep your voice down, lady," he begged. "If they hear you, they will gag you again, food or no food."

But Izzy was going to have her say, so lowered her voice to a whisper.

"Where are you taking me?"

"We are taking you to her."

"Her? Who is her?" asked Izzy

"I know not, my lady, but I am told she is a great sorceress."

"But what do I have to do with all this?"

Huw, suspecting that Izzy knew nothing of the history of Cuddfan, drew closer to her for fear of being overheard and asked, "Do you know anything of our history, lady?"

"I know a little from reading the first few pages of my father's book, but then you and your friends kidnapped me."

"They are no friends of mine, lady!" he replied.

"Please don't keep calling me lady, my name is Izzy."

"I am sorry, lady … augh … Izzy. My name is Huw. Would you like me to tell you a little of our history as I was taught it at school?"

"Well, yes, it might help me understand why I've been kidnapped!" she snapped.

"History has it, that after a great battle with invaders, in which Arthur was mortally wounded, Myrddin, the king's sorcerer, took him and his knights to Ynys Enlli to heal their wounds with his magic. That same magic also endowed Arthur and his knights with the gift of immortality. Myrddin, fearing for the future welfare of the Celtic nation, took rocks and soil from every corner of the island close by, named Ynys Mon and cast them into the great ocean. Then with his most powerful magic, he summoned up a fiery volcano from the depths of the sea that spewed out molten rocks into the air, and continued for seven days and nights, after which a virgin island was spawned, of the same manner as Ynys Mon with all its mountains, hills, forests, and rivers. He called the new land Cuddfan and shrouded the island in a veil of mist around its shores to hide the kingdom from the known world and protect it from invaders. Myrddin brought Arthur here together with his knights from Ynys Enlli. They had a great ship built and transported Celtic people and beasts from far and wide to live in peace in the new realm.

"Myrddin was so weakened by his work, he returned to Ynys Enlli to heal himself and restore his powers. Nimue, the Queen of Ynys Enlli and the keeper of the sacred sword Caliburn was an ambitious sorceress who secretly wanted to conquer Cuddfan for herself. She knew the only person to stand in her way apart from Arthur, was Myrddin. So, on his return, she tried to beguile him in the hope he would reveal the secrets of his magic to her. Myrddin knew that Nimue had an evil side to her because he had the gift of reading minds. But she overcame him one night with her beauty and cunning, and from their passionate union, a female baby was born. They named their daughter Creiddylad, and as she grew up, he began to teach her his magic.

Nimue became jealous of the attention he gave her, so Myrddin, fearing their daughter could be turned to evil ways by her mother, spirited her far away where she wouldn't find her. When Nimue discovered what Myrddin had done, she became full of rage and took up war with him. According to Brother Catamanus, who served Myrddin at the time, they fought for twenty days and twenty nights in catacombs below the ground with their magic. Finally, in hand to hand combat, Nimue surprised Myrddin from behind and held Caliburn to his throat. Myrddin, realising his fate, prised the sword from her hand and thrust the mighty blade through his own body and deep into the heart of Nimue, turning their intertwined bodies instantly to ice. When Brother Catamanus informed Arthur of his death, he was so mourned that he lost himself to his people for twenty years."

"Yes, yes, yes, that sounds very interesting but you're still not telling me why I've been kidnapped," Izzy said impatiently.

Just at that moment a hooded figure appeared in the doorway and interrupted their conversation. "We're breaking camp soon, so get her majesty ready!"

The night-watchman shouted back at him, "She hasn't finished her food yet, give her a little more time."

"Them's your orders. Do as you're told, or else!" the man shouted back.

"I'm sorry, Izzy, we had better do as they say," said the watchman as he took the bowl from her and re-tied her wrists.

"But why take me?" Izzy insisted. "I am only the king's daughter – I have no magic powers."

Huw continued to try to answer her question.

"Apart from Nimue and Myrddin, Caliburn, the sacred sword of the Celts, can only be wielded by Arthur as king. Anyone who tries to grab any part of it in their hands to use its great power will be burnt. You are the daughter of Arthur, and you have inherited the right to hold Caliburn in your hands without injury. Thus Meyric's master believes only you can pull the great sword from the bodies of Myrddin and Nimue and release her from her frozen tomb. You are also the key to departing from Cuddfan, as only you have the power to sail beyond the great mist to Ynys Enlli in your ship, *Nicole*."

It was all beginning to make sense to Izzy now. The future of Cuddfan was at stake. The only way she could stop their plan would be to escape … maybe with the help of the palace watchman? But could she turn Huw away from the treacherous path he had chosen? She was about to ask for his help when the man responsible for driving the wagon came over to tell them they were moving off. It was then that the palace watchman did something quite unexpected to Izzy's mind. He offered to swap places with the driver, and as it was a somewhat uncomfortable experience driving a wagon over rough terrain, he didn't wait to be asked a second time and enthusiastically agreed to the deal. Although this wouldn't make it any easier for Izzy to free herself from her captors as there were four of their number on horseback behind the wagon, it would at least give her a chance to try and coax him into helping her.

Arthur was closer than the villains had expected as he was resolved they would not break their pursuit to rest either man or beast. As they broke through a clearing in the forest, the mighty dragon that George had encountered at the palace, landed in front of their path. Arthur dismounted and walked to meet the creature. To Dan's reckoning, they appeared to be conversing with each other, but he could hear no sounds coming from their mouths. Arthur turned and remounted his horse as the dragon once again took to the skies.

Arthur announced, "A small group of them have attempted to take *Nicole* from her anchorage in the bay, but were stopped by the bravery of the men Owain placed on her for security. According to one of the prisoners, they were to take the boat to Rhosneigr where they planned to meet up with their main party, led by a man called Meyric – the man responsible for Izzy's capture – and they were going to use her to sail to Ynys Enlli. Now that I know what they are about, we can plan her rescue."

"How far are we from Rhosneigr?" asked Daniel.

"Only a few hours' riding from here. It looks as though they were trying to make us believe they were travelling in the opposite direction, then double back to their planned meeting place, but we shall be waiting for them."

"How can you be sure he's telling the truth, Arthur?" asked Dan.

"Because if we found out he was lying, his life would be ended. The thing you have to learn about evil men, Daniel, is that they will never needlessly sacrifice their own lives for their masters."

As Arthur's horse stamped his hooves in the dust in eagerness to continue the chase, Arthur responded to Dan's doubt. "Just to make sure, Bedivere, take six of your best men with Master Goode and follow their track. If you come near them, lie low in secret till we all meet at Rhosneigr." Bedivere, one of Arthur's most trusted and courageous knights, picked out six of his men, and acknowledging his king's bidding rode off, following the lead of Master Goode, deeper into the forest. Arthur pressed his men boldly onwards at a gallop and headed towards Rhosneigr.

Izzy's captors meanwhile were keeping far away from the main tracks to avoid being seen, which meant they had to travel over the rough terrain of the virgin forest floor and use the cover of the trees to remain undetected. The wagon lurched violently from side to side as the wheels negotiated the stony ground. Izzy's ride in the cart was becoming extremely unpleasant, especially as Meyric had forced the watchman to re-tether her hands after their short break. At least she had been spared the discomfort of a gag, which meant she could talk to the watchman. However, being minded that there were four riders behind the wagon observing her every move, she had to make sure that any conversation she had with him went unnoticed, for fear of being silenced for good.

With every sway of the wagon, Izzy cunningly moved her body closer and closer to the driving seat until she could go no further. "What is your name, watchman?" she asked softly.

He was a little surprised to hear her voice from the back of the wagon but welcomed the chance to talk with her. "I am known as Huw."

"Are you married, Huw?"

"I was, but my wife died some eighteen months ago."

"I'm so sorry to hear that," Izzy replied sympathetically.

"Why should you be sorry? It was your mother's doing that she died," he retorted sourly.

"My mother … what did she have to do with your wife's death?"

"My wife was one of the queen's handmaidens, but when she became heavy with child, she was banished from court because the queen would have no reminders of babies, due to you being taken away when you were born. I pleaded with the king, but he refused to argue the point with the queen."

Izzy was still mystified as to why her mother's actions, although heartless, would have caused the death of Huw's wife.

He continued, "I was on duty the night my wife gave birth at home. She was alone, and she and the baby died because of complications. If she had not been dismissed from the queen's household she would have had the right to have the court physician in attendance, and I would now have a son and wife to go home to. It's alright for him and his kind, they are immortal, but we, his people, live only one brief life. Although I remained loyal to their majesties in service, my heart is full of hatred and I vowed that one day I would have my vengeance. Then when I was petitioned by Meyric to assist his men with your kidnap, I felt it was the perfect way to seek atonement for my loss."

All this time while talking, Huw had kept his cold gaze fixed straight ahead, but now, turning to look over his shoulder at Izzy he said, "Now, being close to you and seeing your kindly nature and innocence, I feel greatly ashamed for what I have done."

Izzy was stunned by Huw's sad tale and felt as though she wanted to give him a hug to make it all better. But she knew that the reality of their situation was not part of a fairy tale; this was real life and happening now. She didn't really know what to say next, but feeling that Huw's regret could be harnessed into helping her escape, she said with genuine compassion, "I am so sorry you lost your wife and son, Huw, but I'm sure my mother would never have knowingly set out to harm them in the way it turned out. I will ask my father to exonerate you of your crime towards me if you would help me escape."

"You ask a great deal of me. I doubt your father will wipe away my sins so easily." There was a long pause while Huw debated in his mind what he should do. "I no longer care about my own life now my wife has gone, but if I can, I will assist you to restore your freedom."

For the first time, Izzy thought she could trust him, especially as he would be putting his own life at risk if their attempt failed.

"We will have to choose our time wisely," continued Huw, "these men are not those you would want to cross. They would commit murder for the price of a flagon of ale."

The daylight was beginning to fade as Arthur and his men arrived secretly and quietly in Rhosneigr. They didn't want to alert the local populace to their presence so they dismounted and tethered the horses, together with the wagon, to lines some distance away under cover of the trees in a small wooded glade, then kept themselves hidden amongst the sand dunes that overlooked the beach.

Arthur made it plain that Izzy's safety must be assured before an all-out attack could be launched. They had a good view from their hiding place of the road running down the centre of the long, curved bay. It led all the way down to the water's edge, and Arthur placed his men along the beaches on both sides for an ambush. He sent a handful of men into the fishing village to acquire a local sailboat with orders to take it out to the peninsular. In the darkness, a light from a lantern on the boat's mast coming from the sea would be mistaken for *Nicole*. Arthur knew that Meyric's men, not apprised of the failure of their fellow conspirators to seize *Nicole*, would be expecting to see her approaching from the south, so his idea was to give them false comfort that everything was going to plan. He did not want them to have any notion that he had knowledge of their intentions.

Although Bronwyn, George, and Daniel would have liked to witness the resulting battle close at hand, Arthur's orders were clear; they were to stay at the rear with the wagon and horses. Woe betide anyone who sought to challenge his authority in these situations. Although counsel from his most senior knights was often sought by him, as a seasoned warrior and respected commander his decisions were final and his orders were carried out by his men without question when planning an engagement.

Even though the wagon had stopped at the forest edge, Izzy could hear waves breaking on the shore. Whispering, she asked Huw if they had arrived at Rhosneigr.

"Yes, Izzy, and we must make your escape from here or not at all."

As soon as it was completely dark, Meyric and his men broke cover from the safety of the sheltering trees and led his men down to the beach. He ordered them to rein in their horses and dismount. Walking forward a few paces onto the soft sand, he looked out into the pitch blackness of the sea. One of his men passed him a lighted lantern that he hoisted up into the air with the aid of a spear. One of Arthur's men aboard the decoy boat lit his lamp, and hoisting it aloft, returned their signal; they began to sail shoreward slowly so not to cast suspicions on the identity of the vessel.

The men guarding Izzy from behind the wagon also dismounted and moved forward on foot, leaving their horses grazing on the vegetation at the edge of the trees. Huw saw his chance, so without hesitation he cut Izzy's bonds and helped her from the back of the wagon before placing her astride the saddle on one of the horses the guards had left behind. So as not to spook the horse and alert Meyric of their attempt, he gently put his foot into the stirrup and steadily raised himself up onto the horse's back behind her. Putting his arms around her body and taking hold of the reins, he whispered in her ear, "Hold tight, Izzy," and kicking the back of his heels into the horse's flanks, launched the animal into a full gallop out of the forest and onto the beach.

Everyone was caught by surprise. Arthur could only see the shadowy shape of a rider in the darkness, so he had no idea Izzy was heading straight towards him. Meyric realised what was happening but remained unflustered. He grabbed a crossbow from one of his men, and placing a foot in the deadly weapon's stirrup, drew the heavy string back till it clicked into the mechanism of the trigger. He placed a bolt in the groove and took aim. The insignia on Huw's household tabard was a perfect target even in the darkness, and pulling the trigger he released the lethal shaft on its way, striking Huw squarely in the back with a sick resounding thud. As Huw felt the sharp pain of the bolt piercing his back, he shouted in Izzy's ear to keep going, then losing control of his limbs he released his grip on the reins and slid from the horse's back onto the soft sand, pushing the bolt even deeper into his body. Meyric's men let out a loud cheer of delight. But Izzy, instead of continuing her flight to safety, pulled up on the reins and turning the horse in the opposite direction, rode back to where Huw was lying. She dismounted and knelt beside him, trying to pull him to his feet, but he was too heavy for her. Reeling from the pain, he looked into her eyes as she lifted his head from the damp sand. "Please, please go, Izzy. I am mortally wounded, you do no good to stay."

As Huw took his final breath, something buried deep inside Izzy's being surfaced, and with a cold determination she withdrew Huw's sword from its scabbard, got to her feet and turned her icy gaze towards Meyric. Summoning up all the courage from within her slight body, she ran towards him, dragging the point of the sword in the sand behind her. Meyric calmly started to reload the crossbow, but he fumbled and the bolt slipped from his grip onto the ground. Frantically he dropped to his knees to retrieve it.

Izzy was just a few steps away from him when she took the sword in both hands and let out a blood-curdling scream as she raised it above her head. Meyric looked up towards her as Izzy took an almighty leap into the air, transmitting the full force of her anger down through the sword. But at the last second she hesitated, stopping short a few centimetres above his shoulder. Meyric saw his chance and hurriedly got to his feet. He discarded the crossbow and grabbed the blade of the sword in his hand, at the same time as an arrow pierced his neck and exited the other side spraying blood over Izzy's face. He slumped to his knees in surprise. With the life force of his savage heart draining away, he placed his hands over his wound to stem the blood, and looked into her eyes with a black stare before his lifeless body slumped onto the sand.

Galvanised by Izzy's scream, it was Arthur who had unleashed an arrow from his bow towards Meyric's neck. Then, giving the order for his men to attack, he ran to his daughter's side. Izzy stood in silence, shivering, the sword still gripped in her hand, looking down at Meyric's lifeless body. She slowly turned to face her father, shaking her head in disbelief at the thought of what she had nearly done, then returned her glance towards Meyric's body once again. Arthur, seeing his daughter's state of mind, gently prised the sword from her trembling hand and threw it to the ground saying softly, "It's alright, Izzy, you are safe now." Stunned by her overwhelming emotions, she collapsed into her father's arms. He cradled her blood-stained body in his arms and carried her to safety.

All around them was bedlam as Arthur's men swept through what was left of Meyric's horde. Some had tried to escape the way they came, but Bedivere and his knights were waiting for them. Most gave themselves up without a fight once they had knowledge of Meyric's death. Arthur's prophecy to Daniel that evil men will not die for their masters, proved right.

As Arthur neared the place where Bronwyn and the boys were waiting, Izzy regained consciousness. Still in her father's arms, she looked at him with entreating eyes. "Please take care of Huw's body, Father. I know he was involved in my kidnap, but in the end he sacrificed his life trying to save me."

Considering Huw's treachery against his family, Arthur was shocked by his daughter's forgiving nature, but not wanting to distress her any further, cautiously replied, "You must not distress yourself with such issues, Izzy. I am more concerned with *your* wellbeing. He lies dead where he fell and any retribution for his sins against us is now beyond our judgement."

Izzy, however, was having none of it. She wanted to be sure before she left this place, that Huw's body would be treated with reverence and not discarded like the rest of Meyric's men. Calmly she declared, "I can walk now. Please, Father, put me down …"

Considering her troubled state of mind, he was startled by her announcement, but reluctantly stopped and placed her feet carefully on the soft sand. She was still shivering from cold and exhaustion and wobbled on her feet before regaining her balance. Worried for her condition, Arthur stretched out his arms to support her, pleading with her that it was imperative to get her to the warmth of the wagon.

"I will not leave this place until you make a promise to me that you will treat Huw's body with respect!" she exclaimed fervently.

He nodded. "Yes, of course, if that is what you wish."

She continued, "and see to it that he is laid to rest with his wife and son, wherever that may be."

He nodded again. "Yes, Izzy, I promise."

She persisted, "And promise to bury him with the full honours that are due to him for saving your daughter's life."

Exasperated finally, he exclaimed, "*Yes*, Izzy, I promise! Now let's get you out of here before you die a death yourself and I have to arrange your funeral." Without wasting any more time, he picked her up in his arms and walked hurriedly towards the wagon where Bronwyn and the boys were waiting anxiously for her safe return.

9

Arthur's Secret Plan

Like an expectant father awaiting the birth of his first child, Arthur paced nervously in his private chambers waiting for news of Izzy's condition from the court physician, who at that moment was in her room with the queen. Dan and George, knowing their sister was at last in safe hands, were out on Arthur's balcony taking in the glory of the early morning sunrise.

Arthur had increased security on the royal apartments by trebling the guard. He certainly didn't want a repeat attack on his family. His instinct told him that apart from Huw, someone else in his household was passing on information to his enemies. Although Huw had been a party to Izzy's kidnap, Meyric must have had previous knowledge of her return, and that was known only to a handful of Arthur's closest associates. As soon as he had returned to the palace, he had put his first minister to work questioning the prisoners, looking for any clue that would lead him to the traitor. If there was anyone who could get information out of them, it was him. He had no need for physical torture. Men will say anything to halt the pain, although not necessarily the truth. He used the old ways, taught to him by the ancient Celtic sorcerers like Myrddin, using his mind to cause extreme anguish.

The ominous silence in the room was broken by a loud knock on the door. A guard entered. "The court physician, Majesty," he announced.

The boys rushed in eagerly from the balcony and joined Arthur, who was warmly greeting his physician, now appropriately dressed in a long green gown for his audience with the king.

"Come, John, tell me of Izzy's wellbeing."

"I've given Lady Isabella a sleeping draft to combat her exhaustion, majesty. She is sleeping now. The wounds on her face will heal with time, but who knows how long the mental wounds will take? The trauma of her kidnap and the death of Huw has created a malaise in her."

George stepped forward and asked when they could see Izzy.

John looked down at George and adjusted his spectacles to the end of his nose. "The draft I have administered your sister will cause her to sleep until tomorrow, so maybe she will be ready to receive you then."

Arthur knelt on one knee beside George and put his arm around him. "She is in good hands, George. Bronwyn will let us know when she wakes, and then we can all see her together." He stood and put his hand on John's shoulder. "We are much indebted to you, John. How is Lady Isabella's dog? It would be good if she were there when she awoke."

"She is fine, Majesty. It appears she had not been poisoned after all — merely given a strong sleeping draft. She is with Captain Owain, who has a way with her. I will inform him to bring her directly to your majesty's chamber."

As John was about to take his leave, Arthur whispered in his ear, "Please stay a moment, John, I have a delicate matter to discuss with you in private." Turning round to the boys he said, "Well, that is good news … now I have some pressing affairs of state to attend to, so I have arranged for you both to learn more of our culture."

"I would rather learn more about the dragons," pleaded George.

"Don't be ungrateful, Georgie," retorted Dan. To Arthur he said, "I must apologise for my brother."

"It's no matter, Daniel, I can change plans around at a moment's notice. After all, I am the king!" He laughed, and opened the door to his chambers, instructing one of the guards to take the boys to Lord Bedivere's rooms. "You must tell him we have changed our minds and George would like to meet the dragons."

"Wow! Thank you, sir," cried George in delight.

"Daniel, you are to watch our knights in combat training. Now off with you both, I have a kingdom to run." Dan grabbed hold of George and pushing him through the doorway, thanked Arthur and followed the guard down the stairway. Arthur turned to his physician.

"Thank you for staying, John, I would rather not discuss this in front of the boys. I want you personally to arrange the funeral of Huw the watchman. I promised my daughter that he would be laid to rest with his wife and son, with all honours."

"But Majesty, he is a traitor!" John implored.

"I know he assisted Meyric with her kidnap, but he has fully redeemed himself with Izzy. If I had been more agreeable when he solicited my help, maybe things would have turned out differently. Let me know the details so that we can attend his funeral as a family."

"As you wish, Majesty," John replied reluctantly.

"Thank you, John. Please inform my first minister on your way out that I am ready to receive him."

John bowed to Arthur and took his leave.

Arthur eagerly beckoned his first minister. "Come in, Gawain. What news? Do we have any names?"

Gawain was carrying a bundle of papers under his arm, which he placed on the table. "Majesty, we have names of Meyric's minor associates who were involved in the attempt to overthrow you, but it seems he was the only person who knew the identity of the instigator of this rebellion. Unfortunately, of course, he has carried that secret to his grave. According to his men, he met the person alone and in secret, but they knew that whoever this person is, he must be very powerful, because Meyric was so fearful of the consequences of failure."

"Have you arranged for the arrests of those whose names you have been given?" asked Arthur.

"I think we should delay that for the time being, Majesty. My suggestion is that we would do better to place a spy in their midst."

"Ah!" exclaimed Arthur.

"I have put myself into the mind of this person who is behind all our troubles, and he will now be aware of Meyric's failure, so will need to choose a successor if he wishes to resume his plans."

Arthur found himself warming to Gawain's plan. "And who do you have in mind for this perilous task?"

"Whoever we choose for this charge must be well known to despise your majesty … but do you think you could put your trust in someone who dislikes you?"

Deep in thought, Arthur walked out onto his balcony, and resting his hands on the stone balustrade looked down into the depths of the lake for inspiration. He turned and looked at Gawain enquiringly. "Meyric sought out Huw the watchman because he knew he blamed the queen and me for his wife's death." He thought for a moment, frowning, then went on, "So why not feign a similar situation where someone close to us, who we trust, is publicly dishonoured. This way we weave our own web of deceit to trap this filthy mosquito who wants to infect this land with its vile disease."

"That person would need to put his life at great risk, Majesty. Have you anyone in mind?"

"We will think on it, Gawain. But for now, we must keep this plan between ourselves – even the queen must not be privy to our intentions. If we are to draw this traitor out from the darkness, all must believe our decoy would betray us."

There were several small courtyards in the palace, but by far the largest was the tiltyard where Arthur's knights carried out their daily combat training unless other duties took precedence. Arthur had a sizable standing army that he could call on in time of war from all the twelve manors in his kingdom. His knights and officers were based in the palace and numbered two hundred or so. Once a week, usually on a Sunday, all able-bodied men from each village on the island would be expected to practise their archery skills at a piece of open ground in the middle of each town, known as the butts. As well as using this time to practise, the men trained young boys from the age of five to use a longbow. There was a lot of friendly rivalry between the hamlets in the kingdom as to who had the most skilful archer. Consequently, Arthur turned their desire to be best into an annual competition. The winners of each discipline received prizes and a place on the list of names to be entered into the tournament which took place at the palace every year. Many of Arthur's knights and officers started their military careers that way and earned their spurs through taking part in this sometimes-brutal contest of arms.

George and Dan were blown away by the scale of the courtyard as they entered it from the royal apartments. In front of them was the rear of a richly decorated grandstand supported by carved oak pillars and draped in exquisite heraldic hangings. They followed Bedivere up the steps to the top of the stand, and as they walked out into the seating area, a scene from a Hollywood epic greeted them. Below was the royal tiltyard where mounted knights in armour took it in turns to gallop up one side of the centre barrier with lances, trying to hit a series of small shields fixed on top of poles on the other side. Behind the tiltyard was a series of small fenced areas, known as a Champ Close, where men-at-arms were practising with various weapons in hand to hand combat. The courtyard was surrounded entirely by a variety of workshops and stables, built into the fabric of a circular stone wall.

Bedivere apologised, and asked the boys to make themselves comfortable and observe his knights at practice for a short time while he attended to some urgent palace business. As they watched in awe at the spectacle played out below them, they failed to notice the armed guards entering and standing behind them. A few moments later a scruffy little man dressed in tatty leather clothing and smelling as though he needed a bath, pushed his way abruptly past the guards and enquired in a gruff manner, "Is one of you called George?"

Dan turned round to face him. "This is George, sir," pointing to his younger brother.

"Well, I've been told he wants to meet my dragons."

Dan turned his brother round to face the scruffy little man. "My brother is deaf, sir. If you want to get his attention you must speak to his face so he can read your lips."

"Yes, yes, Bedivere told me all that … the last thing I need is a deaf-mute hanging around when I'm so busy," he muttered under his breath.

"I assure you, sir, my brother is no mute, he can speak for himself," Dan replied angrily. He looked at George and said, "This man is going to take you to see the dragons, George," then in a whisper so the man couldn't hear him, "He's a bit grumpy so I'd watch out if I were you."

George couldn't care less what the man's temperament was like – he was actually going to see a real dragon! He jumped up and down with such excitement that he almost fell into the seats in front of him. The little man turned and began walking back to where he had come from, growling to himself, and beckoned George with his hand to follow. George bowed to Dan with a snigger, then punching the air and shouting, "Yes!" tailed the man past the guards and down the steps.

Apart from the four guards, Dan was now alone; not that he minded. George was known for consistently asking stupid questions all the time, especially during the best bits of a movie. He settled back in his seat and put his feet on the bench in front of him so as to take in the full ambience of the moment in peace and quiet; all that was missing was a bag of popcorn.

Without warning, a pair of smooth white hands was thrust in front of Dan's eyes, blotting out his view of the proceedings. A female voice from behind whispered in his ear, "Guess who?"

His heart missed a beat as he recognised the soft voice, and he turned round to see Angharad smiling at him. "What on earth are you doing here?" he asked.

"Are you not happy to see me?" she pouted as he stood up.

His heart was pounding two to the dozen, but he managed to stutter a sentence. "Of course I am – glad to see you, I mean. Just a little surprised to find you here."

"My father is one of the king's advisors, and as he was summoned to the palace, I thought I would join him and see my friend Bronwyn … I mean the queen. She told me of Izzy's kidnap … how terrible for her … thank goodness she escaped without harm."

"Yes, she has … but I think the experience will haunt her for some time to come."

She climbed over the seat that separated them from each other to sit beside him, and with lowered eyes, said softly, "Actually … I was hoping to see you again, Daniel."

He couldn't resist any longer and pulled her towards him, kissing her gently on the lips. Angharad replied by putting her arms around his neck, bringing them even closer. Suddenly their moment of tenderness was interrupted by a nervous cough. Embarrassed, they hastily separated themselves from their warm embrace and looked behind to see an equally embarrassed Lord Bedivere.

"Lord Bedivere, how good to see you again," a startled Angharad blurted out.

Lord Bedivere bowed to her and replied, "Thank you, Lady Angharad – as always, you are a vision of beauty. Pray, how is your father?"

"Oh, he is in private council with the king. I thought it would be gracious … while I was here … to call on Daniel … and enquire after Lady Isabella."

"A noble thought, my lady. I am sure master Daniel would favour your company more than my own at this moment, so I will take my leave."

He turned to go, and Dan asked, "Maybe you can show me the armouries another time, Lord Bedivere?"

Bowing towards Dan, he said, "Whatever you desire, master Daniel." As he left, Dan placed his arms around Angharad's waist and pulling her towards him, kissed her once more.

The Dragon Master's quarters were more akin to stables than the lavish apartments George had grown accustomed to in his short time in the palace. But he didn't care what the accommodation looked like for he was actually going to meet with real dragons – not ones created by a computer but living, breathing creatures.

The man, known only as the Dragon Master, seemed to George to be a bit short on words, but then he did live with dragons, so he supposed they must communicate in other ways, and not being able to hear anyway, it didn't much matter. He was a short, rather grimy little man with hunched shoulders and not much taller than George. His most unusual feature was his hands which, considering the diminutive size of his body, were enormous.

George thought he would break the ice by asking a few questions. "Where do they live … the dragons, I mean?" he asked, not expecting a civil answer.

The Dragon Master turned and thrust his face at George, who staggered back a couple of steps. "In caves at the rim of the old volcano," he replied gruffly. He began rummaging inside a large old wooden chest. "Ah, here they are," he muttered with a sardonic smile. He pulled out what appeared to be scraps of dirty rotting rags and threw them at George. Thrusting his face at George again he said mockingly, "Put these on, you won't want to mess up your nice courtly clothes, will you?"

George caught the ball of rags and scrunched his face at the acrid odour coming from the parcel, so dropped them on the floor.

The Dragon Master thrust his face at George again and growled, "I've got far better things to do than show my dragons to deaf little boys."

George could see the man was trying to intimidate him and expecting he would run off back to his brother; but he didn't know of the stubborn side to George's nature. He had endured years of bullying because of his deafness and had learned not to submit to antagonism. He was certainly

not going to back down now, even if it meant taking insults from this nasty diminutive little man all day.

"Well, if it's not convenient, I will inform the king you're just too busy to show me your dragons," George snapped, assuming an air of authority.

The man stopped in his tracks and thought for a few seconds. He mumbled to himself and slowly turned round to George again. In as loud and penetrating a voice as he could muster, he said into George's ear, "I guess it wouldn't harm just this once, but you must realise these beasts are wild animals – they prefer solitude – that's why they live way up there. I may be called the Dragon Master by them in the palace, but dragons have no masters. I am someone they tolerate because I understand them and bring them the occasional tasty morsel from the king's hunting grounds ... they are partial to a bit of venison now and then. In fact, I'm taking them some now with Arthur's blessing for their help in retrieving his daughter."

"That's my sister," George exclaimed in delight.

The Dragon Master looked puzzled. "Then you are the king's son?"

"Well, not quite. It's very complicated but we ... me and my brother, that is, are kind of hon...or...ary sons."

Still none the wiser, the Dragon Master bent down and picked up the leather garments George had discarded and put them back into his hand saying, "Son or no son, you still have to put these on. You see, lad, dragons mistrust unfamiliar smells and they tend to lick anything they don't recognise the smell of ... and you wouldn't like to be licked by a dragon, believe me. Not nice, dragon saliva. Only when they get to know you're not a threat to them will they accept you and your smell."

"But they stink!" exclaimed George squeamishly.

"That's the whole idea. They're my old clothes, they smell of me. They're used to my smell, you see, so unless you want to be covered in dragon spit, I suggest you put them on! The quicker you get them on, the quicker we can be off."

George thought it would be a worthwhile sacrifice to make if it meant he was going to meet the dragons. Besides, even if he wasn't sure what dragon spit did to you, he wasn't going to find out the hard way. Quickly he proceeded to change into the damp, crumpled garments consisting of a pair of woollen hose, a filthy linen shirt and a leather doublet. He stood up to check with the Dragon Master that he was suitably attired. The Master looked him up and down then told him to hang on, and delving again into the big chest, came out with a leather cap which he placed on George's head with both hands. Sniffing the air around him he laughed and said, "You'll do. Can't have you coming back to court with no hair, can we?"

For the first time, George felt perhaps he wasn't so grumpy after all. *But what is in dragon saliva that is so awful?* he thought.

There was a loud rap on the door of Arthur's chamber where he and his first minister, Gawain, were in council around the table. Arthur shouted to enter, and a guard appeared announcing Captain Owain and Bella. As they entered the room, Owain instructed Bella to sit. "I have brought Lady Isabella's dog, Majesty, as you instructed. What would you have me do with her?"

"For the time being leave her here with me, Captain," Arthur replied.

"Then with your Majesty's permission, I will take my leave." He bowed, but before he reached the door, Arthur rose from his chair.

"Please wait a while, Captain." Placing his hand on Owain's shoulder he said, "Please come and sit with us, for we would like your counsel."

Surprised, Owain replied, "As you wish, Majesty."

Arthur looked across the table towards the captain. "You are a most loyal and devoted subject, are you not, Owain?"

"Oh yes, Majesty," Owain replied. "I have served you since I was a small boy. My life has been enriched by service to your noble household."

"And your family ... I am told your son is in the service of Lord Bedivere?"

Owain was very proud of his son's position as a young knight and continued telling the king and his first minister about his two lovely daughters at home, who made sure he was well cared for since the death of his beloved wife. Owain himself was captain of Arthur's small navy which included, amongst others, several small sailing vessels and the royal barges. It was his men who had prevented the capture of *Nicole* by Meyric's gang.

"Would it be true to say, Owain, that your family are the most cherished part of your life, and you would lay down your life for their protection?" asked Gawain.

Owain looked puzzled, but replied with sincerity, "I would most certainly do so, Majesty, and I would do without hesitation for your family."

Arthur and Gawain looked at each other with a smile of satisfaction. "I am sure we have found our man in Captain Owain," said Arthur.

10

Dragons' Lair

The Dragon Master drove the small horse-drawn cart, laden with deer carcases, off the barge that served as a ferry, onto the small pontoon at the base of the cliff. By his side was an over-excited George, now dressed in the rags he had been forced to wear. There were guards everywhere, Arthur's security precautions against further attacks on his family.

As the cart made its way slowly towards a fenced enclosure, a gate opened, and the Dragon Master turned and backed the cart into the opening. He climbed down from his seat and opened the access door of a strange-looking lift that would take them up the hillside. It comprised a large basket of wickerwork structure complete with roof, open holes for windows, a gate on one side, and a floor of rough planks. He lowered the hinged board at the rear of the cart, revealing two sacks of apples and several deer carcasses covered in buzzing flies. He grunted as he pulled out the corpses from the cart and carried them one by one on his shoulders, huffing as each one was dropped unceremoniously onto the floor of the lift with a thud.

All this time, George sat on his seat in the cart and watched him struggle until they were all loaded into the basket. The Dragon Master looked up at him, wiping the sweat from his brow with a dirty old rag. "Come on, boy," he said irritably, "you may not be big enough to handle the deer, but you're certainly big enough to bring me those two sacks."

George sighed, mumbling to himself, "Ha! Nothing changes, does it?" Climbing down from the cart, he grunted angrily as he picked up each sack in turn and dropped it in front of his diminutive slave driver. "What do dragons want with apples?" he asked scornfully.

Intentionally avoiding the question, the Dragon Master asked sarcastically, "Have a hatred of hard work, do we, boy?" He closed the gate of the lift and stood beside George, shouting to someone in a pit below,

"Let her go, Bryn!" On hearing the command, Bryn, a well-built boy of about fifteen with rolled-up sleeves revealing man-sized biceps, pulled on a stout lever that opened a sluice-gate and released rushing water onto the blades of a wooden waterwheel. After a few seconds, the wheel gradually began to turn. He waited until it picked up enough speed then pushed another lever that engaged a series of wooden cogs to intermesh with the gear of a capstan. Slowly the rope wound tightly around the capstan's core, and the basket jerked and creaked as it began its slow ascent skywards up the cliff towards the dragons' lair.

George looked over the side of the gate and down to the ground as it moved further away. His glances panned upwards and out towards the island where he had a magnificent view of the palace rising from the lagoon like a medieval cathedral. The creaking wicker basket was now level in height with the royal balcony from where he had caught his first glimpse of the red dragon with Arthur. As ever, he wanted some answers to important questions before his meeting with the dragons, but decided it was best to be polite.

"What's so dangerous about dragon spit, sir?"

"Well," said the Dragon Master, doing his best to keep his face in front of George so he could read his lips, "the surface of a dragon's tongue is covered in hundreds of sharp barbs, like fishhooks, that face back into the throat. It uses these barbs to remove the skin from its prey by licking to get at the flesh below and is capable of stripping a man's skin with one lick. It can also remove any flesh left on the bones. They cannot chew their meat, so the saliva of a dragon breaks down the flesh as they swallow. If you get any of it on your skin, it will burn you terrible. I have seen dragon's saliva melt iron into liquid. Despite their huge size they have very poor eyesight, so rely on smell to hunt their prey. On the other hand, their hearing is very acute – they can hear a rabbit scurry into its burrow from a great height, then home onto it by its smell."

"Wow!" said George. "And the all-important question – do they really breathe fire?"

"Only the males. They produce a pungent air from inside their gut, like we do when we've eaten well." He made a false burp to demonstrate his explanation. George caught the full effect and took a hasty step back. "As they emit this gas, it is ignited by a lightning bolt which is discharged from inside their stomach. They can also use the lightning bolt to stun their prey when in flight."

George was pretty impressed by the anatomical facts of the dragon's eating habits, but the one question that remained had been implanted when he first saw the herons on the island at Menai Bridge and noticed how much they reminded him of dragons. "Just one more question, sir – can they change into *herons* in my world?"

The Dragon Master looked bewildered and replied, "Your world, boy? What do you mean by 'your world'? Don't you come from around here?"

George began to tell him the story of how they came to Cuddfan and how he felt sure the *herons* had something to do with it and changed into dragons when the fog lifted.

"Well, on my soul, I've never heard such a thing!" He winked at George as though he wanted to keep him guessing. "Maybe – it's magic?"

Suddenly George caught a whiff of a familiar smell and cried, "Guano!" The Dragon Master looked at him with a mystified expression. "Bird poo … augh … I hate bird poo!"

The Dragon Master finally understood what George was on about and said, "That's not bird poo, boy, it's dragon poo. You'll have to get used to that smell if you want to be around dragons. I've got a nice side-line selling it to the palace gardener for his herb garden. Swears by it, he does."

George was horrified. He couldn't believe that he would have to put up with the most horrible smell in the world, and wasn't at all sure he could handle it.

The Dragon Master rummaged around in his pouch and pulled out the same old dirty rag he had used to wipe away the sweat from his brow earlier. "Here you are," putting it round to cover George's face and tying it at the back of his neck. "That's better now, isn't it?" he added, standing back to admire his handiwork.

George began to choke. He wasn't sure at all which was worse, guano or the rag. He pulled it down and sniffed the air, but quickly returned it to cover his nose and muttered, "Thank you, sir." He was so busy worrying about the smell he hadn't realised the basket had stopped its ascent. His heart began to beat nervously and he could feel the blood pumping through his veins, causing a whooshing sound in his ears. The Dragon Master had painted such a frightening picture regarding dragons' eating habits that he really wasn't quite sure what to expect. Perhaps he should just wait in the basket while he did his business? He sat in the corner trembling with fear as the Dragon Master opened the gate of the basket out onto the ledge of the cave entrance,

The Dragon Master, glanced down at him, noticing his reluctance to move. "Thought you wanted to meet my dragons, boy … too late to back out now." So George plucked up all his limited courage and moved out timidly towards the ledge, his heart beating nineteen to the dozen. The basket creaked as he jumped the gap between it and the ridge, causing it to bounce against the cliff face. The Dragon Master walked a few metres into the cave and with an outstretched hand rang the bronze bell hanging from a rope. Its sound reverberated deep into the cave, and as the final distant echo faded away, George took a few more brave steps closer towards his destiny. The silence was abruptly broken by a scuffing sound coming from deep inside the cave, as though something substantial was being dragged. Although George could not hear anything other than his pounding heart, he could feel the ground beneath his feet vibrate in sympathy with the recurring thump of something heavy walking towards him. He looked into the darkness, half closing his eyes and beginning to wish he had stayed with Dan. Through his squint he caught a glimpse of the outline of a beast as it stepped out into the light.

To George, it must have seemed as high as a house; its shoulders and wings crouched above its long neck as its red horny head projected out towards him. Its tail, some five or six metres long, swung from side to side as it put one leg in front of the other. The pounding stopped, and the creature lowered its great head towards George, then snorted as it drew closer to his face. He could now feel it's stinking breath on his skin. Slowly he opened his eyes and there he was, face to face with the dragon. George was frozen with fear as the dragon screwed up its nostrils and sniffed him twice, then pulled back its head and opened its mouth to reveal its colossal tongue. George thought *this is it, I'm about to die, it doesn't like my smell.* He screamed, and as he closed his eyes tight shut and covered his face with his hands, he shouted, "Please don't lick my face off!" Unexpectedly he heard a voice from within his mind. "Don't be frightened, George, I will not harm you."

George very slowly dropped his hands away from his face and opened his eyes. The dragon's head was level with his and only centimetres away. Was he dreaming? Was this dragon actually talking to him inside his head without opening its mouth? Instinctively he put his hands over his ears. For the first time in years since being struck down with deafness, he could hear what this creature was saying to him without his hearing aid.

"Yes, George, I am talking to you through my thoughts and reading your words from your mind, so there are no secrets from me."

"Can the dragon master hear you?"

"You mean old Efion ... no, he can't hear me, not while I am talking to you. I concentrate my senses into one mind at a time – but he knows I am talking to you." He slowly looked George up and down and smiled as dragons can. "I see he has played the same old trick on you, making you wear his stinking old clothes to mask your own smell. And did he tell you our tongues will strip the skin off a man in one lick?"

"Yes ... in fact he seemed to take great pleasure in telling me how dangerous you are," replied George, rather peeved.

"Oh, take no notice, it's just an act he puts on. He is very kind to us dragons – it's people he has problems with. Our tongues are like that of a cat, and our saliva is just like your own. As for fire, I am the only dragon that can exhale such horrific venom."

George breathed a sigh of relief. "Thank goodness for that!"

"My name is Ambrosius. I am named after Arthur's uncle. I am the leader of this clan of dragons. We are the last of our kind, and although we communicate through thought with each other, I am the only dragon who can pick up human thought." The dragon laughed as he picked up George's dislike of pungent smells. "Oh, the smell of guano, as you put it, well, yes, I'm sorry for that. If you want to be with us you must get used to it ... and you will."

George, embarrassed by the ease with which the Dragon Master had fooled him, pulled the rag away from his nose and mouth, put his hand up towards Ambrosius's head and stroked along his horny plates. Ambrosius closed his eyes to acknowledge George's affection and turned to face Efion. "You ought to know better than to make a fool of someone so young, Efion. The poor lad was frightened for his life."

"I'm sorry, Ambrosius ... just a bit of fun to brighten my day."

"I sense in the boy a brave heart. Although he feared for his life, he stood his ground and faced me. You should not be so ill-tempered towards him. In his soul he has the makings of a warrior and one day may surprise us all with his courage."

Efion bowed his head, feigning shame, and then turned his gaze towards George, who had returned to the basket and was struggling to unload its cargo. He smiled to himself and pointed to George. "You see, Ambrosius, at least the boy has learnt a little more respect for work from my gentle goading."

"Maybe so, but you must learn to have consideration for him coming from a different world, with different values from our own. Hold back your displeasure with him and be a little more forgiving, then he will learn much from you and our world, as we will from him."

"Well, that's my nature, but I will try, Ambrosius. Now, I must give him a hand to unload the deer carcasses before he hurts himself. They are far too heavy for one so young."

Ambrosius chuckled. "You see, Efion, you are learning already!" He turned his body round and began the arduous trek back to re-join his ladies. He stopped and looked back towards Efion. "Oh, Efion – thank Arthur for me for the victuals, my ladies will enjoy a feast tonight. And thank you too for the apples, they will help restore my inner being."

"They are from the king's own orchard," replied Efion. "Now I must give the boy a hand before he does himself a mischief."

Ambrosius smiled and turned away, heading back into the darkness.

Efion turned to George and queried, "Well, you've met a dragon now, personal and close up – would you like to see him again?"

"Yes please, Efion," George replied.

"Damn him, he told you my name, didn't he?" George nodded. "You mustn't tell a soul, do you hear? Now let's give you a hand with those deer."

George pulled off his leather cap and helped Efion drag all the carcasses and sacks from the basket. When the task was done, he walked into a corner of the basket and sank onto the floor with a deep sigh. He untied the rag from around his neck that Efion had given him and wiped the sweat from his brow. Efion followed him in, and with a broad grin on his face closed the gate, signalling to Bryn below to winch them back to the ground.

11

Time for Reflection

Bronwyn was standing on the balcony of Izzy's apartment under a starlit sky. She watched the full moon rise gracefully above the rim of the volcano. As its silvery beam shone down, reflecting over the still, darkened waters of the lake, she prayed that it would herald a more hopeful period in their lives. She was full of remorse, for it was her actions and her actions alone that had driven Huw, in despair, to seek retribution and put her own daughter's life at risk. She was now more determined than ever to put Izzy's future happiness above that of her own.

Other than the mumblings of the guards on duty in the corridors of the palace, it was eerily quiet. The boys were asleep in their beds, George no doubt dreaming of dragons, and Dan of his lovely Angharad. Bronwyn's gaze turned towards the door as the silence was broken by the sound of muffled voices in the passageway outside. The hinges creaked as it opened and Arthur, as quietly as he could, crept into the room.

"How is she?" he whispered.

"Her tormented dreams distressed her greatly for a time, but thankfully she has been sleeping peacefully for the past few hours."

Arthur beckoned Bronwyn to sit beside him for a while, and as she joined him on the sofa, he said, "We both have been party to our daughter's kidnap in some way, but we must now put all our own bitterness behind us and rebuild Cuddfan in the ways Izzy would want to be part of."

Bronwyn leaned towards him and kissed him gently on the cheek. "I am sorry, husband, for all the pain I have caused you during these past years. I now see that your actions were well-intentioned. Together we will strive to make this a happy place for our daughter to live if she desires to stay, though I fear the kidnap attempt may have blackened her judgement of us and our kingdom so much we will lose her forever."

Arthur, understanding his wife's anguish, said, "Meeting our daughter for the first time in my chamber but a few days ago, I had my doubts she possessed the courage to take up the challenge we had set her. I felt her time away from us had softened her inner being too much. Here was a girl on the threshold of womanhood who seemed far far away from the harshness and reality of our world. Then, on the beach at Rhosneigr, when I saw her risking her own life to slay Meyric for killing Huw, I knew –" he paused and took Bronwyn's hand in his, "– I knew that somewhere inside that slender young body was contained the courageous yet compassionate heart of a woman born to be the future queen of Cuddfan."

"But first, Arthur, you must find out who is responsible for the plot to take Izzy from us. Until then she will feel too insecure to stay with us, may even turn against us and return to her world, the world she knows best. I cannot bear the thought of losing her again." She wept silently.

Arthur looked into his wife's tearful eyes and said softly, "I make a solemn promise to you, my love, to find out who is behind this plot to bring our royal household down."

"Perhaps we should summon my mother here. She will know what to do and she has the magic to help crush the evil that still inhabits our kingdom."

"Your mother has magic enough to bring Izzy back to us, but not the magic of Myrddin. Hers is the magic of potions and charms. His is, or was, the magic of life and death. If he were only alive now, the kidnap attempt would never have happened."

Bronwyn pulled away fretfully. "Yes, but he's not here, is he, Arthur dear? Your promise to safeguard Izzy from danger has failed you, but mostly her. With all your power and men at hand, you couldn't even stop a common outlaw like Meyric from entering the palace and taking her."

"That is my failing and my failing alone," Arthur replied remorsefully. "I admit I was blind to the absence of loyalty in the members of the lower ranks of my household. But I have acted on the chink in my armour and have appointed Captain Owain as head of a special cohort to be Izzy's personal bodyguard. He has chosen every man himself for their integrity and skills in combat. He is a most loyal and kindly man who has proved his worth on many occasions and has agreed to my proposal. I understand from Izzy that he has already earned her respect for the kindness he has shown to Bella."

Bronwyn felt much comforted at hearing her husband's diligence, and glanced towards Izzy as she lay peacefully asleep in her bed. "I have been thinking that Izzy may feel suffocated with all the armoured male entourage around her wherever she goes. I believe she needs to foster new friendships of her own choosing. God willing, if our daughter chooses to stay, it will help ease the pain of George and Dan when they leave to return to the New World. I am sure she would favour companions of her own age around her. Maybe we should acquaint her gently to as many seemly young men and women as possible."

Arthur, sensing his wife's clemency towards him, offered, "Captain Owain has two daughters near Izzy's age, Alwen and Rhiannon, and a son, Tristan, who is in service with Bedivere. There is also Lady Angharad, a close friend of yourself and, it seems, rather fond of Daniel. I propose we spend a few days at the hunting lodge as guests of Lord and Lady Gochwyban and invite Captain Owain's son and daughters to join us. I am most eager to see Izzy's ship *Nicole*. I understand she has many marvellous machines on board. I'm sure this will distract us all from the horrendous events of the last few days."

Bronwyn was, for once, in full agreement with her husband and demonstrated her fellow feeling by leaning towards him and again kissing him, but this time with such feeling that her affection surprised him most pleasantly.

The night seemed long. Bronwyn had finally fallen asleep on Arthur's shoulder but he remained wide awake until the sun heralded the dawn. Then sleep took charge of his body, and giving in to his need for rest, Arthur joined his wife in slumber.

Bronwyn woke first and on discovering that Izzy was not in her bed, shook Arthur's arm with such force he thought he was being attacked, and awoke with a jump. From behind the other side of the door to the water closet, they could hear splashing water. They both stood up and facing the door waited with bated breath for Izzy to reappear. The door opened, and there stood Izzy, her hair wet. She was still sporting the bruise on the side of her face that Meyric had inflicted during her kidnap attempt. She walked up to them both and gave each a kiss on the cheek. "'Morning, Mum, 'morning, Dad," she chuckled. "I'm starving … is it time for breakfast?"

Izzy's cheerful mood took them both by complete surprise and they looked at each other in bewilderment. Bronwyn rushed towards her and gave her a hug saying, "I am gladdened you appear to be so much better, my darling, we were all so afraid for you."

Arthur gently held her chin, looking at her bruised cheek and cut lip and asked if it still caused her pain.

"Not as much as the pain I feel for poor Huw. He sacrificed his life so I could escape. If only we'd waited a while longer, he might still be alive. I know he was a party to my kidnap, but if he'd not been so appallingly treated by you both, he would have remained loyal to you for the rest of his life." Izzy stared at her parents as if willing them to deny her harsh words, but they simply looked back at her with remorseful faces.

Bronwyn took Izzy's hand. "I know I was selfish in the way I treated Huw's poor wife, Izzy. Can you forgive me?"

"I will forgive you both, as long as you promise me you will never treat your people with such insensitivity again," she demanded.

Arthur looked at Bronwyn. "Your mother and I have discussed this matter at some length, Izzy. We are ashamed of our self-centred behaviour and have both made a solemn vow to change our ways."

"That's good!" replied Izzy. "And for my part, I will honour his memory by trying to live up to the person he saw in me that was worth giving his life for. Today is the dawn of a new Izzy Moorefield!" She went into her room and came back with the book Arthur had given her. "I need pen and ink to fill in the first chapter of my new life in Cuddfan."

Bronwyn couldn't believe what she was hearing and asked incredulously, "Does this mean you have decided to stay?"

"I have," she replied, smiling at her mother.

Bronwyn rushed to her side and embraced her daughter tenderly. "Oh, Izzy my darling, I thought you would surely abandon us after what has happened to you."

Arthur joined his wife and daughter in a long embrace. "But pray, Izzy, tell us what has lightened your feelings towards us?"

Izzy began to tell them the reasons for her decision. "I had a lot of time to think while trussed up in that awful wagon. My main concern was how much I would miss my adopted parents, and Dan and George, if I were to stay here, but Gorawen assured me she would arrange for me to come and go as I please, so I could visit them whenever I wanted. Then after Huw told me a little of the history of this kingdom you call Cuddfan, I began to wonder what it would be like if I became a part of it.

"But it wasn't this alone that made me decide to stay. I can't explain it, but when Huw and I tried to make our escape and he was killed by Meyric, something deep inside me snapped and took over my mind. I had never felt that way before. Oh, I was scared, but it's as though something in my head told me I was doing the right thing to kill the man who murdered Huw, even though I stopped short at the last minute. Yes, I know he was party to Meyric's plan, but we were two abandoned souls thrust together in terrible circumstances, and somehow in all this chaos, he gave me the inner strength to carry on after his death. So you see, I believe I am a part of this kingdom, and whether I like it or not, I belong here with you, my true parents." She thrust her parent's hands together in hers and smiled at them.

12

Celebration and Frolics

For a few days things were very hectic in the royal household. Arthur decided to postpone the trip to the hunting lodge as, with Izzy's acceptance to stay in Cuddfan, there was much to be done at the palace. More important was the worry that there were still traitors in the kingdom who would even then be plotting his family's downfall. With the increased security at the palace, it was much safer than the hunting lodge.

Dan and George had been given the option to return home, but both had elected to stay and see their sister crowned queen. It didn't go unnoticed that their real reasons may most likely have been due to their individual experiences of the last few days. Izzy was thrilled knowing they were going to stick around.

Arthur began telling everyone of his plans to present Izzy to the people of Cuddfan. The celebrations were to start with an elaborate banquet at the palace to show his daughter off to his courtiers and retainers. This was to be followed by the grandest of tournaments, where everyone from all over the kingdom would be invited to compete in the skill-at-arms contests. The coronation of their new queen would take place a week later with such splendour and ceremony they had never before witnessed, and the entire enterprise would conclude with a grand tour throughout the land.

Arthur asked Daniel if he would like to take a small part in the Grand Tournament, small being the operative word as it took seven years to train for knighthood. This meant he would have to be kitted out in a 'full harness', Bedivere's term for the armour he would need to wear, mostly for his own protection. Thinking it would endear him to Angharad if he chose to accept, Dan agreed for all the wrong reasons. As the tournament was only a few weeks away, he would have to squeeze his training into a very tight schedule. Not that it was a problem for Dan as he could ride very well, and how difficult could it be to hit a target with a lance at a gallop? He was about to find out. But first he was to join Bedivere and Tristan, Owain's son, in the Armoury to be measured for his 'harness'.

The Armoury was situated in one of the many workshops built into the outside wall of the tiltyard. Each workshop entrance was furnished with a colourfully painted sign over the doorway. The Armoury was the palace's storehouse where all armour and weapons were held and checked for repair or replacement. Next to the Armoury were the armourer's workshops, where items of armour were produced and others repaired by a small team of skilled craftsmen. Next door was the weapons smith where everything from swords to arrowheads was expertly crafted and maintained in the event of war. The saddler made saddles and anything in leather such as belts, sword and dagger scabbards, and straps to attach to the armour. The final workshop was something of a tailor's shop, but instead of making everyday garments, they produced arming doublets and any padding that was worn beneath armour to prevent chafing of the wearer's skin.

At the far end, close to the entrance to the tiltyard and as far away from the workshops as possible, were the stables, and Dan was about to find out why. As he walked around the perimeter of the courtyard, the noise of the continuously tapping hammers was more pronounced the closer he got to the workshops. He was a few minutes early for his meeting with Bedivere and Tristan, so he thought he would watch the armourers at work while waiting. It was most unusual for him to be early for meetings, but since arriving in Cuddfan he had miraculously discarded some of his old, less appealing habits. Besides, he was keen to try on some armour; *very good street cred in the girl department* he thought.

The stone wall at the front of the Armoury's workshops was low enough to allow as much natural daylight in as possible for the men working inside. In the interior, several stout oak benches with iron stakes wedged into square holes ran along the length of the wall. Sitting at a bench was a man beating the surface of a piece of bronze-like metal over a ball-shaped stake with a small flat-headed hammer. It was bouncing so fast on the surface of the plate that its movement was just a blur. The man next to him was joining several small pieces of shaped metal plates together with rivets. The finished parts, when joined to become one piece of armour, moved over each other with remarkable smoothness and precision. There certainly wasn't the clanking noise he'd heard when he watched old films of knights in armour on TV, Dan thought. Behind the two men working on the benches he could see racks of hammers, all highly polished, bearing different shaped heads. By the side of the stands were wooden frames supporting many stakes of different shapes and sizes, again with highly polished surfaces.

At the heart of the workshop was a brick forge with the biggest pair of bellows Dan had ever seen. Two teenage boys, sweat dripping from their brows from the heat of the fire, pumped the bellows in harmony to force a continuous stream of wheezing air into the heart of the glowing embers. A man wearing a scorched leather apron raked fresh charcoal over the blaze, causing a veil of bright orange sparks to dance into the air. A second man, gripping a hefty hammer in his right hand, stood by the side of a stout flat anvil mounted on a section of tree trunk. He too was sporting a blackened leather apron, his sleeves rolled up above his elbows to reveal huge muscles any weightlifter would be proud of. He seemed to be waiting for something to happen. The first man picked up a pair of tongs from the side of the forge and carefully pulled out a flat piece of white-hot iron from beneath the searing coals, rapidly placing it on the anvil. Shards of red-hot metal flew into the air with every blow of the hammer as the other man beat the metal into submission. Dan watched mesmerised as the flat disc quickly began to curve into a bowl shape. He signalled to his colleague to cease hammering and returned the piece of formed metal into the heart of the fire.

As a second-year engineering student, Dan was so intrigued by the process that he didn't notice two men approaching him from behind.

"A magical process is it not, Daniel?" smiled Bedivere.

Dan turned to face him. "Lord Bedivere … I'm sorry, I was so fascinated by the way the metal was being shaped I didn't see you, but yes, it is indeed a magic art."

"I would like to present Tristan to you. He is Captain Owain's son and is undergoing training with my cohort."

Dan stepped forward and went to shake hands, but Tristan, not sure what to do, bowed courteously towards him and Dan, not wanting to seem ignorant, returned his bow and smiled.

"Well, Daniel, I believe you would like to take part in the tournament to celebrate your sister's coronation?" Bedivere enquired.

"Only in a friendly way," Dan replied. "I realise I am at a disadvantage compared with everyone else, but I do have riding experience, mostly gymkhanas when I was younger."

"Gymkhanas, what are these?" Tristan asked.

"In a way, they are a bit like tournaments. We have competitions against the clock to ride around a set course picking up objects from the ground as we ride. We also jump fences. I suppose it's mostly riding skills. We start off riding ponies at a very early age and as we get older progress to horses. It's supposed to be a bit of fun, but a lot of people take it very seriously and spend a load of money togging their kids out in all the gear."

Bedivere looked at Tristan and remarked, "Yes, it does sound very similar. Did you joust with each other?"

"Not quite," replied Dan, "but we did get into the occasional scrap, I suppose."

Bedivere laughed and put his arm round Daniel's shoulders. "Let us go and see how skilful you are on horseback and then we can get you fitted out with a harness."

Back at the royal apartments, Izzy was being measured for her new wardrobe. If the truth be known, she would have preferred to be with Dan and Bedivere. Izzy wasn't really a frock person; her favourite everyday attire at home was jeans and t-shirts. However, she thought there would be plenty of time in the future to get involved in the male-dominated pastime of tournaments. She was actually a better rider than Dan and had many more gymkhana rosettes to her credit. She loved to hack across the open countryside when she had the chance. Having no fear as a child, she got caught up in all kinds of scrapes with the boys at home.

Bronwyn was in her element. She was exactly the opposite of Izzy where clothes were concerned although, like Izzy, she was an excellent horsewoman as she had proved that day when they first met in the gardens of the hunting lodge. That seemed so far away now. Bronwyn had her royal dressmakers in attendance in her apartment. Izzy, standing on an improvised plinth, was wearing a boned corset and complaining that only fat women wore corsets. The royal costumier told her that it was the fashion and no lady of the court would be without one. Izzy told him she had a dislike of dresses, let alone the torturous undergarment she was expected to wear. However, as it was Bronwyn's wish to fit her daughter out in the most exquisite gowns possible, she would stop her moaning and put up with the indignity of standing like a mannequin while being continually draped in different fabrics. Now she knew what it must feel like to be a bride, except she was getting married to a kingdom.

On hand were the queen's ladies-in-waiting who, like schoolgirls, were chatting and giggling with each other. Not one of them could make up her mind which fabrics to choose for the coronation gown. No matter. The first item Izzy would need to have made was a linen toile, which was to provide a basic pattern for the dress, but made of cheaper cloth, linen in this case. This was to make sure that the design fitted her body perfectly. Once any alterations were made, the toile would be unstitched, and the pattern transferred to the more precious and expensive fabrics.

The apartment was littered with all kinds of luxurious cloths, and Bella was having a great time diving underneath them, much to Izzy's amusement, but the dressmakers were getting flustered. They pointed out that these fabrics were really hard to come by in such a small kingdom as Cuddfan. Bronwyn finally lost her patience, and catching hold of Bella by the scruff of her neck ejected her into the corridor where Owain, now Izzy's official bodyguard, was waiting. He laughed and assured Bronwyn he would be most happy to keep her out of mischief's way, especially as it meant him getting away from the women's continuous clacking.

George was thrilled when he found out he would be allowed to stay for Izzy's coronation. She told him that although *she* could go between both worlds at any time, it would be beyond the bounds of possibility for him or Dan to come back once they returned home. She assured them both that she would visit as often as possible; after all, she might be queen of Cuddfan, but they were still her family. That being the case, George decided it was now or never to emulate his heroes in his favourite fantasy books and films, and ride a dragon. He didn't know whether it would be possible or not, but it wouldn't do any harm to ask. He planned to ask Efion, the Dragon Master personally. Although no longer intimidated by him, he was just a bit nervous about how he would react to his proposal.

As he walked across the vast courtyard towards Efion's quarters, he caught a glimpse of Dan riding around the tiltyard. He wanted to keep his plan a secret for the time being so quickened his step.

Efion was busy filling small sacks with dried guano from the corner of the stable. George, trying to pretend he was no longer repulsed at the smell, walked up and patted the old horse in the stall next door and gave him an apple he'd saved from breakfast. "Morning, Efion," he said happily.

"Morning, Master George, and to what do I owe the pleasure of your noble presence this bright day?"

George was surprised by the cheery reply and thought it was a good time to make his request. "You know my sister is being crowned in a few weeks' time?"

Efion stopped shovelling and leaned on his spade. He turned to face George and replied in his usual unbending manner, "I might have heard a rumour, yes."

"Well ..." George stuttered.

"C ...C .. C . Come on, boy, spit it out!" Efion mimicked.

"Well, in my world, when our queen has an anniversary or special occasion, the Red Arrows – they're a very famous aerobatic display team – do a flypast over Buckingham Palace and ... I wondered if I could lead the dragons in a kind of flypast over the king's palace."

"Can you fly, boy?" Efion teased.

"I thought," George muttered, red in the face, "it might be possible for me to ride on the back of Ambrosius."

There was a horrible period of silence, but instead of the usual sarcastic comment, Efion walked over to a decaying chest covered in old sacks. After clearing off the detritus he opened the lid. George walked towards him as he pulled out what looked like a dusty old seat. Efion placed it on an old wooden crossbar and took out a rag from the bag hanging as usual from his belt, and flicking away years of dust and spiders' webs, revealed a handsome red leather saddle. "This belonged to my great, great, great grandfather in the days when he rode Ambrosius into battle against the pirates."

George was speechless. Efion spat on the rag and began buffing the rear of the backrest to uncover exquisite carvings, tooled into the leather, depicting a battle scene of a pirate ship in full sail and dragons flying above.

"When he died, his saddle was placed in this old chest and forgotten. I think he would approve of you riding Ambrosius once more. I have never had the mettle to go up there in the clouds myself. But we will have to ask Ambrosius first as he may not want to carry anyone again –he's getting on a bit … even for a dragon."

Dan had proved to Bedivere that he could ride a horse, but there was still an awful lot to learn. At this stage he was riding in day clothes – being on horseback in armour would be a different matter. He had completed a couple of passes against the shields but was having great difficulty keeping the lance up so failed to hit any of the targets.

He dismounted and walked towards Bedivere, then handed the reins to Tristan, who mounted the horse by leaping straight into the saddle from the ground and galloped to the end of the list where he was handed a lance. The horse reared up on its hind legs and charged straight into a full gallop towards the shields. One by one the small targets were hit down. After throwing his lance to a waiting squire, he returned to where Dan and Bedivere were standing and jumped out of the saddle as the horse came to a stop in front of them. The smile on Tristan's face said it all; the smell of male testosterone filled the air. Bedivere smiled to himself, thinking a bit of friendly rivalry wouldn't go amiss. He had known Tristan a long time and knew he could trust him not to take it too far. But Dan – could he handle it?

"I think you need more time in the saddle with a lance, Daniel. Don't forget Tristan has been doing this since he was eight years old. Let's see – you have just two weeks before the tournament and some of that time is going to be spent away at the hunting lodge, so you must practise every spare moment you have. I will be accompanying the royal party with my cohort as will Tristan here."

Bedivere was interrupted by an approaching man-at-arms who informed him the king would like to see him in his apartment. "In that case, we will take a break for a while," he said apologetically. "Tristan will take you to the armoury to be measured for your harness, and I will catch up with you later." He called over a squire to take the horse from Tristan and return it to the stable. Tristan and Dan bowed to Bedivere, took their leave and headed towards the Armoury.

George and Efion had reached the top of the cliff edge in the creaking basket lift. Instead of the once scared boy huddling in the corner, George, now full of bravado, couldn't wait to meet with his new friend again. He rushed headlong into the darkness of the cave holding a lantern to light his way. Efion smiled to himself as he followed, knowing that Ambrosius wasn't the only dragon in the cave. However, there was no need to worry for when he finally caught up with them, they were deep in conversation with each other.

"Ah, Efion, what do you think of master George's plan to fly with me?" asked Ambrosius in mind-speak.

"Well, as long as you are happy to take the boy. I have the saddle still," Efion replied.

Ambrosius looked George up and down trying to guess his weight. "I think I could take your weight, although the saddle might have to be altered to take my extra girth." He grinned at George. A dragon grin could be mistaken for a growl as it meant showing all its teeth, but George and Efion both knew Ambrosius was definitely not growling. "I think it is about time you met the other dragons, George." He turned to Efion and repeated what he had told George.

Efion nodded and turning to George said, "We must follow Ambrosius into the cave where the other dragons sleep. Now remember that the other dragons cannot communicate with us as we do with Ambrosius, so let him do all the talking, and please keep close to me."

It was slow progress; dragons are swift in flight but extremely slow on the ground. They came to a fork in the tunnel and George could just see a light at the other end of the cave. "That's the main entrance out of the cave when they leave to hunt. This way leads into the centre of the hive where they sleep."

As they neared the centre of the hive, it opened out into a vast cavern. The ceiling was as high as a cathedral. Ambrosius stopped and signalled to George and Efion to wait, and as he continued for a few more steps Efion pointed towards the roof, where dragons were hanging from crevices just as bats do. The stench was awful, and as George held the lantern aloft, he could see the floor of the cave was covered in guano. The sides of the cave were littered with the abandoned bones of various animals.

Efion whispered to George, "This is where I do most of my work, clearing up after them. Dirty beasts, aren't they?" George nodded in wholehearted agreement.

One by one, the dragons slid from their perches and dropped to the cave floor, landing lightly on their feet. They shuffled forward and formed a semicircle around Ambrosius, who began communicating with them. He asked George to step forward so he could introduce him. As he moved to Ambrosius's side, the dragons dropped their long necks down to George's eye level and moved them in a swinging motion from side to side as they observed and sniffed the air around him. They chortled with each other like a gaggle of geese, then raising their heads in unison, leapt one by one back up to the roof of the cave.

Ambrosius turned his head towards George and gave him a gentle nudge that almost knocked him over. "They have given their approval. In fact, my ladies are quite taken with you, George."

"Ladies, you mean all those dragons are female?" replied George.

"Oh yes, we are the last of our breed, and I am the last male. Unfortunately, I am now far too old to father a new generation. There was a time when hunters would come after us in packs with the most horrific weapons. Each male dragon's head was worth a thousand gold pieces for a hunter who was brave enough to tackle us. We would have been hunted to extinction if it wasn't for the magnificent Myrddin, who is, or shall I say was, the greatest Celtic sorcerer who ever lived."

George's face began to turn red with embarrassment as he remembered the fun he had had slaying dragons on his games console. Still, that was only make-believe, and besides, he had now outgrown such childish games. Ambrosius smiled at George and winked because he could read every thought that went through George's head. Efion announced that it was time to get back to ground level, so after George had given Ambrosius an affectionate hug, they headed back to the basket lift.

13

Man of Steel

Every part of Dan's body, including his head, had been measured and recorded so the man in the armoury store could kit him out with full armour, or harness as it is called. Usually, a harness was made to measure, but as there was very little time until the tournament he had to settle for the nearest fit. In Arthur's time, armour consisted mostly of a mail hauberk over a padded gambeson, and a simple helmet called a spangenhelm. Since then armourers had developed a far more sophisticated form of armour in which there was more plate than mail, and each piece had a hardened surface as a defence against arrows, so the individual sections were thinner and lighter. Although most armed combat in peacetime had become more of a sport, Arthur's standing army had to be prepared to go to war at any time, so every piece of armour manufactured in the kingdom had to stand up to the same punishment whether for sport or war.

It wasn't long before the armourer appeared, accompanied by his two assistants, with a varied selection of armour and undergarments. They placed everything on the large table in front of them and took their leave. Even armour had become fashionable items of wear and Tristan discounted some of the pieces as unsuitable.

Dan was bemused by Tristan's fussiness and asked, "Does the shape really matter? Surely it's all about protection?"

"Yes," Tristan replied, "but when we take part in the tournament, we are on show to the whole kingdom, so we must look our best, especially as there will be many young women watching our heroic encounters."

"Well, in that case, maybe I should be the judge of what armour I would look good in," Dan retorted.

Tristan held up his arms and stood back in defeat while Dan pushed his way forward to the table and looked at each piece in turn. He had no idea which part went where, apart from the helmet, but wasn't about to give in and show his ignorance at this stage. The next twenty minutes were therefore spent with him picking through the individual pieces, trying them on where he thought they went and looking at Tristan, who grinned like a Cheshire cat and pointed to the part of the body each piece was supposed to protect.

Finally his choice was made, and two young squires appeared to dress Dan from head to toe in plate armour. The last thing to go on was the helmet, and as it was strapped underneath his chin, Tristan held up a small mirror in front of him to see how he looked. Dan couldn't help going into various poses, thinking that the girls back home would consider him a real hero in all this. Tristan told him to walk around in it for the next couple of hours to get used to it. It was not that it was especially cumbersome or heavy, but Dan had simply never worn anything comparable to it before.

Tristan led him to the tiltyard and put him through some exercises. Every so often he would stop him and adjust the odd strap here and there until Dan felt comfortable. Tristan then instructed one of the squires to fetch the horse Dan was to ride. He whispered something into the lad's ear, who went off towards the stable sniggering. Dan was oblivious to this as he was too focused on trying to impress the small audience which had been gathering around the tiltyard, by attempting to do press-ups in full armour.

As the young man led the black stallion into the tiltyard, Dan noticed it was not the one that Bedivere had picked out for him to ride earlier. This horse was dancing about all over the place; even the squire was having difficulty controlling him. Right away, Dan felt he was being set up for a fall, and a rather painful one at that if he fell off wearing this load of scrap metal. As the stable boy tried to hold the horse still, Dan walked warily towards him and not wanting to appear cowardly, tightly gripped the pommel of the saddle with his left hand and the seat with the other, then placing his foot into the stirrup he raised himself up slowly to sit in the saddle. The stable lad nervously handed Dan the reins and swiftly retreated for fear of being run down. The horse lowered its head and snorted in defiance, lashing out violently with its hind legs. Dan gripped hard with his thighs as the horse lurched forward into a gallop. He held on for dear life as it reared up and then bucked, trying to eject this unwelcome rider from his back.

All of a sudden, the horse stopped dead in the centre of the arena. It stood motionless for a few moments jerking its head up and down in a rhythmic motion while exhaling noisily through its nostrils. Dan prepared himself for the worst, but miraculously, it stopped prancing and turned its head to the right, pricking up its ears. The horse then trotted quietly over to the side of the tiltyard where a figure was standing on the other side of the fence. It was Owain, with Bella by his side. Having escaped from Izzy's dress-fitting session, he had come out for some fresh air. The horse nuzzled his head into Owain's chest as though he was an old friend. Owain leaned forward, whispered something in the horse's ear and blew into its nostrils. The horse pulled away and nodded as though it was acknowledging a command. Owain looked up at Dan. "He should be a lot calmer now, master Daniel."

Dan was amazed and so thankful. Yet again, the calming effect of Owain's voice had saved the day. "I do wish you would teach me your secret, Owain," Dan told him.

"Maybe one day," he replied. "Now I need to speak to my son!"

As Dan rode his horse at a trot round the perimeter of the tiltyard, Tristan headed towards his father. The two spoke together out of earshot, but Dan noticed from where he was that there seemed to be an argument going on. As the two parted company and Owain left the tiltyard, Tristan walked to where Dan's horse was standing quietly, waiting for a command. He stopped and looked up at Dan sitting in the saddle. "I am to apologise to you. If you prefer to ride a less spirited horse, we will change it for the one of Lord Bedivere's choosing."

Dan, not going to be seen as a wimp, replied loftily, "No, that will not be necessary, I prefer a horse with attitude." Gently squeezing his thighs into the horse's flanks, he persuaded it to canter towards the end of the barrier and beckoned the young squire to hand him a lance, which he grabbed and clutched tightly beneath his arm. It was more awkward to hold onto now he was wearing armour, but he had come too far to give up. He turned his steed to face the row of small shields along the length of the barrier. They looked smaller now, but Dan had been quite good at 'tent pegging' in his gymkhana days, so *how hard can it really be?* he thought. He pondered for a moment and gritting his teeth, squeezed his thighs into the horse's flanks, sending him from a standing start into a full gallop. Dan's aim was straight and true; one by one, the shields succumbed to the force of his lance to the accompaniment of enthusiastic cheers from the gathered crowd. He galloped towards Tristan and his squire, brought the horse to a sudden stop that covered both of them with dust from the sandy ground, and threw the lance for the squire to catch, announcing with a smirk, "Is that how it's done?" As he dismounted, he thought to himself that his performance was more luck than judgement, especially as he had closed his eyes during his pass! Maybe, just maybe, it was the horse that did all the work and that whatever Owain had whispered to him, had a magical effect on him?

"What's his name, Tristan?" Dan asked, as he patted the horse's neck.

"He is called 'Trehern', which means 'strong as iron'," Tristan replied.

"Well, I think that's a very suitable name for such a spirited animal. I will ride him from now on." Dan handed the reins to the stable lad and removed his helmet.

Tristan glared at him with some disdain and replied sarcastically, "Lord Bedivere will have to be informed you have rejected his choice of horse in favour of Trehern. He may not sanction it as this horse is greatly prized by him for the stud."

Dan couldn't help himself from retaliating in the only way he knew, and mimicking his father's court voice announced, "I'm sure if I ask the king, he will allow me this one indulgence. I will seek his counsel when we dine this evening."

14

Presentation at Court

For many years Bronwyn had denied Arthur her company, and in doing so had driven him to lock himself away even while he continued with the business of governing his kingdom. This meant there was no reason in their lives for celebration and feasting. Courtiers considered life at the palace to be dull and boring. Most of their time was spent away, busying themselves on their own estates. But things had changed since word got around of Izzy's arrival, and once again the palace buzzed with excitement as courtiers returned, eager to meet their king's long-lost daughter. And what better excuse for a feast than to celebrate the king and queen's newly enhanced relationship and the joyful return of their daughter.

Unknown to Izzy, Bronwyn had secretly summoned her mother, Gorawen, to Cuddfan to tell her the exciting news that Izzy had decided to stay. Wanting to surprise Izzy, she had sneaked Gorawen into the palace the evening before. Izzy had nearly finished dressing for the feast when there was a knock on the door of her apartment. As it opened, standing in the doorway was her grandmother, beaming at her. Entering the room, she ran over towards Izzy and smothered her in hugs. "Oh Izzy, my darling, you look every inch a queen! I'm so happy for you and Bronwyn that you have decided to stay."

"Well, grandmother, you don't look half bad yourself," Izzy replied.

"Oh, this old gown, it's one of Bronwyn's cast offs – she lent it to me for this evening's celebrations. It must have been made for her when she was pregnant with you otherwise it would never have fitted a lump like me."

They both laughed; Izzy was so glad to see her grandmother again.

Everyone was in a jocular mood as Arthur and Bronwyn presented Izzy, Dan, and George to the closest members of the royal court. Of course, everyone knew Lady Gorawen, but were surprised to see her there as she had always avoided such occasions in the past.

The huge dining hall was decorated with elaborate wall-hangings depicting the flora and fauna of the area as well as hunting and battle scenes; a group of eight musicians played from the gallery above. The tables were set out in a circular pattern, so no one person was sitting at the head. Arthur and Bronwyn were sitting together as hosts, and seated next to her mother was Izzy. Gorawen had asked to be seated between Arthur and Bronwyn; she wanted to hear the whole story from her son-in-law about Izzy's kidnap. George had elected to sit next to Izzy, but Dan, wanting to gather as much advice from Arthur on the joust as he could, was seated next to the king. After the discomfiture he had experienced that day with Tristan, he sensed he would require some expert guidance to avoid failure in the tournament, and who better to give a few pointers than Arthur.

As the servants brought the first course to the table, everyone waited patiently until the king had started before they too began to eat. Medieval etiquette was a ritual that was carried out with great ceremony. Each servant had a role to play in serving the food and drink; these were not low-born servants but young male members of the household whose parents were quite often of noble birth. Dan noticed that some of the young men serving at the tables were the same knights he had seen at the tiltyard that very day. As he was offered wine by someone standing behind him, he recognised Tristan's voice. Seeing as Dan was seated next to the king, this time he was on his very best behaviour; it was a little too close to home to pull another stunt as he had done with the feisty steed Trehern.

Izzy was keen to know what her little brother had been doing all day, but not wanting to give any secrets away, George just told her he had been doing a bit of this and a bit of that. She thought how strange, as he was usually so vocal it was almost impossible to shut him up. Izzy wished he would say something as she desperately wanted something different to discuss other than frocks. She tried surreptitiously to attract Dan's attention, but he was deep in conversation with Arthur – discussing tournament tactics no doubt.

Once the food was cleared away by an army of servants, the trestle tables were moved from a neat circle into a sweeping curve to allow for an uninterrupted view of the entertainment Arthur had laid on for his guests. To great applause and laughter, a succession of jugglers, tumblers, clowns, and fire eaters thrilled the court with their skilful acts, daring stunts, and comical sketches.

As the applause for the last performers faded, and the great hall fell silent, a frail, wizened old man stepped out from the shadows and faced his audience. Izzy sensed an aura of tranquillity in his presence; the man's ice-blue eyes shone out like jewels through the mass of snowy-white hair that framed his weather-beaten face, terminating in the long beard that cascaded like a waterfall down to his waist. His name was Heddwyn, a loved and well-respected Celtic poet and storyteller. He carried a gnarled old wooden staff, as long as he was tall. He bowed gracefully to the royal hosts, raised himself fully upright like a young stag about to do battle, and stamped his staff three times on the stone flags beneath his feet, the sound echoing eerily around the hall.

As he uttered the first lines of an ancient poem in the Celtic tongue, the whole court was rapt, and it slowly dawned on Izzy that it was the same rhyme that Aunt Gorawen had recited to her when she was a little girl. It was all becoming clear now that even from an early age she was being groomed by her aunt for this day. The language she had been taught that she thought was Welsh was, in fact, the ancient language of her father's people, Celtic.

Heddwyn's sparkling eyes danced in harmony with the tangled white hair of his eyebrows as he began to tell the story of King Vortigern and the two dragons, one white and the other red, that resided in a subterranean pool beneath the crumbling walls of his castle. Bronwyn quietly translated the words to Izzy, George, and Dan in English as it unfolded until, finally, the exciting conclusion of the tale was reached and Heddwyn, bowing to his audience, took his leave to cheers and rapturous applause.

Izzy turned to her father. "I've been meaning to ask you for a while, Father – your language is beautiful, yet all the people I've met in Cuddfan speak English."

Arthur smiled and gripped her hand. "When all those years ago I asked Gorawen to find a family to bring you up as their own, I explicitly stated that one day when you were old enough to be told, I would want you back. After telling me she had placed you with an English family, I vowed to learn your language so that when you returned you would not feel isolated. On her part, she would teach you a little of our native tongue. I have learnt many languages in my time on this earth to aid my studies of ancient civilisations, in the hope that I could bring a little light from the New World into Cuddfan. You may have noticed the large library in my day chamber; those books were furnished for me by Gorawen. I wouldn't say it was easy for me, but after studying for a year, I came to realise that it was such a rich and noble language and infused with so many of the words from the civilisations I had studied before, that I would make it a second language to our own."

Izzy's eyes lit up. "You did all that for me?"

"You have many new challenges to face, Izzy, and I didn't want to risk losing you through our failure to communicate in a language you are familiar with. It has not been easy to educate everyone; many of the books we have are old and were written in the form of English that might be more familiar to your brother's ancestors. People in my world are eager to welcome change, but at a much slower pace than you have been used to in the world in which you grew up. One of the many reasons I sent you away from Cuddfan was for you to learn the ways of the modern world and on your return, bring a shining new light into the darkness of our isolated kingdom."

Izzy placed her hand on her father's cheek and caressed it with an increasing intensity of the love she felt on hearing the words spoken from his heart. No wonder her father had become such a legend that kings throughout history had so much regard for him they created orders of chivalry based on his courage and honour. Pictures of him as a hero were drawn from fragments of stories of the past, but to her, he was a father whom she was growing to love more deeply as each day passed, a far more caring person than the myth and the legend everyone thought they knew.

The master of ceremonies, a large man resplendent in velvet and silver, standing behind Arthur, suddenly tapped his staff on the floor three times and shouted, "Pray silence for the King!"

The room fell silent; Arthur stood up and coughed to clear his throat. "You must all be aware by now that we, the Queen and myself, have been recently reunited with our daughter, the most beautiful Lady Isabella. But what you may not be aware of is ... that it is my intention to stand down as king of Cuddfan. I have ruled over this great kingdom of ours for some fifteen hundred years and now feel it the right time to pass this responsibility on to our daughter. She will be crowned three weeks from now. After the coronation we will introduce Queen Isabella to all her subjects in Cuddfan with a tour of the kingdom. To celebrate our daughter's return and my time as king, a Grand Tournament is to be held, the winner of which will be given the title of Queen's Champion along with the due respect that goes with this office, including the granting of a new manor." Arthur picked up his glass of wine, looked down towards Izzy and continued, "A TOAST to THE FUTURE QUEEN of CUDDFAN, LADY ISABELLA!" Everyone stood and toasted Izzy.

Izzy looked up at her father in astonishment and whispered to him as he sat down again, "You didn't tell me I was to take over from you and Mother."

Arthur smiled, "Don't worry, Izzy, your mother and I will always be here to advise and counsel you."

Izzy, with a worried expression, replied, "but I'm far too young, Father, I'm really not ready for such responsibilities."

Gorawen looked round at her granddaughter and said sharply, "Nonsense, Izzy! You have the makings of a very good queen. From what I've heard from Arthur you have the tenacity of a lion – excellent common sense – a good head on your shoulders – er, kindness in your heart – and as well as your mother and father, I will be on hand to support you in any way I can."

Before Arthur could answer, a man stood up from his seat and asked nervously, "May I speak openly, Majesty?"

Arthur looked puzzled, but could not deny his plea so replied, "Why, of course, Lord Llewelyn, you know that every man and woman is free to speak openly to the court."

Llewelyn bowed respectfully and began, "I am a loyal subject of your majesty. My ancestors have served and supported you since you became our king. You won the divine right to rule by possessing the sacred sword Caliburn. Now you wish to relinquish your title and pass it on to your daughter. However, it seems to me that without Caliburn to prove her birthright to rule, she would lay our kingdom open to pretenders and rebellion."

Frowning, Arthur sat back in his seat and Izzy could see he was troubled by the comments. Everyone looked to the king to reply. He knew that Llewellyn spoke the truth, but in all the excitement of their plans to crown Izzy, he had forgotten the importance of the sword to reinforce the entitlement to his family's sovereignty. He stood up and addressed the gathering.

"Every man, woman, and child in our kingdom knows that the resting place of Caliburn is outside of Cuddfan on the holy place we call Ynys Enlli. You are also aware that I, as your sovereign king, am the only man who can withdraw the sacred sword from its resting place. But as Myrddin's prophesy stated when he created this Otherworld, if I ever leave these shores it will return to the sea from whence it came. The sword therefore is beyond our reach, and I fail to see the relevance of your statement, Lord Llewellyn."

"I make it, Majesty, because it is written in our laws that any issue to the throne should prove his or her worthiness by seizing hold of Caliburn."

Arthur's anger was mounting beneath his calm exterior, but he knew he had to remain composed and unruffled. He was curious to know who or what had goaded Llewellyn into making this stand. "We thank you for your concern over this matter, Lord Llewellyn, and will give it our careful consideration over the next few days." Hoping he had defused the situation, Arthur clapped his hands together and raising his voice a little, exclaimed, "This is a celebration for the safe return of our daughter, so musicians, please break this silence for us and fill the hall with your music!"

As he sat down, he caught the eye of Gawain, his first minister, who immediately got to his feet and came to the king's side. Arthur whispered into his ear, "I want you to place a watch on our Lord Llewellyn. I want to know every person he has an association with. I fear his plea was planned and made with a purpose."

Arthur smiled, and turned to Izzy. "Now, my daughter, will you dance with your old father."

"But I don't know how to," she replied nervously.

"No matter … no matter … no one will laugh at you, I assure you. Just follow my lead." He offered his hand to her, and Izzy, with some reluctance, stood up and placed her hand in his. Arthur led his daughter to the centre of the hall where they stood for a moment in silence looking at each other. He winked at her and signalled to the musicians to begin. Izzy, watching her father's feet very closely, began to dance with him.

While they were dancing Izzy asked her father, "What was all that about? Why is the sword so important to everyone that I was kidnapped on account of it, and Lord Llewelyn got his knickers in a twist?" Arthur was flummoxed; he had never before heard such a phrase as 'knickers in a twist' and he suspected it was indelicate. But he understood what she was getting at and told her they would discuss it later, in private.

Gorawen turned to Bronwyn and patted her hand. "Well, my darling, I am very tired, it's been a long day. Sadly, I'm not as young as I once was. Please tell Izzy I said goodnight and thank Arthur for a wonderful evening." She rose from her chair and kissed her fondly on the cheek. Before Bronwyn could say anything, she had disappeared down the Great Hall.

Seeing his chance to have some fun, Dan stood up, bowed towards the Queen and asked if she would join him in the dance. "Why, master Daniel, I would be honoured to accompany you," she replied with a warm smile. They walked out to the centre of the floor to join Arthur and Izzy, and before long the rest of the court followed suit. As the evening wore on, Arthur and Bronwyn introduced Izzy one by one, to many members of his court. It would take her some time to remember all their names, but she was enjoying herself being the centre of attention for once.

Dan was getting rather tipsy. His wine glass was being refilled by Tristan every time he placed it back on the table, so he was unaware of just how much he was consuming. One minute he was telling one of the courtiers how he had tamed the great wild stallion Trehern, and the next found him collapsed in a heap on the floor. Izzy ran over to her brother and looked at him with no little contempt at embarrassing them all in front of the court, but Bronwyn came to the rescue with two guards, who helped him up from the floor and escorted him to a suitable place out of public view to be sick. Bronwyn assured Izzy that he wouldn't be the last or indeed the only man to be taken by the illness that night. Izzy laughed and put Dan out of her mind as she re-joined the party.

George by this time had found a suitable place to curl up, and had fallen asleep. This had been one of the best days of his life. None of his friends would believe him when he got back home, but he didn't really care anymore. If George had his way, he would stay here for the rest of his life, even if it did mean he would have to get used to the smell of guano.

The royal party retired to their apartments. Dan had been helped to his bed by the guards and Arthur carried George, who was still fast asleep. He was rather enjoying his time as a father, having never known what it was really like to have children running round him. As Izzy tucked George into bed and kissed his cheek, Arthur whispered for her to join him in his chamber.

Izzy walked into the king's chamber to join her father and was greeted by Bronwyn, who served them both with a late-night drink made from herbs from the garden. They sat around the fire to warm themselves from the evening chill that blew in through the balcony window. Arthur asked Izzy if she had enjoyed the evening.

"I had a fantastic time, thanks, Father – 'ace' as we say in my world."

"I must get used to the way you speak, Izzy."

"And you must teach me more of our wonderful language – so I can understand what people are saying behind my back," she replied jokingly.

"You wanted to know more about the sword Caliburn and why it is so highly regarded by our people?" Izzy nodded.

"There are many different stories as to its origins, but I only know the one that Myrddin told me when I was a boy. It was wrought from many rare and wonderful metals from the earth and symbolised the struggle of the Celtic people to be ruled by one of its own. It has no master. I know from first-hand that it is the only weapon to hold the power of life and death over an immortal. To even grip the sword, you must be worthy of its loyalty. Sadly, as Lord Llewellyn well knows, it is no longer within our sight. The only reminder we have of its great power is the scabbard."

Arthur rose from his seat, walked over to a chest, and opening the lid pulled out a long object wrapped in a woollen blanket. He shut the chest and stepped back, taking his seat next to Izzy. He placed the parcel on his lap and slowly unwrapped it. Izzy and Bronwyn were taken by surprise by the beauty of what they saw. "This is the scabbard that once contained the great sword of our people. No one knows of its existence but me. When Myrddin fought Queen Nimue and killed her and himself with Caliburn, his assistant Brother Catamanus witnessed the great battle and brought the scabbard back to me for safekeeping. It has magic powers of its own, and together with the sword it will make whosoever has the right to possess it, invincible."

Izzy picked up the scabbard and dropped it immediately back into Arthur's lap, letting out a muted scream. "I wasn't expecting that, it felt alive!" Arthur smiled. Now knowing what to expect, she picked it up again, but this time held onto it. "Wow! I can feel something surging through it into my body."

Arthur chuckled. "It's a wondrous feeling, is it not, Izzy? The scabbard has become one with you. It senses your lineage and entitlement to the Celtic throne."

"Surely then this is all the proof we need, Father? We don't need the actual sword," Izzy replied, placing the scabbard on the table.

"I'm afraid that will not be enough. Although the scabbard responded to your touch, it is only something you can see and feel. The sword is more powerful and impossible to grasp unless you are the rightful heir, and it will burn the hands of the unworthy who try. More importantly, if you or I were to wield the sword, it would ring out a most sonorous sound that all can hear. Thus it is the only proof our law accepts – and that, the ultimate confirmation of birthright, has to be carried out during the coronation ceremony. But the sword is out of our reach, indeed out of the kingdom, on Ynys Enlli."

Izzy recognised Ynys Enlli as the Welsh name for Bardsey Island. "Why is it out of reach?" she asked.

"It is in the New World – your world. I cannot leave this land even though I am immortal. As I told the court, if I leave these shores, Cuddfan will no longer exist. Thus, I am prevented from leaving the kingdom by Myrddin's magic, and as I am the only one who can take possession of the sword, it is lost forever – which means you will not be able to prove your right to the throne of Cuddfan."

"But *I* am not tied here! Gorawen told me I could pass between the two worlds any time I desire, and if the scabbard reacted to me then surely the sword would too," replied Izzy excitedly. "After all, someone kidnapped me to do exactly that."

"It is out of the question – it is far too dangerous. We know not what will happen once you have drawn the sword. You may unlock Nimue's evil on yourself, and for all we know, on Cuddfan too." Arthur looked at his wife and could see she was about to break down. "What I am about to say to you must remain between us. It is vital for certain plans we have secretly put in place that no one knows. Gawain has good reason to believe that Myrddin and Nimue's daughter, Creiryddlydd, may have been the person responsible for your kidnap. She certainly would have inherited both her parent's magical powers and would also be an immortal. We know not where Myrddin took her when he spirited her away. I didn't want to tell you this before as I knew it would worry you."

Izzy pondered for a few seconds, staring down at the scabbard. Then in a moment of unexplained inspiration, she reached out and grasped it in both hands. Closing her eyes, she concentrated into it all her innermost thoughts. Its energy began pulsating through her body in waves, forming pictures in her subconscious. Two thousand years of history flashed into her mind's eye, including the final moments of Myrddin's life, but far too fast for her to realise what she was witnessing. However, what she saw next threw her back into her chair with a jolt. She opened her eyes wide and jumped to her feet, looking down at her parents. "The scabbard has shown me the way. I will go to Ynys Enlli and retrieve Caliburn."

Bronwyn had heard enough. She jumped to her feet and placed her hands on Izzy's shoulders, pleading with her. "You have only just returned to us, Izzy. You could have been killed at the hands of Meyric and his band of thugs. I will not allow you to risk your life again over a stupid sword!" Tears began rolling down her cheeks. She turned to Arthur for support and cried out in anger, "For pity's sake, Arthur, forbid her to go. You are still king! You have the power to change this ridiculous law. I will never speak to you again if you allow this to happen."

Arthur sprang to his feet, took her in his arms and tried to comfort her. He turned to Izzy, shaking his head. "No, Izzy! I will not allow you to risk your life for a stupid law. I am the king, and I can change laws."

Izzy came into her parents' embrace, grasping each of their hands tightly in hers. "It is for that very reason I must reclaim the sword. If you change the law to suit yourself, it will ever after be a cause of suspicion and will be levelled against you. Even you must realise that as long as it's out there, there will always be a threat of someone using it against us."

Arthur sighed deeply. "This is all the family I have and I do not want to lose either of you. You have inherited your mother's beauty, fire, and stubbornness, and from me a determination to do what is right for our people. To decide now would be foolhardy. I will sleep on it and let you know my answer after we have attended Huw's funeral."

Bronwyn couldn't contain her feelings any longer and in floods of tears ran from the room, slamming the door shut behind her. Suddenly a chilling breeze blew the door of the balcony wide open and agitated the flames of the fire into a frenzy. In the distance, the distinctive warlike cry of a dragon encircling the night sky could be heard.

15

Fools and Heroes

George was in a deep sleep when Izzy burst into his room. She went over to his bed and shook him. "Come on, sleepy head, wake up!" she yelled.

He awoke in a daze, and sitting up rubbed the sleep from his eyes. "What's all the fuss? I was in the middle of a dream."

Izzy sat on the bed and looked into his bloodshot eyes. "I need your assistance, little brother."

"Me ... why me, what do I have to do?" he replied.

"You have met with Ambrosius, the great dragon, haven't you?"

"Might have ..." he said evasively.

"Don't come that with me, George, I am your sister, remember."

"Oh, all right, I have met Ambrosius ... why, what of it?"

"I want you to introduce me to him."

"Why, what do you need to see him for? He's *my* friend."

"I cannot tell you why yet, Georgie, but you mustn't discuss this with anyone else ... not even Dan. We have to keep this between you and me."

Finally, George agreed to her demands. "Ok! But I will have to ask Efion first. When do you want to meet him?"

"I am going to attend poor Huw's funeral this morning, so shall we say after lunch?"

For once Dan had risen from his bed before everyone else. He was keen to get himself fit for the tournament and decided to go for a run before breakfast, even though he was sporting a rather nasty hangover from the night before. Luckily for him, Bronwyn had left a foul-tasting drink by his bedside with a little note underneath the glass saying, 'drink me before you rise. Bronwyn'. He had taken it, and although the taste of it almost made him sick, it seemed to be working. By his third lap round the courtyard he was beginning to feel a lot better. It was just as well his headache had stopped pounding inside his skull as the palace was now waking up and the workshops around the courtyard were rapidly becoming busy with the dissonant sounds of strident hammering.

His tenth lap was interrupted by Bella, who came bounding up to him, stopping him in his tracks. A few metres behind was Owain. "Good morning to you, master Daniel … feeling better, are we?"

"Ah, well, yes, the queen left a drink for me to take – pretty horrible but it seems to be working."

"I am intrigued why you are running round and round for no purpose that I can see?"

"Ah well – there is a purpose – it's to strengthen my body and improve my breathing for the tournament."

Owain smiled at him. "Excellent, master Daniel, but maybe you should be running within your armour, to get used to it." Dan chuckled, thinking Owain was jesting with him, not realising he was serious.

The next statement from Owain surprised Dan as he appeared to be reading his thoughts. "You think I jest, master Daniel, but I mean it. You should wear your armour until it becomes part of you. Now, if you have a moment, I will properly introduce you to your horse, Trehern."

As they walked into the stable, they were met by the hectic scene of horses being fed and watered before being exercised. As they approached Trehern's stall, Dan could see why he was so highly prized by Lord Bedivere. Although he was fully occupied feeding, his eyes and ears were alert to what was going on around him. Owain walked into the stall alongside Trehern and immediately the horse responded to his presence. He beckoned Daniel to join him and gently took hold of his hands, placing them over the horse's muzzle while whispering into the horse's ear and looking into Daniel's eyes. Dan felt a pleasing calmness come over him and he was conscious of the stallion's heartbeat blending with his own. Pulling his hands away from the horse, Owain whispered, "Now you are one with Trehern. You will never have to speak a command to him – he will do exactly as you bid from your thoughts. You must now ride him straightaway to cement your bond with him."

He helped Dan to mount and told him to relax his arms to the sides of his body and grip the unsaddled horse with his thighs, then think his command. As he thought of moving forward, Trehern moved ahead. He thought of reversing, and the horse retraced his steps. Dan was amazed. Owain asked him to keep what he had experienced to himself and tell no one of the powers he had demonstrated that morning.

It was Izzy's wish that Huw should be laid to rest beside his wife and son, who were buried in the graveyard of a small church close to the palace. As the funeral cortege, complete with a guard of honour of some twenty men-at-arms, entered from the south side of Aberffraw, and the church came into view, Izzy could see the volume of support Huw had earned during his lifetime. The whole village had turned out to pay their last respects to a local boy who had touched all their lives at some time with his generosity and kindness. She was so glad she had persuaded her father to honour Huw for saving her life rather than vilifying him for his part in her kidnap attempt. The details of his role in the plot were kept a closely guarded secret, known only to those close to the king. In the minds of Huw's friends and fellow villagers, he was a hero who had lost his life trying to save their king's daughter.

As the royal party left, they were enthusiastically cheered by the crowd. It was the first time they had set eyes on Izzy and all were eager to catch a glimpse of her. To them, she was a goddess who would one day be their queen. It confirmed in her the enormity of the responsibility that would be laid on her shoulders by the simple task of placing a crown on her head.

Dan was so excited at the thought of riding Trehern again, he decided to forego breakfast altogether. Before Owain left, he had told him that the more he got involved with Trehern's welfare, the stronger the bond would be, which meant taking over the role of stable boy. With this in mind, Dan had collected Trehern's grooming tools and spent an hour or so making his coat shine before saddling him for some serious riding. Since the tournament was announced, the tiltyard had been a hive of activity, all the young men around the palace being eager to prove their worth in the joust and win the prize of a lifetime. Consequently, Dan drew a lot of attention as he walked out from the stable with Trehern following closely behind him without the use of reins. He couldn't wait to show off his new skills, so as soon as he entered the tiltyard, Dan commanded Trehern to stop while he walked forward several paces and turned to face him. With all eyes now focused on this pair, Dan commanded Trehern to walk towards him. He stopped directly in front of him, and to everyone's amazement, bent one leg, lowering the front of his body nearer the ground, close enough for Dan to step into the saddle and take up his riding posture. Trehern raised his body slowly up into a standing position to make ready for his master's next command.

From the side of the tiltyard came a slow continuous hand clap, and as Dan turned towards the source of the disparaging applause, Tristan came out from the shadows clapping his hands together with slow, determined smacks and shouting sarcastically as he walked towards him, "Bravo! Bravo! Obviously, you are a natural, master Daniel." He stopped clapping and bowed. "Surely you no longer need the help of a mere mortal like me?"

Dan was dumbfounded; he couldn't understand Tristan's attitude towards him. What had he done wrong, and what did he have to gain by trying to chastise him in this manner in public?

Tristan continued his tirade of sarcasm. "Well, why don't we see just how good you are at the joust?"

Dan bent down from the saddle and pleaded with him in a soft tone to stop this nonsense, but Tristan goaded him even further and strutted around Trehern in a circle, trying to humiliate him in front of the gathering crowd, shouting, "I see you are afraid to take me on, master Daniel!"

Dan lost his composure at this and galloped over towards the stand of lances, where he swooped down to gather one in his hand. He turned on the spot and charged back towards where Tristan was standing. "Very well, Tristan, let's see what you've got!"

Tristan yelled for his horse to be brought to him, and after waiting impatiently for few minutes mounted it, galloped towards the stand and, snatching a lance from his squire, ordered him to remove the small shields from the fence. He galloped back to pull up within a few centimetres alongside a now fuming Daniel. Tristan shouted at his squire for two shields to be brought out to them, but instead of rushing to do his master's bidding, the boy stepped forward and looked up at the two warring young men. "Please, sirs, you cannot joust without armour! If nothing else, at least wear your helmets – I implore you."

Tristan kicked the squire hard in the chest, knocking him off his feet. "How dare you question me, you insolent boy! Do as I command or you will feel the sting of my whip!"

Dazed, he looked up at his master from the ground in bewilderment. This was not the young man he had happily served for the past five years; he couldn't understand the sudden change in his temperament – he had always had a kind and generous nature. Fearing the consequences, however, he jumped to his feet and ran to the stable to fetch the shields. Things had gone too far for either of the headstrong adolescents to back down now, and as the squire returned, breathless from running in haste with the two shields, they each snatched one in turn and galloped out to either side of the tiltyard. The young squire, shaking his head, legged it towards the safety of the fence.

Daniel by this time was beginning to panic. Clearly, having no armour for protection, one of them could get killed, but as he contemplated giving in, Tristan was in full gallop and heading towards him. Suddenly a horse and rider appeared from nowhere and jumped the fence, clearing it by a few centimetres. It was Lord Bedivere who, returning from Huw's funeral, had heard the commotion as he entered the courtyard. As Bedivere charged from the side at full gallop towards Tristan, Dan threw down his lance and watched as horse and rider collided into Tristan's mount, knocking both rider and horse into the fence and onto the ground. Bedivere jumped from his saddle, and as a young squire ran out to take hold of the reins, picked Tristan up from the ground by the scruff of his neck and pushed him screaming towards Dan, who by this time had dismounted Trehern.

Bedivere was so furious at them both he yelled, "No one, and I mean no one," as he grabbed Dan by his collar, "jousts without the protection of armour. I will bang both of your stupid heads together." Releasing his iron grip, he glared at them contemptuously. "You are both supposed to be above such stupid behaviour. I will not have anyone showing off in front of my young squires." Dan stared at Tristan in silence and bowed his head. "Now return your mounts to the stable, and when you have done rubbing them down, I will see you both in my quarters."

Efion was engrossed in polishing the dragon saddle when George walked into the stable. "Ah, master George, you should be doing this, not me."

George picked up a blanket from the side and threw it roughly over the saddle to hide it. Efion shouted at him, "What are you doing, aren't you pleased I'm working on it for you?"

Looking very secretive, George whispered, "Sorry, Efion, I have someone who wants to talk to you and I don't want her to see the saddle."

He suddenly twigged. "Ah, I see, and would that person be your sister?" George nodded in agreement. Efion tapped his finger to his nose and winked at him. "Is she waiting outside?" George nodded again and running out to the yard, grabbed hold of Izzy's arm and pulled her into the stable.

Efion removed his hat and bowed, "I am honoured you seek me out, Majesty, how can I serve you?"

Izzy, still wearing the black gown she'd worn for Huw's funeral, smiled at Efion and thanked George, hoping he would leave them in privacy, but he wasn't moving. She intimated with her eyes and flicked her head, but still he wouldn't go. She finally ordered him to wait outside. He stood his ground and said, "No! If you want to speak to Ambrosius you will have to speak through me. They are very dangerous creatures, you know, and they will lick your face off if they don't like your smell!"

Efion let out a haughty laugh. "I have taught you well, master George." Izzy looked confused and gave George a disapproving frown. Efion put his hand on George's shoulder. "Please leave us a moment, master George. I'm sure your sister has good reason to talk to me alone."

George looked hurt that he should be discarded in this way, and very slowly and reluctantly shuffled outside, but placed one foot out and the other inside. He shouted, "I will be just here if you need me."

Seeing George was still within range, Izzy moved closer to Efion and turned her back on her brother so he couldn't read her lips. "I need to talk to Ambrosius urgently, Master Efion. I cannot stress how important it is to speak to him alone."

"You have not discussed this with master George?" he replied.

"Why do you say that?" she asked.

"Only because when you communicate with Ambrosius, it is done in silence." Izzy looked baffled. "Ambrosius reads and talks to your mind. No one can overhear you. Your brother knows this. He is just a little worried you might be trying to take his friend from him, that's all."

"Ah, I see. No, it's nothing like that. I can't tell you my reasons for wanting to talk to Ambrosius, I can't even tell my brothers. You can assure George from me that I am not trying to take his friend away from him. He seems to respect you very much and will trust your word over mine."

Efion shook his head. "I think it would be kindly and wise to include your brother in your first encounter with a dragon. For it was he, Ambrosius, who confided in me that, despite your brother's callow appearance, he sensed the courage and wisdom of a warrior in his heart."

Izzy was surprised by his comments. She had known Georgie from the day he was born, and although she loved him dearly, she never really saw him as anything other than a selfish little boy who enjoyed computer games and cartoons. "If you think that is best, I will do as you suggest, Efion. Maybe I will see my brother in a new light!"

Gawain, Arthur's first minister, was ushered into the king's chamber. Arthur walked towards his friend with an outstretched hand, beckoning him to sit. "What news of Lord Llewellyn? Have you found anything that might connect him with any of the names procured from Meyric's men?"

"I feel it is too soon to make any judgement on his allegiance. I have questioned him in a friendly manner and it seems his outburst at the feast was without provocation. In fact, he believes his words were not his own but came from bewitchment."

Arthur was astonished. "And what of your thoughts on the matter – do you believe him?"

"As you know, Majesty, there are very few people who can impede the truth with my methods of questioning. Yes, I think that he believes he told me the truth, but I have instructed my men to watch him closely in case he has deceived me."

"The more I think on it," Arthur said with a sigh, "the more I suspect you are right about Creiryddlydd. She is Myrddin's daughter and would have inherited his powers of mind-invasion. But as to her whereabouts we are in the dark, so we must be on our guard at all times. We should be open to any possibilities and look inside our closest allies as well as our adversaries in case she has turned them to her own mind."

"Let us hope the subterfuge we have put in place entices her from the shadows before it is too late. Is the plan well in hand?"

"Yes, indeed it is. I am sorry I cannot divulge the details at this stage. It is not that I do not trust you, but as with a spider's web, its first few threads are delicate and can be broken by the slightest breeze."

Gawain knew that Arthur had no choice but to keep his plans to himself. The least who were privy to his stratagems, the better.

"Now," said Arthur, "I would like to discuss security arrangements for Izzy's coronation."

Tristan banged on the door of Bedivere's quarters and a voice from within bellowed to enter. Tristan, followed by a crestfallen Daniel, entered the room, and together they stood with heads bowed in front of a very angry Bedivere. Beside him, and to witness the proceedings, was his second-in-command, Sir Aeddan.

Bedivere looked up at them both. "I am much disturbed by your behaviour to one another in front of my young knights and squires. I am most angry at you, Tristan. I thought of you as one of my best, and for that reason I followed the king's bidding to honour you with the task of training Lady Isabella's brother for the joust. And as for you, master Daniel, I was assured by his majesty you were of good character and fit for training as a knight. I even gave you leave to take my prize stallion for your own occasion. To say I am distressed by your actions would belittle the displeasure I feel." He pondered to himself for a moment, staring coldly into the eyes of his two charges, though more for effect than necessity. With a stern face he delivered his decision. "I have thought awhile on this matter and sought the counsel of the king. We have decided to put you both to punishment until you prove to me you are worthy of continuing my sanction as knights. You will no longer lodge in your allotted apartments but with the apprentices of the armourer. For the next seven days you will both toil in his workshops and do his bidding." Tristan and Dan looked down, away from Bedivere's steely gaze. "Do I make myself clear?" he said in a raised voice.

"Yes, sir," was the muted reply in unison.

"Have either of you anything to say as to my judgement?"

"No, sir."

"Then you will take your bedrolls from your quarters together with some suitable attire and report to Master Emrys, the king's armourer, for duty." The boys glanced at each other with hidden repugnance and then turned to face Bedivere's grim countenance. "Now be gone from my sight," he said, pointing towards the door.

They bowed and turned to take their leave, but before they reached the door Bedivere spoke once again. "And gentlemen, if we have a repeat performance of your unruly actions, I will personally take a horsewhip to both of you. Now get out!"

As they closed the door quietly behind them, Bedivere leant back in his chair and grinned at Sir Aeddan. "Reminds me a lot of myself when I was their age. I still remember the taste of the horsewhip my master gave me – on many occasions!"

16

A Secret Plan

Izzy gazed out over the lake as the basket lift made its slow ascent up the side of the cliff face. George felt guilty for lying to his sister about Ambrosius, and tugging her elbow to attract her attention from the view. "I didn't mean what I said back there, you know … about Ambrosius."

She looked down at him and smiled. "I know, George. Efion explained to me how close you and Ambrosius have become." She knelt down beside him and gazed at his face. "You see, your big sister needs help from your friend Ambrosius, help that nobody else can give, and because my father has enemies who would harm me, I have to keep it a secret between Ambrosius and me and not tell anyone, even you, dear brother. If anybody got to know you knew my secret, they would kill you to get it. I know you wouldn't tell them, but I can't put you in that situation."

He hugged her and replied gravely, "You know you only have to call on me, and I will be there in an instant."

"Yes, I do know that, Georgie," she replied, unaware she would have to call on her young brother's help sooner than she realised.

The basket came to an abrupt halt as it reached the top. George opened the gate onto the ledge and stretched out his hand to help Izzy step over the gap. She smiled at him for being so thoughtful, then suddenly screwed up her nose as she got a whiff of guano.

"Oh – that," declared George nonchalantly, amused at his sister's reaction, "occupational hazard of working with dragons, I'm afraid. You'll get used to it," he added, offering her a cloth to put over her nose.

Efion chuckled quietly to himself as he lit the lantern and led them towards the hive. As usual, Ambrosius had sensed a presence and had come to meet them halfway. George asked her if he could talk to Ambrosius first and introduce her, but the wily old dragon knew before they even met each other who she really was. As Ambrosius had told

George, you couldn't keep any secrets from him. George spent a few minutes in Ambrosius's presence with a little small talk discussing their expectant flight. Izzy watched wide-mouthed as her little brother talked to a real dragon. George had talked about it enough, but nothing could have prepared her for the reality of seeing one herself for the first time. As George stepped back into the shadows, he urged his sister forward to stand before Ambrosius, and as Ambrosius's voice dimmed inside George's head, he knew they were talking with each other.

"Hello, daughter of Arthur, your brother tells me you need to speak with me." Izzy was amazed by the experience of having Ambrosius's voice inside her head and opened her mouth to speak. "There is no need for you to speak aloud to me, my child. I can read your answer from your mind before you can form the words with your lips."

"Then I see I will have to be very careful with what I am thinking in front of you, Ambrosius. It's a pity I can't do the same!"

"If you could do that, my child, you would have knowledge of my secrets and I fear your young mind could not withstand the effects of such power. Life for humans would be so much simpler if you all had the power to read each other's thoughts – a world without lies."

"I don't think so," replied Izzy. "Men would soon learn to deceive with their thoughts as they now with their mouths."

"Ah, you are enlightened of man's failings – and from one so young! You are truly your father's, or should I say your mother's, daughter. I understand you need my help to retrieve the sword Caliburn?"

Izzy was shocked at Ambrosius's ability at reading her thoughts even before they formed words in her head.

"Female minds are somewhat more complex than the male of your species, but because your minds can ponder on many thoughts at once, I can predict your words in anticipation of what you want to say."

"Caliburn's scabbard has shown me the last moments of the life of Myrddin and Nimue. It also showed me those who witnessed their deaths, and besides Brother Catamanus, there was another. I believe that was you, Ambrosius. You brought Brother Catamanus back to Cuddfan."

"That is so, little princess. I relive that moment often, with great pain in my heart, and you want me to take you back to that place where evil sleeps, perhaps waiting for you to awaken her?"

"My parents have both forbidden me to retrieve the sword, but it seems I can't be accepted as queen unless I hold it in my hand. To me, it's not the symbol of power everyone seems to think it is, but a symbol of my birthright to govern my people. You are the only living being that knows the location of the sword on Ynys Enlli. I beg you – will you do this for me and for our land?"

"This task could prove most perilous for both of us. Ynys Enlli is in the New World and a great distance from the protection of Cuddfan. Who can know what lies beneath the ground after centuries of decay? The man Meyric, who kidnapped you to gain the sword, was just a pawn in a game being played by someone with much more power than we can ever imagine. Is Arthur's daughter ready to deal with such evil?"

"Arthur's daughter will do whatever it takes."

"That being so, your mission is mine. We will need time to prepare. We can only leave Cuddfan at night, and it must be under cover of darkness. Only when there is no moon can I enter your world as me."

"You mean carrying me on your back will prevent you from changing form into a heron as you did when you brought my brothers and me into your world?"

"You were very observant, even in your time of distress."

"No, it was George who believed you were dragons right from the time we arrived in Menai Bridge. At the time I thought it was just a small boy's vivid imagination, but now I know somewhere in that little brother's head of his, is someone extraordinary."

"Although you and your brother are not born of the same blood, you both share a bond with this land and he, like you, will help mould this kingdom into the world Arthur saw in his dreams as a young man." Ambrosius stretched and flexed his wings. "Now I will speak with George alone, for you will need his help to prepare yourself for this undertaking. Although tender in years, his courage and loyalty to you will eclipse many of those who now swear allegiance to your cause."

Izzy thanked Ambrosius for his wisdom and stepped back towards George, who had been sitting on a rock wondering what conversations his sister was having with his friend. "Ambrosius would like to speak to you now, Georgie," she said with a smile. He jumped to his feet, but in his enthusiasm to hear what Ambrosius had to say to him, slipped and fell headfirst onto some dried dragon poo. Ambrosius grinned, and opening his mouth, he gently gripped the collar of George's doublet between his front teeth, lifted him up into the air and put him back on his feet.

As they entered the basket lift for their return trip to the ground, a fly hovered around George's head and landed on his nose. Izzy couldn't help but laugh and holding her own nose with her hand said, "Occupational hazard, hey Georgie?"

She gave him back the rag he'd given her earlier. Wiping away the worst from his face he said calmly, "On a more serious note, Izzy, Ambrosius has asked me to make certain secret arrangements for you. He hasn't told me what the two of you are up to, but I am to tell you to be ready when the moon has turned its head to the heavens and to bring with you the scabbard. He said you would understand. He has sworn me to secrecy, which I will honour with my life."

Izzy replied fondly, "If you weren't so smelly, little brother, I would give you a big kiss!" For once George was glad he had guano on his face.

17

Justice be Done

Tristan and Daniel had not spoken a word to each other since their appearance before Lord Bedivere. Each had gone to their respective apartments, changed into working attire and collected their bedrolls.

Dan took one last look at his room and sighed. The way he was feeling at that moment, he could quite happily have walked away from this old world with its stupid outdated values of chivalry and Bedivere's form of so-called justice. It would be a lot less trouble to head back to *Nicole* and wait for George there in comfort. Then he remembered the lovely Angharad and sighed again. On second thoughts, he was being a bit of an idiot and seven days wasn't really that long. Dan closed the door and made his way to the Armoury. As he rounded the corner outside the workshops, he noticed that Tristan had already been put to work on a bench, polishing a piece of armour; he didn't look pleased. With a similar lack of enthusiasm, Dan went through the entrance, whispering to himself, "I just hope you're worth it, Angharad."

A tall, well-built, middle-aged man with muscular arms and thick wrists walked towards him. He introduced himself politely, but looked dour and humourless. "You must be master Daniel?" Dan nodded and thought that he wouldn't want to get on the wrong side of this fellow. "I am Master Emrys, please come this way." He beckoned Dan to follow him and led him into a dormitory at the back of the workshop. He pointed to a grubby mattress on the floor. "This is where you will sleep while you are in my charge."

Dan looked around at his new accommodation. To say it was simple living would be an understatement and he was not impressed. He placed his bedroll on top of the dirt-stained mattress, but before he could spread it out, Master Emrys had grabbed hold of his shoulder in a vice-like grip. "You can do that later, lad, now please to follow me to your place of work."

He thrust a leather apron into his hands as he hurried him to an area of the workshop away from Tristan. A young man of about sixteen was sitting at a bench punching small holes into hundreds of tiny plates. He spoke abruptly. "These are holes for lacings. Master Alwyn here will instruct you what to do." He looked Dan square in the eye. "I don't want no scrappers either, understand!" and disappeared up a flight of stairs leading to an office of some kind on stilts. Dan watched as he came to the window and stood motionless, peering out over the noisy workshops like a prison guard.

"Don't mind him, he doesn't like having people in his workshops who don't have the skills to be an armourer. He was told by Bedivere to take you two and lick you into shape. He doesn't like being used as a pawn … I'm Alwyn, by the way."

Dan replied, "I must admit, I would rather be somewhere else right now. My name's Daniel." He put out his hand to shake with Alwyn but there was a shout from the back of the workshop. "Get on with your work!"

Alwyn whispered to Dan, "I'd better show you what to do. As long as we're working, he won't shout at us, right?" Dan nodded, and Alwyn explained, "I am punching holes in these plates so they can be attached by laces to an arming doublet. When I punch the holes, a little sharp burr is left on the other side which will, over time cut the lace and the plate will fall away leaving a gap for the tip of a sword blade or arrowhead to get through. Your job is to take that burr away and make it smooth so it won't cut. Although the task looks simple, it's important. If you were to leave the burr in place you could be responsible for someone's death." He showed Dan how to deburr the hole and Dan thought how easy his task was going be – until he saw a box on the floor containing thousands of little plates each with two holes to be smoothed. "Being apprentices, we get all the nasty little jobs the armourers don't like doing. They say it's all part of our training, and they had to do it when they were apprentices."

Dan asked, "How long does an apprenticeship last?"

"Seven years. Then you become a journeyman working for different armouring shops."

Dan was shocked. "Seven years sleeping on the floor back there? No way!"

"Oh, we get one day for our pleasure every week."

"That's kind of them!"

Alwyn tried to change the subject. "Was that you in the list this morning with that black stallion?"

"Did you see me?"

"I was watching while I was eating my lunch. You were outstanding. I think that other knight wronged you, he should never have challenged you without armour."

"Well, that little stunt brought me here to share your bench."

They chatted on while they continued to work. Dan had at least found someone he could talk to as an equal who wasn't out to show off or try to make him feel inferior.

That evening, in the privacy of the royal apartments, Arthur and Bronwyn decided to have a family conference with Izzy. They were eager to tell her their plans for the coming two weeks. Izzy, however, was not in the mood for niceties after she discovered Dan had been sentenced to one week's hard labour in her absence. She confronted her father, shouting at him in a very discourteous manner. "What gives you the right to judge my brother in one of your kangaroo courts without discussing it with me first?"

Surprisingly, it was Bronwyn who stuck up for Arthur. "How dare you speak to the king in that way! He is your king as well as your father and you will show him the respect he deserves. You are not aware of the facts that forced Arthur and Bedivere to make the decision to punish Daniel and Tristan. I assure you, if they had been lesser mortals, they would have been publicly flogged!"

Izzy was not going to back down, but before she could speak Arthur stepped forward and put his hands on her shoulders. Gazing kindly at her he said, "Before you judge me, Izzy, why not ask Daniel what he feels of the punishment?" Izzy stopped in her tracks as Arthur continued, "I give you my word, if your brother feels he has been wrongly judged he can be released this instant and join us for supper."

Arthur called in one of the guards and instructed him to take a message to Daniel at the armourer's workshops and to present Lady Isabella's invitation to dine with her there and then in the king's chamber.

As they waited for the return of the guard, Izzy paced up and down the room huffing and puffing and occasionally giving her parents black looks. Finally, the guard returned and relayed Dan's reply to Izzy.

"If it pleases your majesty, your noble brother told me to thank you for your kind invitation, but he will not be joining you for dinner as he has been a bit of an idiot and has to pay his dues." Izzy stood speechless for once, and turning to her parents apologised for her outburst.

18

A Short Break

Arthur and Bronwyn's decision to take a short break from royal duties and spend a few days as guests of Lord and Lady Gochwyban was met with great enthusiasm by Izzy. She was getting bored with being cooped up in the palace. She knew her father had her safety at heart, but being surrounded by guards all the time restricted her usual free spirit. It would not, however, be much of a break for her father because other than taking part in his favourite sport of hunting, he and his knights had to oversee the final plans for the Grand Tournament. George had insisted on staying behind at the palace; he was far too busy learning to fly with Ambrosius and besides, he and Efion had to prepare for Izzy's secret quest.

Dan, on hearing the news of his sister's trip to the hunting lodge was keen to accompany her as it was there where the love of his life, Angharad, resided. Although he hadn't finished serving his punishment with Tristan at the armoury, Arthur, after an appeal from Izzy for clemency, had finally agreed to release both of them from their purgatory on the condition they both swore an oath that there would be no repeat of their silliness.

It was pouring with rain when the royal party left the palace in a fleet of barges. Arthur and his first minister had planned the holiday in every detail, not leaving anything to chance, and security was very tight. They were accompanied on the barges by fifty men-at-arms. Dan joined Tristan as part of Bedivere's royal guard, which had set out from the palace on horseback earlier to meet the royal party at the hunting lodge.

As the barges neared their destination, the sun, as if by royal command came out, and the rain stopped. As the lines of the royal flotilla were secured to the quayside, Lord and Lady Gochwyban, together with their daughter Angharad, came down to the jetty to greet their royal guests.

Lord Bedivere and his knights had arrived earlier. They formed a mounted guard of honour up to the lodge. It was a magnificent sight as the royal party passed through the lines of mounted knights whose banners fluttered like writhing serpents in the gentle breeze coming off the river. Dan looked down from his mighty steed Trehern, and winked at his sister as she passed. Izzy thought how resplendent her brother looked in his armour. She wasn't the only one to be impressed by Dan's dashing appearance! As they entered the lodge, members of Lord Gochwyban's household formed a double line to welcome their royal guests into their master's home.

The early morning sun rose above the forest canopy, bathing the sandy stone of the lodge in a warm orange glow. The once empty courtyard was beginning to fill up as a string of saddled horses was led out from the stables and lined up in a semicircle in front of the lodge. Before their masters had risen from their beds, an army of stable boys had tirelessly polished every square millimetre of harness, and groomed their masters' mounts to glossy perfection for this special occasion. From a path at the rear of the house, the Master of Hounds, together with the king's falconer, brought their eager charges to the centre and paraded them for all to see. A small army of men dressed in varying shades of green and carrying an arsenal of weapons for the hunt, marched quietly to the side. Finally, a pair of bay mares, each carrying two large wicker baskets filled with all manner of victuals and refreshments, were led out to join the waiting entourage.

Arthur was the first to come out through the door. He stood silently at the top of the steps for a moment, observing the spectacle before him. He smiled with satisfaction and nodded his approval. Putting on a pair of soft leather gauntlets he stepped out into the sunshine. A stable lad stepped forward with his horse.

"A great day for the hunt, is it not, Aled?"

"Indeed, your Majesty," he replied as he held the horse steady for the king to climb into the saddle. He waited for Arthur to make himself comfortable, then handed him the reins.

"Thank you, Aled," he said with a smile. "Now go and tell our hunting party their king is impatient to be off."

As his fellow hunters ran out to join him and mount their steeds, Arthur turned his horse round and galloped off towards the forest track shouting, "The last one to the hunting grounds will sleep in the stable tonight!"

Izzy, Bronwyn, and Angharad, accompanied by knights and men-at-arms for protection, left a couple of hours after Arthur's hunting party had set out. Izzy had accepted Owain's kind invitation to visit his cottage on the coast to meet his daughters. Although she had become very friendly with him since their arrival in Cuddfan, she really didn't know much about his private life and had no idea what reception to expect. Owain had advised her to ride, as he thought it would be a pleasant change from being transported by coach or boat. Not that she minded either way, but to get back in the saddle and be in control of where she was going would be very welcome indeed.

Izzy felt very safe in Owain's company. They rode side by side with Angharad and Bronwyn, chatting all the way. He was very proud of being chosen by the king to be Izzy's personal bodyguard and took his position very seriously, so throughout the journey kept very close to her side, keeping an ever-watchful eye out for anything or anyone suspicious. He had split his retinue into two, fore and aft. At the first sign of trouble, those at the rear could swiftly form an impenetrable wall around their royal charges while those forwards would deal with any attackers.

Travelling with an entourage of some fifty men caused a bit of a stir with the locals; news spread fast, so a lot of people turned out along the way hoping to get a glimpse of both their present and future queens. All but a few cheered as they passed, some pressing small garlands of flowers into their hands. It was the first time Izzy had experienced the warmth of her father's more mortal subjects.

Owain's cottage was situated on the seashore of an estuary, and as they entered the lane leading to the house, they were warmly greeted by Aelwen and Rhiannon, Owain's daughters, together with their honey-coloured dog Megan who came bounding up to meet her master. He was so thrilled that Izzy had agreed to meet his family. They too, like everyone else in Cuddfan were eager to meet her. As everyone dismounted and the horses were corralled into a paddock adjoining the house, Aelwen and Rhiannon brought out refreshments for their guests.

Once fed and watered, the party relaxed on the beach overlooking the estuary, all except the men-at-arms who had the task of keeping Izzy safe.

Anchored about two hundred metres offshore was *Nicole*. It was the first time Izzy had seen her since the day they arrived and she couldn't wait for a chance to get aboard again. In particular, she was eager to gather her toiletries together and take them back with her, especially her shampoo. Medieval soap was excellent for washing one's hands but useless for hair. And then there was her underwear. Celtic women didn't wear anything underneath their gowns other than a long linen petticoat called a chemise, which made it a bit chilly in the draughty corridors of the palace. But as Arthur was keen to see *Nicole* for himself, she would wait for her reunion with the yacht to gather all the personal items she wanted.

Meanwhile, back at the palace, George and Efion were busy preparing the dragon's saddle for his first flight with Ambrosius. Old straps and buckles had been replaced by new, longer ones; the last thing Efion wanted was the saddle breaking away from Ambrosius in flight. Although George had flown in aeroplanes many times on holidays abroad, nothing could prepare him for the adrenalin rush he was about to experience when Ambrosius took to the air.

By the time the basket lift reached the edge of the cave, the rain had stopped, and as the clouds parted to reveal the warm sun, Efion and George pushed the handcart carrying the saddle into the hive. As George wanted to keep his flight a secret from those in the palace, they had arranged to meet Ambrosius at the other entrance on the far side of the mountain. Launching from there would be more discrete.

As usual, Ambrosius sensed their approach and was waiting for them as soon as he heard the trundling of the handcart. As he lowered his neck and head close to the ground, Efion placed a numnah at the base of Ambrosius's neck and explained that its padding would help take up any slack caused by Ambrosius's scales. George helped him lift the saddle into place and Efion attached the straps round Ambrosius's body. Finally, everything was set for him to mount. Before he did, Efion had one final surprise for George. Taking something from a scruffy little sack off the handcart, he pulled out a leather helmet which he placed on George's head. "This is my great-great-grandfather's original helmet that he wore when he rode Ambrosius against the pirates. It now belongs to you."

George, ecstatic and overwhelmed by such generosity, gave him a hug. "Thank you, Efion, it will always remind me of you and Ambrosius."

Efion helped George into the saddle and adjusted the stirrups for his legs, then strapped him into the safety harness. There were no reins, just hand grips on the horn of the saddle. Ambrosius asked George if he was ready and raised his neck slowly into his standing position. He walked to the edge of the cliff ledge. "Hold on tight, my boy," Efion shouted. Before he could reply, Ambrosius launched his massive body off the ledge. George let out an almighty scream as they hurtled dangerously towards the ground before Ambrosius unfurled his mighty wings and swooped to just a few metres above the canopy of the forest below.

"Wo...w!" George cried with his heart still in his mouth.

Ambrosius flapped his wings and within seconds they began to gain height. There was no ride on earth that could compare to the exhilaration of being on a dragon's back, and before long they were soaring high above the island, skipping from cloud to cloud. George could just make out some of the landmarks below.

"Now we are high enough what sort of things would you like me to do?" asked Ambrosius.

"Well," said George, "can you twist in a complete circle?"

"Like this?" Ambrosius tucked his wings tightly into his body and dropping out of the sky twisted his body to make a full turn, then levelled out just above the trees. George could see why he was wearing a safety harness – if he wasn't, he would now be buried headfirst in the forest floor.

They were out for hours, soaring high above the vaporous clouds, trying out all manner of manoeuvres that George planned to use in his flying display. This required minimal effort from George, but Ambrosius, being old and having to do all the work, was exhausted, so they decided to call it a day and flew back to the tranquillity of the cave. George couldn't contain his enthusiasm and all the way down in the wicker lift, animatedly described to a smiling Efion, the exhilaration of flying on a dragon's back.

The sound of the rippling waves lapping gently on the seashore, combined with the heat of the midday sun, was enticing Izzy to go for a swim. The trouble was, there were no such things as bathing costumes on Cuddfan. The alternative was skinny dipping, but as her father insisted she should never go anywhere without the guards ... well, that was out of the question. Then Bronwyn rather daringly suggested they remove their gowns and venture out in their chemises.

The beach wasn't all sand, in fact it got quite muddy nearer the water's edge. But that made it even more tempting. They abandoned their gowns and ran down the beach barefoot in their white chemises, followed by Bella and Owain's dog Megan, who both barked nonstop at the waves and splashed back and forth to their mistresses. It wasn't much fun for their armed guard, though, having to negotiate the muddy beach in their regalia and sweaty armour.

As Bronwyn and the girls ran along the beach, the slimy mud kicked up from their heels and splashed all down their backs, covering their clean white shifts with dark grey streaks. Izzy loved the feeling of the mud oozing between her toes and looked back at the seven sets of footprints they left behind them: two dogs, the queen, and four girls ready for some well-earned fun. Izzy picked up a handful of mud and called Rhiannon who, on turning round, received the missile straight in her face with a splat. Wiping the slime from her eyes she burst out laughing, and that was it: all-out war. They gave no quarter to each other, and in no time at all they were just five grey silhouettes running up and down the beach and into the water. Bella and Megan didn't escape either and as the afternoon wore on, the giggles, barking, and sounds of their splattering feet on the muddy beach filled the air, much to the amusement of the guards seeing their present and future queens enjoying the simple pleasures of mud fighting.

This fun-filled afternoon of girlie high-jinks would remain in Izzy's mind for the rest of her life. Bronwyn too would remember this day. Her dream of sharing her daughter's simple pleasures with her friends had finally come true. In only a short time she felt that their bond as mother and daughter had become closer than she could ever have wished. Their giggling didn't stop all afternoon, even when they washed each other down in the courtyard with buckets of icy cold water from the well, much to the amusement of Owain and his guards who politely turned their backs.

Although hunting was a pastime reserved more for kings, it did have the added advantage of providing food for the table. In that respect, the hunting party had been very successful in bringing back a couple of stags, one wild boar and lots of smaller game. Everyone taking part had thoroughly enjoyed the chase, especially as their king seemed to be his old self once again. It was always the custom to end the day's sport with a great feast in the evening, but as there were so many of the court in attendance, it would take place the following evening as it took several days to organise such a feast. Lord Gochwyban, had anticipated Arthur's request and wisely set things in motion a week before their arrival.

While most of the household were involved in preparing the food, Arthur took the chance to take a closer look at the Moorefield's yacht. Accompanied by Dan, Izzy, and Owain plus the usual dozen or more guards, the barge headed towards the place where *Nicole* had been anchored since their arrival. Izzy couldn't wait to get aboard and was the first to jump off the barge. As she opened the hatch, the horrible smell of rotten food hit her. The fridge had stopped working due to the lack of power and the food left on board had gone rancid in the heat.

As Izzy and Dan tried to clear the boat of spoilt food and the awful smell, Arthur paced up and down the deck in awe. He was intrigued by all the instruments that festooned the cockpit. Izzy thought it was a great shame she couldn't show him everything working. Going below deck, there was even more gear to be seen, and although to us a sea toilet wouldn't stir any of our emotions, to this Celtic king the mechanical mechanism was fascinating. Arthur had become an enthusiastic amateur engineer since ruling Cuddfan and in fact the complicated gates that guarded the tunnel leading to the palace were of his design. Since his kingdom had been locked into the time warp that Myrddin had created with his magic, he had also set up colleges and schools to keep the Celtic culture and crafts alive.

While Izzy gathered together the bits and pieces she wanted to take back with her from her cabin, Dan removed the covers from *Nicole's* diesel engine to show Arthur an example of modern Swedish engineering. He was astonished at modern man's ingenuity and went down on his knees to get a closer look. Dan suddenly had an inspired thought – as the only malfunction on the boat was the electrics, and as a diesel engine, unlike petrol engines, doesn't require electrical power to produce combustion, he could start it manually with a starting handle. After scrambling around in the emergency tool kit, Dan found what he was looking for and placed the rusty old starting handle into the socket end of the crankshaft. After several attempts it burst into life, causing the stern of *Nicole* to disappear in a cloud of thick grey-black smoke from the exhaust. This sudden eruption of the power of the engine sent everyone running for cover until Izzy reassured them it was quite safe.

Dan asked Owain to help him manually raise the anchor and Izzy took the helm. On Dan's signal, she put *Nicole* into gear and slowly moved forward. As Izzy steered *Nicole* out into the sheltered bay, she beckoned her father to take the wheel. Arthur's face was a picture; he was really impressed that such a small assemblage of metal could deliver enough power to drive a boat of *Nicole's* size through the water with such ease. It was a shame the kingdom didn't have any filling stations, thought Dan, so he could take Arthur further out.

Arthur's schoolboy enthusiasm for *Nicole's* magical powers never waned and he chatted continuously to Dan all the way back to the lodge. Izzy watched them, smiling to herself that a mundane piece of modern machinery could cause such emotions in grown men. For her, the bag of personal items she clutched in her hands was far more important to her than some oily old engine.

19

A Date with Destiny

As the wicker lift ascended the cliff face into the darkness of a moonless night, Izzy's mind was full of trepidation at the thought of what she was about to do. She was clutching Caliburn's scabbard, as Ambrosius had told her it would protect her if she was wearing it. Although both her parents had forbidden her to go, she knew that there was no alternative. Yes, Arthur had the power to change the law, but Izzy wanted her people to accept her as a rightful heir to his throne in the time-honoured way. Besides, knowing Ambrosius would protect her, she felt reassured she could come to no harm. It was only on the way up to the hive that Izzy had informed George and Efion of her intention to retrieve Caliburn. They would accompany her as far as the cliff's edge, where she and Ambrosius would leap into the darkness on their journey to Ynys Enlli to regain the precious, all-important Celtic artefact.

George and Efion opened the gate and pulled the handcart carrying the saddle, over the ledge. George lit the lantern and led them into the tunnel. Except for the squeaking wheels of the cart, it was deathly quiet. The atmosphere was tense; the normal jovial conversation they often shared was non-existent, the only communication between them now was the occasional anxious glance at each other.

As they neared the end of the tunnel, they could see the faint silhouette of Ambrosius showing up against the night sky. They stopped and exchanged greetings, but as Izzy was not her usual bubbly self, very little was said. George and Efion got to work immediately and placed the numnah and saddle on the base of Ambrosius's neck, Izzy strapped the scabbard to her waistbelt. Picking up the gas lantern she had secretly retrieved from *Nicole*, she waited nervously for a sign from them that she could mount the great dragon. Finally, after a few tentative moments, Izzy was beckoned to climb into the saddle, and after attaching the safety harness around her, Efion stood back with George. She turned round to face them as Ambrosius stood up. "I wish you were coming with me, little brother," she said with a tremble in her voice.

"If the saddle was a bit bigger I would be beside you now, but don't worry, sis … Ambrosius will look after you," he replied reassuringly.

Ambrosius's voice entered her head. "George is right, my little queen, I will take care of you. All you have to do is sit tight until we arrive on Ynys Enlli and then I will speak to you again and guide you to the resting place of the great sword Caliburn."

Because she had simply had no opportunity beforehand for a dummy run, preparations for her coronation taking up so much of her time, Izzy was desperate that her flight with Ambrosius should be a success. She wanted above all to retrieve Caliburn before the tournament so people could see for themselves, and word would get around to the doubters, that she was a worthy queen. She gripped the handle of the saddle as tight as she could while Ambrosius walked to the edge of the ledge. She turned round to her brother and Efion for the last time and thanked them. In reply they wished her good luck, and as Ambrosius launched his body into the darkness they ran towards the ledge to catch a last brief glimpse of them, but the blackness of the night had already swallowed them up.

Ambrosius had chosen wisely to leave when there was no moon. He knew that once he passed through into the New World, he would no longer have the protection of the veil of Myrddin's magical mist that surrounded Cuddfan, and light sources from the land could expose them and raise the alarm. They would have to avoid Ynys Enlli's lighthouse which stood on the southern tip of the island, but as his destination was Mynydd Enlli, a mountain on the north side, it shouldn't pose too much of a problem. He had spent some time in the New World cloaked as a heron, so he was fully aware of modern transport and the need to keep his wits about him to avoid contact with things such as helicopters that often populated these skies at night.

Although Izzy couldn't make out the landscape below, she could hear and smell the sea. Within half an hour of leaving the shores of Cuddfan, they entered the mist that surrounded the kingdom and she could feel the damp air on her skin. As they broke out into the open night sky of the New World, Izzy was keen to discover where in the world Cuddfan was, but it was far too dark for her to take bearings. Through the darkness in the distance she could see the bright circling light of Ynys Enlli lighthouse. Ambrosius veered to the left and Izzy could just make out the familiar lights of the Lleyn Peninsula. They had often sailed *Nicole* at night through these waters and for a few moments she felt a wave of homesickness.

Without warning Ambrosius began to lose height and tilted his body so his legs were hanging beneath him. He began to flap his massive wings in a figure of eight as the ground came ever closer beneath them. The landing was so gentle Izzy didn't realise they had finally touched down.

"We are here, my queen," he said, "now come where I can see you."

Izzy understood what he was asking and releasing herself from the saddle, she climbed down and walked in front of him. She looked up. "Thank you, Ambrosius, for bringing me here. Now it is my turn, so if you tell me where I am to go, I will recover the sword and we can get out of here."

Ambrosius chuckled to himself; *such bravery and in someone so small*, he thought to himself, *she reminds me much of her father. How innocence of what is to come can give a human being such courage!* "You are sure you want to do this?" he asked.

"I didn't come this far just to back out now. Tell me where to go, and I shall retrieve the sword," she replied impatiently.

Ambrosius lowered his great head to look into her eyes. Their faces were so close she could feel the warmth of his breath on her face.

"I sense your impatience masks your fear of what you might find down there, my child. Fear not, I will be with you every step of the way."

"I'm sorry, Ambrosius. I am just a little tense. You say you will be with me every step of the way, but how?"

"Before I answer your question, there is something I must do. Please trust me for what I am about to do."

"Of course, Ambrosius … but time is running out."

"Patience, child, now roll up your sleeve."

Izzy looked at him puzzled, but did as he asked. Ambrosius kept his gaze on her eyes and dropped his jaw slightly revealing a row of sharp teeth. In a split second his head darted forward, and he bit hard into her arm. Izzy fell backwards onto the ground in pain, gripping her injured arm. She was shocked by what had just happened, and as the blood trickled down over her hand from the small wound, she looked up at Ambrosius and asked shakily, "Why did you do that?"

"I am sorry, but if I had warned you of my intention you might have flinched, and I could have bitten your arm off. If you look at the wound, it is quite small. Now you must take your dagger from your belt and plunge it into my foot hard enough so it bleeds."

Izzy looked at him puzzled, but getting up from the ground, took the little dagger from its sheath and plunged it between Ambrosius's armoured scales. As she carefully withdrew it, a small fountain of blood spurted out of the incision.

"Now you must unite our two wounds quickly, so our blood flows together."

Again she did as instructed without question, and as their blood merged, she felt a strange sensation flow through her body. She didn't have to ask Ambrosius why because she instantly felt the reason; Ambrosius and Izzy's minds were now joined as one. She could actually read his thoughts and see in her mind what he could see with his eyes. Now she understood what he meant when he said he would be with her every step of the way.

"You will have to go below ground to retrieve the sword, and once I lose sight of you our communication would have been lost, but now our blood flows as one. From now on we will see what each other sees, even though we are parted. The tunnel you are about to enter has many paths, and as it is too small for me to lead the way I must guide you from here."

Izzy found her newly endowed power challenging to control at first, a bit like having eyes in the back of her head. However, being inside Ambrosius's mind was comforting because she no longer felt she was alone. He was, though, restricting access to his memories; he knew that such power would be far too much for Izzy to cope with.

After several minutes of guidance and advice from Ambrosius on how to direct her newfound power, Izzy was ready to enter the maze that she hoped would lead to the chamber where the intertwined bodies of Myrddin and Nimue had rested for hundreds of years. As she ignited the gas of the lantern, it exploded with a hissing roar to produce the brightest of lights, and she took the first few tentative steps of her journey into the unknown.

As she moved forward, the light from the lantern danced along the ground. With Ambrosius giving her instructions in her head she moved towards an outcrop of rock in front of her and soon began to sense herself gradually descending below ground. The soft sward beneath her feet turned to stone, and before long she realised she had entered a tunnel. After several paces, she came to what appeared to be a series of steps that took her even deeper into the bowels of this subterranean world. The temperature in the tunnel was a lot warmer than she had expected, which was a good thing as it seemed to go on for ever. The silence was eerie. Thank goodness Ambrosius's voice was always inside her head, spurring her ever onwards.

Gradually the tunnel began to widen out, and before long she found herself in a large cavern. The ceiling seemed as high as a house, but the one thing she noticed straight away was that the temperature was getting colder; her breath was now visible in the light of the lantern. In the cold, the scar on her arm from Ambrosius's bite was becoming less painful. She lifted the lantern as high as she could and turned full circle to throw the light all around her.

The walls of the cavern were covered in great sheaths of ice that draped down to the floor like fabric. Long icicles gripped the roof and hung like pointed teeth. Suddenly there they were, although she could see only a faint outline through the greenish translucent slab of ice. The light of her lantern reflected into her face, temporarily blinding her. Her heart pounded in her chest.

"Can you see them, Ambrosius?" she asked.

"Yes, my child. Remember you are my eyes, so you must move closer so I can see and tell you how best to take the sword."

Izzy walked nervously towards the couple locked in their deathly embrace beneath their icy tomb. At first she was hesitant to look directly at either of their faces, but she was inexplicably drawn to Myrddin. His eyes were closed as if he was in meditation rather than fighting for his life. His appearance was of an ageless man; there were wrinkles, yes, but not as deep as could be expected from a man of his reported age. His long silver hair was thick and still had lustre. Izzy's glance finally rested on Nimue's face. She expected to see a wizened old hag, but was surprised to see a woman of beauty. It wasn't difficult to see why Myrddin was so attracted to her. However, unlike his, her face was contorted with hate and surprise.

Izzy could sense Ambrosius's sadness inside her mind as she walked around the two icy figures frozen in time. She, too, couldn't help feeling a twinge of sorrow for them. Gazing at the ice, it was difficult to make out exactly where the sword was, but from the story she had been told she knew that Myrddin must still have it grasped in his hands. She could just see the pommel of the hilt poking out below the surface of the ice and the point of the blade sticking out from Nimue's shoulder blades, but it too was completely encased in ice.

"Izzy, you must do exactly as I say for fear of awakening the evil that lies beneath the ice."

"You're not making it any easier for me, Ambrosius," replied Izzy with a sigh. "I could do with less of the doom and gloom."

She prepared herself, because although Ambrosius would guide her, she alone had to release Myrddin's grip on the sword to pull it out of their bodies. She placed the lantern on the ground and instinctively put one hand on the scabbard, gripping it tightly as though her life depended on it. She closed her eyes for a moment concentrating on Ambrosius's guidance, then plunged her right hand deep into the frozen ice. As her hand broke the surface, Izzy could feel the ice melting and the cold water trickling down her skin. She pushed it even further into the frozen mass, finally touching Myrddin's hands. Her stomach flipped over as she felt the texture of his frozen skin in the palm of her hand. She opened her eyes. Slowly his grip on the sword released, revealing it in all its glory. What she didn't see was Myrddin's eyes open for a moment and look down at her as the warmth of her hand met his icy one; then they closed again.

Her body was filled with a strange emotion as she grasped the hilt with her hand. As she pulled it slowly towards her, it began to ring, softly at first then filling the cave with a single note like that of a tuning fork, finally ebbing away to silence. It moved a lot more easily than she had expected, but as it was drawn out through the two bodies, she was suddenly overcome by a severe pain in her chest as if the sword was passing through her own body. There was an agonising scream inside her head and a sudden realisation that she might be feeling pain from Ambrosius. As soon as the sword was free, she turned her attention to getting out of the cave as quickly as possible.

Placing the sword into its scabbard, she took one last look at the hapless pair encased in ice. She was half expecting to see the entire block melt in front of her eyes and the two figures brought back to life, but with relief she saw the ice turn to glass, enclosing Myrddin and Nimue's bodies forever, just as before. Picking up the lantern, she quickly retraced her steps towards the entrance of the tunnel. She could no longer feel Ambrosius in her mind, only pain. She was beginning to worry now. Had evil forces attacked Ambrosius while she was below ground? What was waiting for her when she got back to the surface? Luckily, Izzy's memory was sharp and she had little difficulty in finding her way back to the entrance.

As she neared the surface, she put out the lantern and placed it on the ground. Drawing Caliburn quietly from its scabbard, she prepared herself for the worst. The feeling of power the sword gave her was unmistakable and she instinctively willed it into silence; only when it was wielded with purpose would it ring out. She didn't want to alert any enemies to her presence, so like a praying mantis, her movements were slow but decisive.

Through the darkness, she could see that Ambrosius was not standing as she had left him. She walked cautiously towards him, clutching Caliburn in her hand, ready to repel any attacker. Ambrosius raised himself up onto his legs in front of her and turned to face her. As he tried to reassure her that nothing was wrong, she grew wary. He told her to climb into the saddle, but she knew there was something strange happening and she wasn't convinced that he was being honest with her. However, she realised it was not the time or place to argue, so placing Caliburn back into the scabbard she clambered into the saddle.

Ambrosius didn't seem himself at all, in fact he appeared to be uneasy on his feet. Maybe coming back to the place where Myrddin met his death had shaken him? As he prepared to take off from the ground his acute hearing alerted both of them to the sound of flapping wings. His senses told him they were that of another dragon, but before he could take evasive action, out of the darkness an unfamiliar black dragon swooped down, eyes glaring, and landed a few metres in front of them, preventing their escape. The dragon was smaller than Ambrosius but they sensed its hostility. Izzy pulled Caliburn from the scabbard and raised it in the air. It began to ring, and the other dragon, hissing like a snake, turned its gaze towards her. Its evil stare was cold. Izzy knew what it had come for but she knew she would never give it up. She felt something or someone trying to enter her mind, but Ambrosius's presence resisted for her and instead, tried to invade the mind of their aggressor, but its power was far too strong even for him, and he was prevented from doing so. It opened its mouth and, snorting, struck out with its heavy head, trying to knock Ambrosius over, but he anticipated it and jumped quickly into the air. Izzy nearly lost her grip on the sword with the sudden jolt but managed to hold onto it. Realising she would be no help in this contest of brute strength and that dropping the sword could mean losing it forever, she replaced it into the safety of the scabbard and held onto the saddle for dear life as the two dragons veered from side to side, each waiting for the right moment to strike.

Ambrosius, for whatever reason, was too weak for a long-drawn-out fight. He knew that if he stood his ground now, he might not have the strength needed for the return journey home. He raised his body into the air and jerking his head back as if to strike, opened his mouth to release a ferocious twenty-metre-long flame with such force it covered his adversary's entire body; the black dragon staggered back in surprise and fell to the ground. Ambrosius went in for a killing blow with his tail, but his weakened condition slowed his speed, allowing his opponent to jump to its feet. Izzy braced herself for return fire, but it never came. Instead, the dragon turned tail and took flight into the air.

The sky was beginning to lighten, dawn was but an hour or so away. Ambrosius knew they would have to leave immediately or be at risk of discovery. He was still weak, but managed to launch himself into the sky and gain as much height as possible. Hopefully, once they were in the air above Cuddfan, he would be able to glide back to the safety of the mountain. He knew the dragon could reappear at any time and attack them in flight, so kept his mind and eyes alert. Ambrosius didn't want to alarm Izzy, but she had to be aware of what he knew. He was sure that the dragon that attacked them with such violence was a changeling, a very powerful changeling. He knew that whoever it was, was female, as changelings, although able to change into any sort of being, could not change their gender. If it had been male, the dragon would have had the power of fire, and his battle with it would have turned out differently.

20

Death and Glory

The sun was peeping over the horizon as they flew over the shoreline of Cuddfan. In the distance Izzy could see the mountain fast approaching as Ambrosius glided over the forest canopy. He feathered his wings and dropped his tail to slow his descent, and as the cave opening came into sight, lowered his legs to land gently on the ledge. No sooner had they touched down than George and Efion came running out to greet them.

Izzy climbed out of the saddle, but as her feet touched the security of the ledge, Ambrosius slumped onto the ground. His usual bright red colouring had faded to a light pink and his breathing was so shallow it was difficult for them to hear it. Izzy felt his pain and knew something terrible had happened to him while she was below ground. George was devastated and went to Ambrosius's head, trying to communicate with his dearest friend. But his eyes were slowly shutting as his life ebbed away. Efion put his arm round George to try and comfort him as, without warning, Ambrosius took his final breath of life. George burst into tears and looked at his sister for answers, but she too was in shock and succumbed to her own emotions, dropping to her knees beside her brother to mourn the death of such a brave and noble creature.

Efion shook his head in disbelief; he had thought Ambrosius to have many years left in him. But there it was, and what was about happen to him next – he had witnessed the death of a dragon once before – he knew would be very hard for Izzy and George to accept. So as they knelt in front of Ambrosius, Efion pulled George and his sister gently to their feet and said softly, "You must be brave, both of you. This will be difficult for you to understand, but we must now leave Ambrosius, for it is customary with dragons that when they die they will be consumed by the rest of the hive so as to be reborn again in them." He took out a knife, cut the straps to the saddle, and pulled it away from Ambrosius's lifeless body. Still in tears, his heart numb, George helped him lift it into the cart, and as they slowly made their way along the tunnel, Izzy could hear Ambrosius's body being dragged into the hive by the other dragons.

The success of retrieving Caliburn was soured by the sudden and unexpected death of Ambrosius. But as Izzy was about to be crowned queen, she knew she would have to rise above her sadness. For George it was different; he had lost his friend and was heartbroken. It would take him a long time to accept his death. He wanted to know everything that had happened so he could piece together his last hours and in doing so, possibly understand the reason for it. Izzy stayed and comforted her brother throughout the day in the privacy of her apartment. She told him everything, exactly as it had happened, until finally they both fell asleep side by side.

The next morning Arthur, who was totally unaware of the drama that had unfolded the night before, was busy discussing his plans for the Grand Tournament with Lord Bedivere and a group of artisans in the courtyard. This was to be the most spectacular event in Cuddfan's history, so it was crucial for him personally to get every detail right.

They were interrupted by a flustered Bronwyn. "May I please have counsel with my husband alone for a while, gentlemen?" she asked. Lord Bedivere and the artisans bowed respectfully and moved away beyond hearing distance.

Arthur took her arm and whispered, "Why, my love, what on earth is the matter? You appear displeased."

"I have just come from Izzy's apartments," she whispered. "She has the sword!"

A shocked Arthur replied, "What – how? She promised me she would obey our wishes." But from his wife's expression he could see that not all was well. "What is it, is she injured?" Bronwyn relayed the story to him just as Izzy had told her.

"I must go to her," Arthur declared.

"No, she is much tired from the journey, dear husband. Except for her great sadness at the death of Ambrosius, she is in good spirits at retrieving Caliburn. I have given her a light sleeping draught and left her to rest. She will come to us when she is ready," replied Bronwyn.

News of the retrieval of Caliburn was still a closely guarded secret. No one in the palace knew of its return other than Arthur, Bronwyn, and Lord Bedivere. Arthur was astonished when Bronwyn broke the news to him and was eager to be reunited with it once more, but he took Bronwyn's advice and let her sleep.

Early next morning Izzy was brushing her hair and deep in thought when Arthur knocked on the door and walked into her apartment. She stopped, and putting down her hairbrush, jumped to her feet to greet her father with a tender hug. Arthur, unused to such outbursts of affection, welcomed Izzy's growing fondness for him and was fast becoming used to her quirkiness and enthusiasm for life. Nonetheless, he pulled back a little from their embrace and looked gravely at her. "I should be very angry with you, Izzy, for disobeying me. To put your life in danger again after all you have been through … just for the sword."

"Please don't be angry with me, Father," she pleaded putting on a puppy dog expression. "I saw from holding the scabbard that Ambrosius knew its hiding place and he agreed to take me to Ynys Enlli on his back. He promised he would protect me, so I weighed up all the pros and cons in my mind and thought that there was no other way to convince people of my birthright, so we went for it."

"And what of Ambrosius? He lost his life in your attempt! You must realise, Izzy, that when you become queen you will be responsible for the lives of those around you as well as your own."

"I know, and I'm truly heartbroken that he sacrificed his life protecting me – but come, Father, see for yourself whether it was worth it or not." She grinned at him with excitement and took hold of his hand, pulling him towards her bed. Releasing his hand, she dropped to her knees and reached under the bed to pull out a long parcel wrapped in a plain woollen blanket, which she placed on the bed. She sat beside it and peeled back its covering to reveal the scabbard, in which reposed the powerful and coveted sword. Arthur looked into his daughter's fervid eyes, bent down and slowly drew the sword from its natural resting place. He raised it into the air and immediately it began to ring. As it echoed through the air, he was overcome with emotions long forgotten as he felt its power course through his body once more, rekindling memories of his time as a young man. He closed his eyes and took a few moments to relive the past in his mind. Opening them again to look at the beauty of its form, he smiled, and replacing the sword in the scabbard presented it back to Izzy, who stood up and kissed her father on the cheek. "There, Father, was it not worth the risk for Caliburn to be here where it belongs?"

"Perhaps so, Izzy, but what if by removing the sword from the bodies of Myrddin and Nimue you began a reaction you weren't aware of? And what of the dragon who threatened your return? Supposing it had overpowered Ambrosius and killed you? And what of that wound you carry on your arm?"

Izzy tried to calm her father. "Ambrosius," she reassured him, "told me the scabbard would protect me as long as I wore it. I just wish it could have done the same for him. As for the wound, Ambrosius gave me that – a dragon's magic to enable us to see into each other's mind. When he died, he left my mind." Izzy stopped in mid-sentence and looked into space for a moment. She continued, "You know, the strangest thing is that I have once again begun to feel his presence in my head. Maybe it's his ghost?"

Her concentration was lost for a few seconds while she thought of him and then said, "As for that other dragon, yes, I felt its evil stare penetrate my mind, but thanks to Ambrosius's courage I survived the ordeal. However, he did tell me something on our journey home which troubles me even more." She eyed her father. "He told me that he recognised the dragon as a female changeling, able to alter its shape and form at will. Even though he overpowered it, the aura of its evil presence terrified him and it was very likely responsible for his death. I'm not sure that if we were faced with this creature again, we would be so lucky."

Arthur looked soberly at his daughter then smiled and gave her a hug. "Well, at least you are safe for the moment, and as you say, it is better here than in the hands of our enemies, whoever they are. But we must be on our guard. I feel this is not yet over."

Dan was oblivious to Izzy's expedition, the reason being his mind was on other things. He had grown very attached to Angharad and with the king's permission had stayed on at the hunting lodge when everyone else returned to the palace, on the promise that he would carry on his training for the tournament. Besides, Arthur thought, the less time spent in Tristan's company might help to cool their overzealous rivalry. Although they had both agreed in public to be friends, everyone knew that Tristan disliked Daniel intensely. The root of the matter appeared to be that Tristan had once courted Angharad and had hoped one day to make her his bride. But since Daniel's arrival, his dreams for happiness had been shattered. Dan, however, was serious about keeping his promise to Arthur and Bedivere and swore that any rivalry between them would be saved for the tiltyard. But he knew that Tristan was not so inclined to meet him on friendly terms and was sure that if their paths were to cross in the tournament, he would have to defend himself from serious injury, maybe even death.

Angharad's father, Lord Gochwyban, having once been the king's champion in his youth before retiring to the more sedate occupation of running the hunting lodge, had promised Arthur to help Dan hone his skills in the art of foot tourney and archery. Although Dan had become quite an accomplished rider at the joust with the help of his mount, Trehern, he still had a lot to learn to master some of the necessary skills of hand-to-hand foot combat.

A temporary Champ Close, a small fenced arena ten metres square, had been erected in a quiet corner of the gardens. Dan thought Lord Gochwyban looked quite comical as he walked into the combat zone dressed in ill-fitting armour. It was a while since he had had a reason to wear it and had indulged in the delights of feasting more than perhaps he should have. Dan, on the other hand, thought himself very heroic in his shiny new armour and considered that he might have to show this overweight old man some leniency, especially as Angharad was looking on. The last thing he wanted to do was to show up her father in front of her.

In one corner of the arena was a wooden stand supporting an array of deadly looking weapons. Lord Gochwyban walked over and picked up the most fearsome-looking one, a stout ash shaft about a metre and a half long with an axe head on one side and a hammerhead on the other, and at the end, a lethal square metal spike about twenty centimetres long.

"This is a staff weapon, master Daniel, aptly named the poleaxe. In battle, this weapon can cave a man's head in with one blow, helmet or no helmet. The spike can pierce through metal armour as though it was made from paper."

Dan felt the axe's razor-sharp edge with his fingers. "Isn't this a bit too brutal to be used in friendly competition?"

"Yes of course. It's a most effective companion on the battlefield and a weapon of choice for many a knight on foot, but in the Champ Close, you allay the full might of its function by trying to hit any part of your opponent's armour-clad body with such skill and dexterity as will cause him to yield. For each strike you will be awarded points at the Knight Marshal's discretion as to whether it is a killing blow or not. The Knight Marshal's purpose is to ensure that this close-quarters combat is of a gentlemanly nature, and he awards points to each opponent as he sees fit. His only defence is a wooden staff which he will use to chastise anyone should they resort to foul play. You must choose your armour wisely for this combat as it requires further reinforcement to protect you from the kind of injuries this weapon is capable of inflicting from an overzealous opponent. Blows to the head are forbidden, although that doesn't prevent knights from doing so – blood can become inflamed in a fever to triumph over one's rival." Lord Gochwyban handed the poleaxe to Daniel and selected another one from the stand for himself. "Well, my boy, let us see what you have. Don't hold any quarter. Give it all you've got."

Dan nodded confidently and lowered his visor as Lord Gochwyban waited for his first move. Dan swerved from side to side to try and outwit his opponent, then raising his axe above his head, aimed at Gochwyban's shoulder and brought it down with speed. Gochwyban simply stepped to one side, and as Dan's poleaxe whistled passed his body, the momentum pulled him forward and buried itself up to the shaft in the soft earth. As Dan tried desperately to pull it out, Gochwyban twisted his body swiftly and tapping him gently on his back with the point of the spike, chuckled, "My point, I think."

Angharad laughed; she knew what Daniel was thinking and would have been very surprised to see him get the better of her father. She was right, and even though Dan was shocked by the speed of her father's reaction, he decided that it was just a fluke; he was a lot younger and fitter than Lord Gochwyban who would doubtless soon tire, owing to his age and portly proportions.

They stood opposite each other once more and after some fancy foot-shuffling Dan attempted to thrust the point of the axe into Lord

Gochwyban's stomach, but again he avoided the jab by stepping sideways and bringing his own axe down onto the back of Dan's neck as he overstretched himself. "Another point to me, I fear," he said with friendly laughter.

After several attempts at trying to outwit Lord Gochwyban, Dan finally gave up and collapsed on the ground. Sweat was pouring from every part of his body. Wearing the heavy armour had taken its toll, unlike his opponent who was as fresh now as when they had started. Gochwyban offered his hand to Daniel and pulling him to his feet said, "Your biggest mistake is using too much movement and energy when you strike. I can predict your moves before you make them because you visibly prepare yourself with far too much effort."

Dan bent forward, trying to catch his breath. "Yes, I see that now," he said, taking his helmet off and dropping it on the ground.

Angharad, on seeing Daniel's state, picked up a jug of water and rushed over to where he was standing. She poured some out into a horn beaker and offered it to him with a sympathetic smile. He gulped it down and grabbed the jug, pouring its contents over his head. "That's better, thank you, my angel," he said, shaking his head and showering her with droplets of water. She let out a girlie squeal and stepped back out of reach. Dan looked at her dotingly and smiled as she took the jug and beaker from him and strolled back to the fence.

Lord Gochwyban coughed noisily to avert Daniel's gaze from his daughter and said abruptly, "Please pay attention, Daniel."

"I'm sorry, my mind was on other things."

"Yes, well, I understand, but you must never let your mind be distracted by such things when you are in combat. A skilled opponent will make full use of any lapse of concentration. It could make all the difference between winning and losing – or worse, between life and death." He now had Daniel's full attention and continued, "You notice I always allowed you to make the first move, and because of your inexperience you opened yourself up to my counter-attack. That allowed me, with one simple move and minimal effort, to deliver the killing blow. You also present far too much of your body to your enemy, giving him a bigger target."

Daniel, embarrassed by his false assumption of his teacher's fitness, replied, "I must admit, sir, I am amazed at how easy it was for you to defeat me. I really thought our age difference would give me an advantage over you. I obviously have a lot more to learn."

As the afternoon wore on, with the help of Gochwyban, Daniel slowly began to make enough improvement to at least put up a good defence. But he realised painfully that if he wanted to have any chance in the tournament, he would have to be able to attack as well as defend.

There was still a great deal of work to be done before the tournament could finally get underway. A full list of the contenders had been posted in every town and village, and because they were expecting so many people to attend, Arthur and Bedivere decided to build a new tiltyard in Llangefni due to its central position in the kingdom. Much of the building work had now been completed, and although it was only a small market town, it had a vast expanse of flat open ground on the border with the next village, perfect for building their magnificent new arena with enough room to erect hundreds of tents and pavilions to house the competitors and spectators.

Once the news got out that the tournament was being held in Llangefni, people from all over the kingdom journeyed to the town. Many had arrived already, setting up encampments and market stalls, eager to make sure of the best position for trading. It was beginning to have a definite festival feel about the place. Tents and pavilions were spreading everywhere, creating lots of little villages, each one having a sense of its own community. The tournament was scheduled to last five days, the last day being reserved for the presentations and the Grand Finale. This didn't mean that Izzy would have to sit through the whole five days of competition, but she would be expected to open the proceedings with her father and attend the final day, which Arthur promised would conclude with a spectacular ending.

George was still mourning the death of Ambrosius and no longer felt any enthusiasm for the tournament or Izzy's coronation. In trying to understand what had happened, he spent days leading up to the event with Efion, busying himself with simple chores. The Dragon Master too was grieving, but as he understood a great deal more about dragon culture and tradition than anyone else, he seemed to be less affected. However, he had recently discovered something very magical and wonderful that he had thought till now was pure myth and legend, and he wanted to share his revelation with George. It concerned something no other human being had ever witnessed before. He had hinted to George before they left the ground that what he was about to observe must be kept a closely guarded secret between just the two of them.

Efion had spent most of his life in the service of dragons so had never had much opportunity to socialise with human beings – until George came along, that is. Having never married, he had no one to pass on the role of Dragon Master to. The grumpy little man had grown very fond of George, who was becoming more like a son to him than an annoying little deaf boy. Although George was to return to his own world shortly, Efion secretly wished that he would stay and become his apprentice, as he had been his father's.

The clouds opened with a sudden torrential downpour as they closed the gate of the lift and began their ascent to the hive. George thought the sound of the rain rebounding on the roof was reminiscent of wet days on *Nicole*. Then he had been quite happy to sit below deck playing his electronic games, slaughtering dragons while everyone cursed him for his incessant chatter. My, how differently he viewed life now since abandoning such childish ways.

The lift shuddered as they reached the top, the sudden jerk shaking the excess water off the roof in heavy droplets that cascaded down to the ground below. George opened the gate while Efion lit the lantern, and as they made their way silently towards the hive, Efion thought that knowing what he knew, would probably change George's view of life forever.

Dragons usually slept during daylight hours, so George was surprised to hear movement and a strange clacking noise as they approached and walked into the cavern. He opened his mouth in astonishment at the sight that met his eyes, and turned to look at Efion, who smiled back at him. "I came here the day following Ambrosius's death to make sure his ladies were all right and saw what they were doing. My father had told me stories of this, but I never thought I would ever witness it for myself."

On the floor of the hive was a nest some three metres in diameter, neatly built of interwoven twigs and bracken. Sitting on the nest was one of Ambrosius's ladies' clucking like a mother hen, warning them to keep away. George looked up at Efion and giggled inquisitively. "Why have they built a nest?"

Efion looked down at George and gave him a warm smile. "You will see, George, you will see," he teased him. "But for now we must leave them alone to do their work. We will come back in a few days, and if I'm right, all will be revealed."

21

The Tournament

The day of the Grand Tournament finally arrived and members of the household were busying themselves getting ready to depart the palace for the hunting lodge. Izzy hadn't seen either of her brothers for a while and was naturally missing their company, especially George. The last time she saw him was just after Ambrosius died. Still blaming herself for his death, Izzy had hoped to see him before they headed off, but she needn't have worried. For reasons known only to him and Efion, he was in high spirits again, and although he would miss most of the tournament, he had secret plans forming in his mind with a view to the Grand Finale. As for Daniel, Izzy knew he was a contestant and that she would probably have a chance to bump into him at some point during the tournament.

Arthur was deep in conversation with Gawain and Owain at the base of the stairs of the Great Hall, waiting patiently for the ladies to arrive. Suddenly the room echoed to the sounds of female chatter, and as the men turned their gaze towards the top of the stairs Izzy and Bronwyn, together with their ladies-in-waiting, gracefully descended dressed in their state gowns. Everyone was transfixed by Izzy's beauty in her dress of red silk and gold brocade. Wearing the thin plain gold torc around her neck that her mother had loaned her, she looked every inch a fairy-tale princess. Arthur walked up to greet his daughter, taking her hand as she reached the bottom step and said proudly, "Izzy, you are a sight to behold. You …"

He was interrupted by George running across the hall. He stopped in front of them and looked at his sister. "Wow, Izzy, you look fantastic!" He bowed, "Sorry, must dash!" and disappeared in the other direction.

Everyone laughed as Arthur looked at Izzy for an explanation. "What was all that about?"

"Who knows? I've given up trying to understand how my little brother's mind works!"

Still mystified, Arthur took hold of his wife and daughter's hands and led them down to the jetty where they boarded the royal barge that would take them to the hunting lodge. From there they would ride on a series of beautifully decorated chariots to Llangefni and the Grand Tournament. The royal household would be staying at the lodge for the duration of the tournament to save them the journey to and from the palace every day.

As the royal procession neared Llangefni, they could hear the sounds of the expectant crowds awaiting their king's arrival. In front of the two six-horse chariots and leading the way into the lane that led to the arena, fifty men-at-arms in full ceremonial livery marched on foot six abreast. On each side of the road facing inwards were many knights in full armour, mounted on their mighty steeds draped in brightly coloured comparisons, each man proudly carrying their own heraldic banner aloft. As the men-at-arms entered the main gate, the crowds waved in anticipation, while drummers and trumpeters announced their arrival. They cheered as the chariots came through the entrance. Izzy couldn't believe the warmth of the reception accorded by her father's subjects. They pulled up in front of the royal box while squires rushed out to help the ladies in their finery alight from the rear of each chariot and ascend the steps to the royal box.

Once everyone was seated and the fervour of the crowd had died down, Arthur rose to his feet and officially opened the tournament by ordering the release of a hundred white doves to signify the peaceful nature of the games. As they flew across the heads of the audience and into the skies, a gauntlet was raised on a flagpole to signify the official start of the proceedings. It would stay there for the duration, not unlike the flaming torch of our modern Olympic games. The crowd erupted with cheers and applause as the contestants entered and paraded past the royal box to form a complete circle inside the arena. The Abbott walked out into the centre, and all fell silent as those on foot went down on one knee, and mounted riders lowered their heads as he delivered a blessing for those taking part. Then with more loud cheers from the crowd, the contestants left the arena to ready themselves for their part in the competitions.

The tournament was split into several disciplines: riding skills; archery; bills; sword; battle-axe; and the joust. Each section would have an overall winner and points from the skill-at-arms contests would be awarded to each contestant and added to their scores. For obvious reasons, only knights were permitted to enter the joust, but all-comers were welcome to take part in the archery, and although many of Bedivere's young knights considered themselves skilled bowmen, the competition was fierce – many working men from the hamlets were the real experts. A colossal spectacle had been planned to close the games, which Arthur and Bedivere had been working on together in secret.

The first competition to open the tournament was the 'Ring Joust', which tested the accuracy of a rider with a lance and was open to anyone who owned a horse. Here a rider demonstrated his skill at the gallop by picking up several small rings placed on the barrier. The more rings a rider picked up on his lance, the more points he was awarded. Bedivere often used this contest to spot the talents of boys who were born into less noble families who had the potential to become knights, and for this reason it was very popular with young squires who were hoping to be selected for his patronage.

Daniel, awaiting his turn in the quiet of the corral out of public view, was standing by Trehern and feeling very nervous about competing in public for the first time. Although he had done this sort of thing dozens of times on gymkhana competition days when he was younger, something was putting him on edge. As an honorary knight, he had been given two squires whose roles were to take care of his every need while in the competition. Their names, Will and Watt, sounded like characters from a comedy sketch, but as their names suggested, both were blessed with the ability to make people laugh, both by their appearance and by the way they worked together – or not, as the case sometimes was. Dan suspected that Tristan might have had something to do with the choice of squires for him.

Will and Watt appeared from nowhere to tell Daniel he was five minutes away from his moment of glory in the first round. They helped him mount and led him and Trehern to the gate to stand in line. Once in the saddle Daniel felt a little more confident, and as Will smacked the horse's flanks, he was off. Responding to being in the glare of the public, Daniel got into his stride and rode at a canter around the arena to warm up himself and his horse. He collected the lance from Watt, who had rushed to the stand to be ready for his master. Daniel grabbed it from him without stopping and rode towards the royal box where he bowed towards Arthur, Bronwyn, and his sister. Angharad blew a kiss to him and shouted, "Good luck!" He winked back at her and turned to face the end of the tiltyard, feeling a warm glow inside as Trehern galloped towards his starting place.

Daniel looked down at the long row of rings balanced precariously on the top of the posts of the barrier. His aim would have to be perfect to secure each one on the end of his lance; a few millimetres out and the rings would be knocked to the ground. He had practised this many times, and although he had become reasonably proficient, he'd never managed to get all of them. He crouched his lance tightly against his body, focusing his mind's eye on the last ring. He didn't need spurs with Trehern and with a gentle squeeze of his thighs, the horse went into a gallop down the line. One, two, three, four, five – by now the crowds of spectators were counting the rings – six, seven, eight, nine rings went up the lance in quick succession. Now for the final most difficult one of all which was half the size of the others. "Ten!"

As Trehern pulled up at the far end of the tiltyard, the crowd erupted and rose to their feet; it was the first full house of the day.

Daniel rode triumphantly towards the Knight Marshal to present him with the lance and the ten rings. He removed them and counted them out loudly in front of the crowd, then held them aloft to confirm the count. The crowd cheered as Dan threw his lance to Will and in gratification, leaned forward to pat Trehern's neck. Punching the air, he rode around the tiltyard to acknowledge the crowd's pleasure in his success, and out to the gate where Tristan was eagerly waiting his turn to go on. Daniel gave him a friendly salute as he passed him on the way through, but was greeted by a defiant black stare that sent a chill down his spine. Daniel now knew for sure that Tristan was determined to turn the tournament into a personal grudge fight between them. He was aware of Tristram's dashed hopes regarding Angharad and assumed that was the reason.

Leaping from his saddle, Daniel immediately put his arms around Trehern's neck, giving him a well-deserved hug before handing him to Watt to return him to the stable. He then rushed out to the competitors' viewing area to watch Tristan. He knew they were reasonably well matched, but as Daniel had found out, it all depended on the day.

Tristan was ready, and as his horse started the run, the crowds counted down the number of rings. "One, two, three, four, five, six, seven, eight, nine …" Daniel closed his eyes and waited for the ten, but all he heard was a collective groan from the crowd as Tristan caught the edge of the last ring with the point of his lance and knocked it to the ground. That was all he needed to see. He ran back to his quarters and punching his fist in the air, yelled, "Yes!"

By the time the last contestant began his run, Daniel was still the only rider to get all ten rings. Should there be a dead heat, they would have to run again, only with smaller ones, and he knew very well that he wouldn't be so successful a second time round, so was silently praying for the last man to fail. Fortunately for Daniel, his prayer was answered. Although the trophies and prizes would not be awarded until the final day of the tournament, the crowd demanded to see their Champion of the Rings perform a victory lap. And he wasn't about to disappoint them. He beckoned Watt to bring Trehern from the stables, and in a triumphant humour rode into the arena at a gallop, waving his arms to the crowds as he went round, finally stopping in front of the royal box to receive a pennant from his sister to place outside his pavilion.

"I must admit, Dan, I didn't think you were going to beat Tristan, even though I know how hard you've worked. I'm very proud of you," Izzy said with a broad grin.

"Likewise, sis!" he replied and glancing towards Angharad to blow a kiss, signalled to Trehern to rear up on his hind legs then turned to take one more lap around the arena with the pennant flying in the wind.

Thus ended the first day of the tournament, and as the royal party left to return to the lodge, the crowds dispersed into their own camps that were scattered around the fayre, to prepare and cook supper. Small campfires sprang up to add to the rich tapestry of hundreds of brightly coloured tents, and as the wisps of grey smoke drifted heavenwards in the warm evening breeze, the fiery glow of the sun finally ducked below the horizon, gradually shrouding the land in darkness. Small flickering lights began to pepper the enchanting landscape as lanterns were lit, echoing the shimmering stars of the clear night sky. The air filled with the sounds of laughter and music as people celebrated the end of the first day of the tournament, all helped on, no doubt, by a little liquid refreshment.

A small informal supper had been prepared in the hunting lodge for Arthur's household. *One can have too many feasts*, Izzy thought, and was glad on this occasion to relax with her friends and family and not have to dress up just to eat. She missed twenty-first-century clothes, especially jeans and t-shirts, to slob around in when she was on her own. However, she was growing accustomed to the fashions of her new life and was prepared to make a few sacrifices. Everyone was feeling very relaxed after supper. The first day of the tournament had gone without a hitch, so spirits were high, helped along by several glasses of Lord Gochwyban's excellent wines.

The cheerful buzz of conversation was interrupted by the entrance of a woman, a hood covering her head, who came in unannounced. She walked boldly up to where Arthur was sitting. At first, he didn't recognise his unexpected guest and wondered why his guards hadn't stopped her before she got so near. He jumped to his feet, as did his close companions in readiness to repel this cloaked intruder, although not one person was wearing a sword, as per Izzy's wishes.

"Why, Gorawen, how good to see you," the king said on realising her identity, but in some astonishment.

Izzy immediately rose from her seat to greet her grandmother but stood back from giving her a hug when she sensed something strange about her demeanour. *How odd* she thought *she hasn't removed her hood in front of us.*

Gorawen had all the appearance of being furious about something. She pulled a surprised Gawain from his seat so she could sit next to Arthur and clutched nervously at her hood with one hand, as though desperate for it not to slip. "I will speak with you alone, Arthur," she ordered.

Lord Gochwyban walked towards Arthur. "Please use my day chamber for privacy, Majesty."

As soon as Gochwyban had closed the door, Gorawen launched into a tirade of verbal abuse at Arthur, concluding with, "How dare you send my granddaughter to retrieve Caliburn without informing me?"

Arthur was shocked at her outburst. He knew Gorawen could sometimes be a little feisty, but to interrupt the evening with such open hostility and in front of the court was unforgivable.

Izzy, meanwhile, was feeling very upset by her grandmother's behaviour. For one thing, she was desperate to hear news from her of Alison and James. She had also felt an uneasy sensation when Gorawen entered the room – she couldn't explain why, but it felt as if something or someone was invading her mind, the same feeling she had when Ambrosius first read her thoughts on Ynys Enlli. That, though, was a pleasant warm feeling, unlike the cold malevolent presence she sensed now.

The door to the day chamber flew open and Gorawen reappeared, slamming the door shut behind her. She stood for a while still clutching her hood, looking out at the horrified courtiers until her gaze came upon Izzy. She muttered a few words under her breath, and Izzy felt a cold shudder down her spine broken only when Arthur opened the door and stood behind her, causing her to depart down a flight of steps at the side of the room.

From Arthur's mood, Bronwyn could see her mother had ruffled his feathers somewhat, and tried to calm him down.

"I know she is your mother, Bronwyn," snapped Arthur, "but her outburst was inexcusable and has unsettled the whole evening. I am afraid I lost my temper with her."

Izzy, concerned for her grandmother, asked, "What did she want to see you about, Father. Why did she seem so angry?"

Arthur turned to face her, and not wanting to divulge too much in front of the courtiers, whispered, "She wanted to know why I hadn't told her about …" he stuttered, trying to find the right words, "you know … your little adventure the other night."

"But I never told anyone I was going, so how did she find out?" replied Izzy. "And why was she wearing that horrid hood?"

"There is no keeping any secrets from that woman, she has spies everywhere. I don't know why she didn't remove her hood, Izzy. She kept it up all through our meeting – probably a device to intimidate me."

22

Death and Rebirth

In all the excitement of the tournament, not one person except Izzy had noticed George's absence from the celebrations. Although he didn't know it yet, George was about to discover the secret of life, death, and immortality. Efion had hinted at what was happening to the dragons but hadn't told him everything he knew. Now even he was about to be amazed by the miracle that awaited them both in the hive.

The clacking sound of the dragons grew louder and louder as they approached the centre of the hive. Efion stopped and raised his lantern into the air and George's heart missed a beat in anticipation. In the dim light they saw a dragon sitting on the giant nest. She caught sight of them and raised her head in the air, letting out an ear-piercing screech to the other dragons roosting in the cave roof above to acknowledge human presence. Without warning the clacking stopped, and the dragons dropped from their perches to the ground, completely encircling the nest. George wasn't too intimidated by now at being surrounded by dragons, nevertheless he gripped Efion's hand tightly for reassurance. The dragon sitting on the nest raised her body and plodded over to join her sisters.

Efion took George a few steps closer until they were at the very edge of the nest, and both gazed in amazement at what they saw. George didn't know what to expect as Efion hadn't let on to what the dragons were doing, but even he was surprised to see not one, but two eggs lying in the centre of the nest. Each egg was about two metres long and covered in a translucent crust; from within, a green glow emanated. After a few seconds, cracks began to appear in one of the eggs. A head burst through the surface and flopped onto the floor of the nest. Then with a sudden burst of energy, the baby dragon broke free from its prison completely and began slowly unfurling its wings. After a few moments, its translucent body changed colour as its heart pumped blood through its veins.

"Why hasn't the other egg hatched?" whispered George.

"I don't know," replied Efion, "I was only expecting one egg, never thought there would be two."

One of the female dragons lowered her head, tenderly picking up the young hatchling in her mouth and carefully placing it between her back legs. Then she dropped her head and nudged the remaining egg. It started to wobble and a small hairline crack appeared on the surface, releasing a foul-smelling, glowing green gas that completely covered the egg. It rippled like a green sea and slowly settled into the bottom of the nest, revealing the shape of a naked boy covered in red scales from head to toe, standing where the egg had been. Both George and Efion looked at each other in utmost amazement; this was certainly not what they had expected. Within minutes, the boy slowly grew into the stature of a man, raised his head towards the heavens and reached out with his hands towards George and Efion as if stretching for the very first time. He lowered his head and opened his eyes to reveal a beautiful green light that cast two beams onto their faces.

The final day of the tournament had arrived, and the atmosphere in the arena was electric. Izzy and her ladies had been absent for the archery and the skill-at-arms competitions but had kept up with the scores. Angharad had, however, attended every event to show her support and loyalty to Daniel. Izzy, on the other hand, wasn't keen to see her brother possibly get slaughtered by superior, more skilled knights. As it turned out, Daniel made a good account of himself, and although getting a severe beating from Tristan in the Champ Close, still had all his limbs. However, he was determined to show his true mettle in the joust, which was the final discipline and test of a true champion.

Arthur opened the final day's proceedings by announcing the position of the finalists. Daniel's name was in the top three, and although popular with the crowds, had not done too well at archery. Tristan had only beaten him by a point in the poleaxe although Daniel had put that down to his certainty that Tristan wanted to kill him. However, the stage was now set, and the first pair entered the lists. This was the sport of knights and the only competition that ultimately counted.

The competitors were each allowed three lances, and the object was to unseat their opponent. If unsuccessful, he was awarded points for hitting the breastplate, or fewer points for the shield, which each knight carried. Staying in the saddle was very difficult considering that the impact speed could be as much as forty miles an hour. As the day wore on, there were two contestants left with equal points: Daniel and Tristan. This scenario was not what Daniel wanted, and as they got ready for their final pass, he looked up at Angharad for the inner courage love might bestow on him.

Daniel squeezed his thighs to set Trehern at a gallop and focused his lance through to the other side of Tristan's body as Lord Gochwyban had taught him. The tip of his lance hit Tristan square on the right side of his breastplate. The force of the blow shattered the lance in hundreds of tiny splinters and lifted Tristan out of his saddle like a rag doll. He hit the ground with a terrifying crunch. The crowd went wild, but as Daniel rode triumphantly around the arena, there came a slow realisation that his adversary wasn't moving.

He pulled up and dismounted, throwing his broken lance to the ground. But before he could get there, Owain had rushed out from the side, crying out in horror as he cradled his son's lifeless body in his arms. It was apparent now that Daniel had delivered a killing blow. As he ran over to attempt to console Owain, he was greeted by a tirade of verbal abuse. He stood motionless, trembling in shock at taking a life, looking on as two stretcher-bearers appeared and removed Tristan's body.

Bedivere rushed down to join him and tried to comfort him, but Daniel was inconsolable. He assured him there was always the risk of injuries in jousting; such was the nature of the sport it was almost accepted as the norm by those competing, and tragic as it was for Tristan to lose his life, a champion had been chosen by elimination and the tournament had to carry on. Besides, said Bedivere, if Lady Luck had favoured Tristan, it could have been Daniel lying dead in the dust.

To allow the crowds to calm down, and Arthur and Bedivere to take stock, a two-hour break was declared. After that, the prizes would be awarded and the final closing ceremony would take place. This lapse allowed Daniel some time to try and find Owain and offer his sincere regret over the death of his son, but he was nowhere to be found. He was told he had commandeered a wagon and disappeared with Tristan's body, together with his two daughters, Izzy's ladies-in-waiting.

Arthur was sympathetic to Owain's grief but openly angry that he had deserted his post and taken Izzy's attendants without confiding in him. All this had upset Izzy very much, for Owain was more of a friend than her personal bodyguard and she totally understood that his loyalties should be with his dead son. She knew from bitter experience what Dan was going through and hoped they would both see it as nothing but a tragic accident.

A special pavilion had been set aside away from the public gaze, where any of the family could take refreshment during the week's event, and so Bronwyn took Izzy there to reflect on matters a while. They were joined by Angharad, who had persuaded Daniel to join them. Arthur was now in a secret meeting with Bedivere, Gawain, and his ministers. No one else knew the agenda, but something had alerted the king enough to warrant him doubling the guards on his family.

Most of the crowd had remained in their seats for the enforced break, so as the sound of drums and trumpets signalled the start of the finale, a great cheer went up. Arthur and his family once again took their seats, and as the knights entered and lined up in front of the royal box, emblazoned with banners flying in the evening breeze, Arthur stood up.

The crowd's cheer fell silent as he began his speech. "My noble subjects, this tournament is to celebrate the chivalric order of knighthood and mark the passing of my reign as your king. It is also a celebration of the forthcoming coronation of our royal daughter Lady Isabella as queen." He paused nervously and cleared his throat. "We are all saddened that the last joust in the competition cost the life of a loved and valued knight. But it reminds us all of the true dangers of combat, whether it be on the deadly field of battle or in the chivalrous arena of the tournament. We hold no blame to the knight I now name as the Queen's Champion – Lord Daniel of Moorefield."

The crowd erupted as Daniel rode into the arena on Trehern and up to the royal box where he dismounted, and handing his horse to Watt, walked forward to be greeted by Arthur and his sister. He knelt in front of them. Bedivere handed Arthur a newly forged sword and scabbard. Arthur drew the sword and knighted Daniel as Lord Moorefield, Protector of the Queen. Daniel rose, and Arthur presented the sword and scabbard to him as a sign of his knighthood. Daniel then received a kiss of approval from his sister and a silk banner emblazoned with the royal standard. He turned and faced the crowd, holding his sword aloft as they cheered. Buckling the scabbard around his waist and lightly jumping onto Trehern's back, with the banner in his hand he began to canter round the arena to receive the approval of the crowd. He was halfway round when a rider jumped the closed gate of the arena and galloped recklessly across, pulling up short in front of him. It was Owain, red-faced and half drunk. He shouted and cursed Daniel, accusing him of the murder of his son. Arthur sent Bedivere and several guards to protect a distraught Daniel from Owain's rage. They dragged Owain from his horse and took him still struggling and screaming vengeance from the arena. Bedivere told Daniel to dismount and join the king.

As the sun set beneath the horizon, several squires came out from a corner of the arena with flaming torches and one by one lit a series of beacons all around the perimeter. Suddenly the stage was awash with light, and as the gates opened, music sounded, charging the atmosphere with electricity.

A voice bellowed out: *"In the fifth century a troubled Briton was left to the wolves as its Roman conquerors retreated back to Rome."*

Children dressed in dark clothing ran from all corners of the arena into the centre, and a small army of men dressed as Saxons marched in and pretended to slaughter them.

Again, a voice bellowed out: *"Our country was invaded by warring armies from foreign lands. Saxons, Norsemen, Jutes, and Angles all wanted to take our land from us. They brought death and destruction once again to our shores."*

Another army representing the Britons marched in, and a large-scale mock battle took place.

Again, the voice of the narrator rang out: *"Our land was divided into small tribes who would rather war with each other than take up arms together against these violent invaders – until – "*

Through the gate trotted fifty riders, each carrying a blazing torch. Once within, they proceeded to gallop around the arena until they stopped at some unseen signal and moved inwards to encircle the invaders. The riders then turned about-face to their audience, and as they galloped out to the perimeter of the arena, everyone in the centre had disappeared! The crowd cheered mightily.

The narrator continued: *"In the sixth century a great warrior united his people and smote down their enemies with the help of his mighty sword named Caliburn, and the incomparable sorcerer, Myrddin."* Again, the crowds cheered.

Smoke billowed out from the centre, and from a hole in the ground, two figures rose up. The audience went wild and cheered. One was a warrior carrying a sword, the other an older man with long silver hair carrying a gnarled staff in his hand.

"Together he created a kingdom called Briton, having its subjects under one rule, and reigned peacefully as king for twenty-one years. Then evil and the greed of others broke the peace, and a great battle ensued."

The smoke became thicker in the arena, and from opposite ends Celtic warriors dressed in mail and carrying shields marched slowly towards each other to clash in a mock battle. As the smoke dissipated into the night sky, bodies lay on the ground.

"Our king and his loyal warriors lay mortally wounded on the battlefield until .."

From one end of the arena, a cart in the shape of a boat with sails made its way into the centre. Six handmaidens climbed out and picked up a number of the bodies, placing them into the vessel, which then moved out of sight.

"They were taken to a secret place to be made whole again by Myrddin's magic. It was here that he set about creating a great kingdom from the sea, which he named Cuddfan, from which he was to rule his people for all time."

A small mound appeared in the arena and erupted into flames. As the fire died down, a flagpole ascended the heavens; upon it hung an enormous red banner emblazoned with a golden dragon breathing fire.

The crowds by this time were all on their feet, applauding and cheering madly as all those taking part in the pageant returned to the arena. Izzy turned to her father and said, "You kept that quiet, Father! It was fantastic, absolutely unbelievable!" and she hugged and kissed him.

"It's not over yet, Izzy" he replied as he grabbed her hand and led her into the centre of the arena and asked everyone to watch the skies.

As they all looked upwards in silence and great expectation, the unmistakable sound of dragon wings flapping could be heard, followed by a whoosh as a dragon swooped down over the crowds and flew in a complete circle just above the heads of the spectators. Twisting into a roll, it landed gently a few metres in front of Arthur. It was none other than Ambrosius and George. The audience was spellbound by the spectacle.

Izzy too was for once speechless as George climbed out from the saddle and walked towards them carrying a long box, which he presented to Arthur. George then bowed, and with a broad smile winked at Izzy before he returned to Ambrosius and stood triumphantly by his side.

Arthur opened the box and pulled out Caliburn, complete with its scabbard. Presenting it to the crowds, he unsheathed it and thrust it high into the air for all to see and hear as it rang out loud and clear.

He replaced it into the scabbard and gave it to Izzy. "Now show them, Izzy," he said.

She looked at her father in astonishment and slowly drew the sword from its scabbard. With tears in her eyes she held it aloft as it rang out in recognition of her birthright.

The crowd erupted into rapturous applause, chanting "Queen Isabella" repeatedly.

But Izzy and Arthur's triumph was short-lived; from out of the darkness a black dragon swooped low over their heads and landed a few metres away from where they were standing. Thirty guards or more rushed in and surrounded Arthur and Izzy, raising their spears in readiness to propel an attack. Ambrosius raised his head and hissed at it in a defiant show of strength. Izzy quickly recognised it as the dragon which had attacked her and Ambrosius on Ynys Enlli as it still carried the scarring that he had inflicted on the left side of its head and neck. She instinctively strapped Caliburn to her side. A low haze descended, and as it dispersed, everyone could see that the dragon's form had undergone a transmutation and was unmistakeably a woman. Arthur, followed by Izzy, pushed their way through the protective fence of the guards to get a closer look. It was Gorawen, staring coldly at Izzy, her face heavily scarred down one side, hence the reason it had been covered with a hood at the hunting lodge.

"I have come for what's rightfully mine. Give it here, child, and I shall allow you to live."

Izzy stood by the side of her father motionless, her hand firmly gripping the hilt of Caliburn. Imperceptibly she began to draw it from its scabbard but was stopped when something grabbed her wrist from behind, preventing her from revealing its deadly blade.

"Delay that, my brave queen," a soft voice came from above her head.

She looked down at what had prevented her from drawing Caliburn from its scabbard, and was horrified to see it was not of human form. Certainly, it was a hand in shape, but covered in red scales with sharp talons protruding from its fingers. She tried to turn to face her assailant but found herself unable to move a muscle. The figure released its grip and stepped out from behind her to reveal himself to Gorawen.

"Hello, Creiddylad, daughter of mine. My, how much you've aged!"

Gorawen was stunned and stumbled back several steps from him muttering, "Impossible, I don't believe it, I thought you were dead." She turned rapidly on her heels, shape-shifting again into the form of the black dragon, and took flight into the darkness of the night sky.

The strange figure turned round to face Arthur and Izzy. Slowly he lowered his hood, revealing himself to them. His head and face were completely hairless and covered in faint red snake-like scales. But the most compelling aspect of his appearance was his deep-set emerald-green eyes that shone with the intensity of fire. Although his outward appearance had been transformed, Izzy recognised the features of the man trapped in the ice in the cave on Ynys Enlli; it was Myrddin.

23

Preparation for Battle

The finale of the tournament had undoubtedly been a day of surprises. Arthur had returned to the hunting lodge earlier, together with Myrddin and his most trusted knights, to discuss the threat that faced them, and was on hand to greet the rest of the royal party when they arrived.

As they pulled up at the entrance and Izzy, Daniel, and Bronwyn stepped down from the coach, they were presented with another unexpected revelation. Standing next to Arthur was Owain, Tristan, and his two sisters, Aelwen and Rhiannon. Izzy and Daniel were dumbfounded, as was Bronwyn, and looked to Arthur for an explanation.

"Please forgive us for our subterfuge." Arthur sighed heavily. "It was necessary for reasons you will all understand when I explain later. But first let us eat as we have many serious matters to discuss."

As they all gathered in the Great Hall, servants brought out plates of food and giant jugs of water, placing them on tables around the room so they could help themselves. Although wine would have customarily been served as liquid refreshment for a meeting of the royal court, there was now a greater need for everyone to keep a clear head on account of the gravity of their king's announcement.

When they had finished their meal, Arthur stood up and coughed nervously. "Where do I begin?" he said, conscious of the enormity of the task in hand. "Firstly, I owe a very sincere apology to all those who thought brave Tristan here was killed during the tournament – especially Daniel, who considered himself responsible for it. As you can see, he is still breathing and very much alive. We had to weave a web of deceit to try and draw out our traitor from the darkness. Owain was to be used as bait in the hope that whoever the traitor was, they would present themself to Owain and make use of his desire for vengeance. We had to make it believable that he would turn against us. For that purpose, Tristan began by publicly creating a rift between Izzy's brother Daniel, and himself, which would ultimately result in his supposed death in the joust. This would then present Owain with reason to revenge his son's demise by turning traitor." He glanced down at Daniel and smiled apologetically. "We had to convince our enemy that events were true so they would be drawn into our trap. Consequently, some of the pieces on our chessboard had to be unaware they were part of the deception. Only three people, other than myself, were privy to our plan. However, our traitor has already revealed herself to us, so there is no longer a need to carry on with our pretence."

Arthur looked down at Bronwyn and placed his hand tenderly on her shoulder. "If you are not already aware of her identity, she is no other than my wife's mother, and my daughter's grandmother, Gorawen. But that is not her real name. Myrddin, who has joyously been returned to us, has identified her as his daughter, Creiddylad, and her mother is no other than Nimue, which explains why she desires Caliburn so much."

Bronwyn put her arm round Izzy's shoulders, pulling her closer. Izzy looked into her mother's eyes as they both tried to smile through the tears that revealed a past tenderness for memories of happier times.

Arthur continued, "As you can see, my wife and daughter are heartbroken. We are all greatly troubled by what manner of evil has transformed a once loving mother and grandmother into the she-wolf she has become. But pray believe me when I tell you that we are united as a family and are prepared to do whatever is necessary to prevent Creiddylad from seizing power. Myrddin has warned me that she is extremely dangerous having inherited great magic from her parents – himself and Nimue. Yes, it is true, she has kept her real identity hidden from us all. If it were not for Myrddin's miraculous return to us, we would never have known."

Bronwyn and Izzy were still trying to come to terms with the fact that they were descendants of the evil Nimue, the most powerful and malevolent sorcerer in history. Maybe this would explain why Creiddylad had been turned into the vile and sadistic woman she had become. *Who knows what evil traits I have inherited from my mother,* Izzy thought miserably. *What heinous feelings are lying dormant in my subconscious, waiting to be awakened to infest my soul as it has with my grandmother? But I am Arthur's daughter – surely I have inherited enough of his inner strength for righteousness and goodness to dilute any wickedness that may be inbred in me? But what of my mother? She has no idea who her father was and has never asked. Are his virtuous genes strong enough to overwhelm the evil that may flow in her blood?* These questions continued to haunt both mother and daughter, but for now, all thoughts of what could be had to be pushed to the back of their minds.

Arthur lifted his glass and took a few sips of water to lubricate his throat. "I was just as surprised as everyone else when Myrddin appeared at the tournament this evening. Since that time, I have had council with him, but I am not yet privy to the power of the magic that brought him back to us. I am much pleased, and thank God for returning him to us at a time we need him most. It is with some lament, however, that I inform you he has discovered that, during his wondrous transmutation from the grave, he has lost some memories of his past and is no longer in possession of the great magical powers he once held. His outward appearance too concerns him greatly, and he believes that only by returning to Ynys Enlli for a time, can he hope to restore himself to wholeness again. But before he pursues that quest, he has assured me he will stand beside us and fight to the death, if necessary, to rid us of the evil that is threatening our kingdom. He has left our presence for a short time to attempt to reinstate his former being, but has informed me that we must prepare ourselves for war. He has also warned me that like Nimue, his daughter will not give up until she gets what she wants."

Arthur took another gulp of water from his glass, then bent down to kiss Bronwyn on the cheek, but she swiftly turned her head so her lips met his in a show of support. Arthur gripped her hand tenderly and kissed her brow before straightening up to finish the final part of his speech. "As you saw tonight, Caliburn is again returned to us, thanks to our courageous daughter. She did this with the help of my old friend Ambrosius who sacrificed his life to bring them safely back to us. With magic I do not understand, he too has been reincarnated into the creature he once was. I also know that if it were not for the courage and love of my daughter's younger brother George, most of the joy of what transpired today would never have come to pass. He is, as I speak, attending to the personal needs of his beloved dragons."

Arthur paused to refill his empty glass and drink its contents before continuing. "Now, my noble friends, we must ready ourselves for the dangerous task of war against an enemy whose strength and form we know not. Nor do we know how or where they will come at us. Therefore, we have decided, since Creiddylad's eyes are set on taking the great sword Caliburn from us, we will use it as bait to entice her out to a place of our choosing – Rhosneigr."

This was the very place where Izzy's kidnap was concluded, a part of the kingdom he knew that with careful planning his army could defend. Rhosneigr had a broad sweeping bay with a deep, expansive sandy beach protected by a long line of immense sand dunes offering a barrier to any invader.

Time was now of the essence, and Arthur sent his knights to arm themselves for battle. He ordered that the women and children of the court be taken back to the palace together with those too frail to take up arms. The palace was a fortress, and if all else failed, was the perfect place for a last stand. Bronwyn was determined to stay with her husband no matter what, and although she tried to persuade Izzy to return to the safety of the palace, knew in her heart that she would want to take her place alongside her father.

George had returned to the palace with Ambrosius so he could gather the dragons together and prepare for war. Efion had armed George with leather armour and a sword, which he told him he was only to use for defending himself should he be separated from Ambrosius. George told him firmly there was no chance of them being separated, not if he had anything to do with it. Efion was to travel to the hunting lodge by cart. George and Ambrosius had offered him a lift, but he didn't fancy flying and wanted to keep his feet securely planted on the ground.

Ambrosius swooped low over the forest to see the continuous trickle of carts and boats heading to and from the palace with their precious cargoes. Instead of returning to the lodge, George decided to fly his 'flight' of dragons as he now called them, on a sortie around Cuddfan. His duty was to patrol the skies and report to Arthur should he see anything suspicious.

Efion, having arrived at the lodge by a more sedate form of transport, felt entirely out of his depth in the presence of the royal court, but he was there on essential matters, to collect food for his dragons from the king's hunting grounds – a big responsibility for a man of such short stature. However, after talking to Izzy, he had acquired a small army of helpers to assist him in selecting and killing a few deer from Arthur's prized herd.

Izzy sensed Ambrosius's presence getting stronger, so she ran out into the grounds of the hunting lodge to see the dragons land one by one, followed by her brother and Ambrosius. She rushed over to greet them as George jumped from the saddle like a seasoned warrior, resplendent in his newly acquired armour. Izzy noticed George's left arm was bleeding a little, but before she could speak, Ambrosius answered her. "Yes, George and I am now as one force, just as *we* are – you and me. I know as always you have many questions for me, my little queen, but they will have to wait for another day. George and I will be your eyes and ears. You will know what we see when we see it, and we will experience what you see, as long as you remember to keep your mind open to us at all times."

"It's so nice to have you back, Ambrosius, I missed you," Izzy replied.

"Not as much as me, sis," replied George. It really worked; the three of them could communicate with each other through their minds, without talking. It was a bit disconcerting though; it was strange enough when there was just the two of them, but now there were three.

A lone black dragon circled the darkened sky over the small island of Ynys Enlli and landed near the little clump of rocks that hid the entrance to the tunnel leading to the tomb of Myrddin and Nimue. As it neared the opening, the dragon shape-shifted into Creiddylad. She knelt down to break off a branch from the bush at the side of the path. This she ignited with her magic to light her way into the darkness of the tunnel, but as she did so she noticed the lantern that Izzy had left on the ground in her hurry to leave. "Thank you, Izzy," Creiddylad said to herself. It hissed into life as she pressed the button to ignite its pure white flame and made her way down into the depths below. As she approached the glass crypt that had entombed her parents, even someone with her considerable magical powers would have felt uneasy. It was only thanks to Izzy and Ambrosius that she had at last discovered her mother's final resting place and could devise a plan that would release her mother from her icy grave. But it had all gone wrong when the ice was transformed into an impenetrable glass tomb by Myrddin's magic. Now the only way she could free Nimue was by regaining Caliburn and using its powers to destroy the glass and reunite mother and daughter once more.

She bent down, placing the lantern on the floor of the cave, and walked over to the translucent block of green glass. She was astonished to see Myrddin's body still in her mother's embrace. What form of magic had he used to inhabit two bodies at once? She raised her arms and placed her hands flat against the surface of the tomb. It was scolding hot to her touch and would have burnt the skin of any mortal to the bone – another of Myrddin's devices to prevent anyone tampering with it. Not that this was any sort of hurdle for Creiddylad. She closed her eyes and chanted words from a long-forgotten language, swaying her head from side to side. A foul-smelling black mist rose from the floor of the cave, at first swirling around her feet then enveloping her and the tomb in a vile embrace.

A voice entered Creiddylad's head. "At last, my daughter, we meet. I have waited far too long for this moment. It grieves me that we are not standing together to rid ourselves of our enemies."

"I did my best, Mother, but Myrddin is too clever for me. He has outwitted me. I underestimated his powers and the determination of my granddaughter. I was shocked to see him at the tournament – I thought he was dead, and now Arthur is gathering his army against me. What shall I do? I do not have the powers to fight them."

"Do not blame yourself, you have done well, my child. I too was fooled by his cunning when he thrust Caliburn into our bodies. Each alone may not be able to defeat him, but together in mind and spirit we will generate such power that it will destroy Myrddin and Arthur forever."

"How can we do that, Mother? I need Caliburn to break the spell that Myrddin has set around you. Izzy will not give it up willingly and Arthur has surrounded her with an army I have no powers to defeat."

"When I beguiled your father with my passion, I persuaded him to teach me the secrets of his great magic. I secretly wrote them down in a book which I kept hidden away from him. When you were born, I placed the book in a golden casket so it would not perish, and for safekeeping buried it beneath his favourite apple tree here on the island. He was always fond of apples. He told me they were the secret to his great wisdom, so even had he known about *my* book of secrets, I knew he would not think to look there. I will tell you where to find it. You must search out the tree and retrieve the casket from beneath its entwined roots."

"Surely after all this time the tree will have died and withered away?"

"No. This tree is enchanted with powers from the Celtic druids of our ancestors. Myrddin told me that he fed its fruit to Arthur and his knights to heal them from their mortal wounds. The tree itself has great powers of immortality, so you will find it still standing."

"How will the book help me defeat Arthur's army and prise Caliburn from Izzy's grasp?"

"The charms and spells within its pages will provide you with the powers to raise an army of your own. Now you must make haste, my daughter, and seek it out. I have grown weary of my imprisonment in this dank mausoleum that Myrddin has cast for me. Oh, how I long to feel the warm blood of life flow through my veins again."

Arthur's army left the lodge for Rhosneigr in the early hours of the morning before sunrise. It was quite a sight as hundreds of mounted knights and foot soldiers in a torchlight procession snaked their way along the narrow lanes to the coast road. Arthur, Bronwyn, and Izzy rode at the head of the army closely followed by Bedivere, Tristan, and Daniel all arrayed in full plate armour. Izzy proudly carried Caliburn by her side, as was now her right, although her father wasn't happy at the thought of her wearing it in public. He knew it was the one thing that Creiddylad desired the most and would go to any lengths to get. However, as always, her insistence on doing things her way won the day, but only after promising she wouldn't go anywhere without her personal bodyguard by her side.

Eventually the darkness of the dawn was gently washed away by the sun as the procession joined the coast road to Rhosneigr. As it slowly rose above a vermillion-tinted sea and set forth its corridor of flame towards the land, it enhanced their brightly polished armour into a shimmering orange glow. Who would have thought that such a beautiful morning could be the harbinger of a brutal war that threatened to bring death and destruction to Cuddfan?

By the time they arrived at Rhosneigr, the wagons and men from the palace had already unloaded their cargos and were busy raising pavilions and setting up field kitchens. The logistics of feeding and watering such a large army in the field was enormous. The last thing any commander would want in a long-drawn-out conflict was for his men to be without food. By late afternoon, all the tents in the encampment had been pitched and everyone was preparing to eat their last meal of the day before settling down for the night. The smoke from their campfires and the smell of food wafted on the strengthening breeze coming from the sea.

Izzy couldn't settle; she had far too much on her mind for sleep to come, so went for a stroll on the beach to stretch her legs – guiltily, as she was without the protection of her personal guard. As she walked, she felt a presence behind her and turning quickly, saw Bella bounding up towards her with Owain following close behind. Bella barked loudly at the sight of her mistress, piercing the sounds of the breaking surf on the seashore. Izzy dropped to her knees to welcome her beloved dog into her open arms, but in her exuberance she charged headlong into her mistress, knocking her over onto the damp sand, and licked her face. Izzy burst out laughing as she hugged her close.

"I thought you might like to have her company at night, Majesty. She will keep you warm from the evening chill."

Owain stretched his hand towards Izzy and gently pulled her to her feet. Bella stood in between them panting, looking up at Owain as if to say she was sorry for her outburst. Owain affectionately patted her head and turned to Izzy. "The king wants me to ask if you will join him and his knights in his pavilion to discuss his battle plan."

"Why, of course, Owain," Izzy replied with a smile.

As they walked back towards the encampment Owain told her, "I am to return to my post as captain of the king's navy. The king has assigned Tristan and Daniel together as your personal bodyguard."

"Oh, has he, he didn't ask me," she replied jokingly. Then in a moment of tenderness, she stopped and put her arms around his neck, pulling him close. "I will miss your company, Owain."

The captain, somewhat embarrassed by his future queen's show of affection, gently pulled away and took her hands. "I will miss you too, my lady, but I am sure we will see each other from time to time when all this is over. After all, my daughters are now officially appointed your ladies-in-waiting. Maybe one day you will again do me the honour of being a guest in my little house on the shore."

Izzy recomposed herself, wiping away the single tear that had escaped down her cheek, and carried on walking. "I haven't had a chance to thank you and Tristan for the loyalty you showed my father in his clever plan to unmask our traitor. I must admit, you fooled all of us in your little scheme." She poked him gently in the ribs with her fingers and smiled. "I'm not sure I can forgive you for deceiving me!"

As they walked into the pavilion, Arthur and Bedivere, Tristan, Daniel, and his knights were discussing the final elements of their plan. "I think that we have it, gentlemen ... ah, Izzy, I am glad you could join us, I would like to go through our plan with you." Bella thought this could be a long night, so found the most comfortable spot in the tent and curled up for a bit of shut-eye.

Arthur had laid out a parchment map of the area in the middle of the floor of the pavilion and placed chess pieces on it to represent the various positions of his army. With sword in hand as a pointer, he described in detail his grand plan. "We have no idea when, how, or where Creiddylad will make her first strike, so if she decides to mount an assault from the sea, I have asked Owain to blockade the entrance to the bay between the jagged rocks that spread out to sea either side of the beach here," pointing with the sword. "Owain has ordered his men to acquire anything that will float and sail them out into the bay. Each boat will carry our best archers. At best, the blockade will prevent the enemy from reaching the beach. At worst, it will, pray God, delay them long enough to allow time for the army to take up defensive positions here and here," again pointing with his sword.

"You must use *Nicole*, Father," Izzy suggested, glancing at Dan for approval.

"No, Izzy, I cannot allow that, she is too precious to risk being damaged," Arthur replied.

"Not if Owain was aboard," countered Daniel. "He could command his men from her decks. She is fast under sail and has the advantage of the engine if necessary to get her out of trouble."

Owain glanced at Izzy and could see she was keen for her father to make use of *Nicole*. "I think it a most splendid idea, Majesty. I promise I will look after her and bring her back to you in one piece."

"Very well, I can see I am outnumbered." Arthur grasped Izzy's waist and kissed her cheek. "Thank you, Izzy, and thank you, Daniel." He coughed and continued, "Now, where were we? Ah yes – in case they attack from the land, we have placed a thousand men to our rear, behind the whole length of the dunes. Beyond these sandy hillocks is mostly flat marshland surrounded by thick forest. Any army who attempts a surprise attack here will fall prey to the deep quagmires that populate this area – they have been known to swallow a man whole in seconds, an agonising death, wouldn't you agree, gentlemen?"

Everyone nodded in agreement and Bedivere said, "We have posted sentries around the whole perimeter of the camp, Majesty, with strict instructions to report anything out of the ordinary to their captains."

"Then I am sure we will all sleep well in our beds tonight, Bedivere. I suggest you all return to your quarters and get some sleep."

They all bid Arthur goodnight and left his pavilion with hope in their hearts that all would go well when their enemy finally made her move. Izzy woke Bella from her slumbers, and as she walked over to her father to kiss him goodnight, he took her hand in his and looked quite sternly at her. "I want you to promise me, Izzy, that when the battle begins you will stay by my side. Please don't go off on one of your lone crusades. Creiddylad is coming for Caliburn, and when she does, she will strike with a venom you have never yet witnessed. I have fought many battles in my lifetime and in the heart of the mêlée that ensues, courage and bravery is no match for the evil she will unleash upon us. We can only hope to triumph over her together, side by side – not alone."

Izzy hugged him tightly. "Yes, Father, I promise."

"Good … now off to bed with you."

Sleep was not an option for such a great warrior as Arthur, and although he had commanded all others to bed, he himself still had work to do. Myrddin had returned and joined him in his pavilion to pass away the wee small hours in meditation, a practice they had done many times when Arthur ruled as king of the Britons, many centuries before.

For a boy of Georgie's age sleep was easy, it was staying awake that was the difficult thing. Before he came to Cuddfan, he was known as 'lazybones', who preferred to slaughter dragons and monsters on his games machine rather than help with chores. Yet here he was, patrolling the skies well after midnight on the back of Ambrosius, accompanied by his flight of dragons. But it was now far too dark for him to see anything. Besides, he had worked with little sleep for the past few days and was feeling completely shattered. In the distance, he could see the inviting glow from the small campfires dotted in amongst the sand dunes at Rhosneigr, so he decided to call it a day and, reminiscent of bombers coming in from a midnight raid, landed his retinue gently on the beach one by one.

George dismounted Ambrosius and told him to get some well-deserved shut-eye. The dragon was still chuckling to himself at Georgie's turn of phrase when his little warrior made his way towards Arthur's pavilion to make his report like a seasoned commander. He walked past the guard, removing his helmet and tucking it under his arm as he entered the tent. Myrddin and Arthur were both relaxing in campaign chairs, deep in conversation, catching up on old times no doubt. On a little table by the side was a half-empty glass of red wine and a bowl of ripe juicy apples, one of which Myrddin grabbed and bit into it.

"Now I know why Efion took sacks of apples to Ambrosius," George announced.

Myrddin and Arthur hadn't noticed him enter, so were a little startled by the interruption.

"I wondered where you had got to, George, come and sit down beside me," Arthur said, pointing to a cushion he was resting his feet on. George attempted a little bow. "No need for any ceremony here, George, you're family," he remarked.

George removed his sword from his belt and plonked down on the pillow. What do you mean about apples?" asked Arthur. "I'm intrigued."

"I think our little warrior here is more observant than we give him credit for," put in Myrddin, winking at George. "You must learn to keep secrets, my young Dragon Master."

On seeing the puzzled look on Arthur's face, Myrddin tried to change the subject, but Arthur interrupted him. "Myrddin, tell me, what is it about apples that's so important and why should it be kept a secret?" he asked.

"Oh ... very well ... but you must promise not to divulge what I am about to tell you," Myrddin replied grudgingly. "The power of our magic is only effective because it's kept secret."

George and Arthur enthusiastically nodded in agreement.

"What you should both know about dragons is they are very simple creatures with brains that are tiny compared to ours. Every day is the same for them – they hunt, they kill, they eat, they sleep, day after day. But Ambrosius is different because before I thrust Caliburn into mine and Nimue's bodies, I transferred my soul into his heart for safe keeping until the time was right for me to be reborn. He was never aware I had invaded his senses except for gaining a few new powers from me, like thought-speak … and a liking for apples," he said, winking at George.

"When Izzy drew Caliburn from its resting place, the shock of pulling the sword from my body was too much for Ambrosius to bear, resulting in his death. When he was consumed by the other dragons, he and I were reborn again. But as you can see, living inside a dragon's head all those years has come at a cost. Some of me has seeped into him, and some of him has seeped into me."

"Does that mean you can fly and breathe fire, just like Ambrosius?" asked George, hugely thrilled by the possibility.

"I think I will keep that secret to myself, young Dragon Master," Myrddin replied, pointing his scaly finger to his nose. "Now, to more important matters! I have brought you a gift, in appreciation for the part you played in bringing me back to Cuddfan."

Myrddin stood up and reached down to pick up a sack from beneath his chair. He fumbled to undo the drawstring and sighed, "It's challenging, having talons for hands. I am still working to rid myself of this appearance, but until I return to Ynys Enlli and restore myself, I will have to get used to them, and unfortunately you will have to get used to seeing me like this."

George jumped to his feet. "May I?" pointing at the sack.

"Why, yes, of course, thank you," replied Myrddin handing it to him.

George took hold of the bag. It was heavy in his small hands. He untied the drawstring and carefully pulled the opening apart. Peering inside, he gasped as he pulled out the object hidden within. It was a bronze helmet of immense beauty. Its skull was divided into quadrants separated by engraved bars of Celtic knotwork. Each quadrant was covered in tiny scales of silver and so too were the two cheek pieces hanging from small hinges attached to the skull. Its reinforced brow was decorated in the form of two dragons divided by a nasal bar of finely carved knotwork.

Myrddin took it from him and placed it on his head. "Mmm …", he said, standing back, "I think it will require a little extra padding to fit your head, George, but my, how gallant you will look astride Ambrosius."

George was overcome and flung his arms around Myrddin's waist. "Thank you, thank you, it's the best present ever!"

"It was crafted by a legendary Celtic armourer, who many centuries ago made it for a courageous young dragon rider such as yourself. He was the craftsman who created Caliburn's scabbard. It has the same magical powers and protects whosoever wears it from harm."

So much for Georgie's plan for an early night, but he did eventually fall asleep perched on the cushion between Arthur's feet, admiring his new helmet, until Arthur gathered his little warrior up in his arms and gave him to one of his guards to return him to his quarters.

24

Into Battle

As dawn greeted Arthur's sleeping army a damp cold sea mist slowly moving towards the shore alerted the guards, and suddenly the camp was full of activity. George came running out from the tent he shared with Efion wearing his newly acquired helmet. Efion had stuffed it with one of his smelly old rags for extra padding, but it still wobbled from side to side as he ran, almost obscuring his view, and as he fumbled with the buckle of his sword belt, he tripped over a small rock, falling headlong in front of Ambrosius. "Why Master George, you do look very dangerous this morning," he said with a chuckle.

"Huh!" George replied, getting to his feet. "This wasn't quite the effect I had in mind, perhaps I need more padding?" But he soon saw the funny side and burst out laughing as he climbed into the saddle. Within a few moments they were airborne, and as George and Ambrosius flew beyond the sea mist, they got their first glimpse of the enemy. An armada of all manner of ships was heading straight towards Owain's blockade. As Ambrosius swooped down to get a closer look, they gasped in amazement as the enemy's fleet was nothing but a load of rusting and rotten hulks covered in seaweed and barnacles. Creiddylad had finally amassed herself a navy. Using her newfound powers from her mother's book, she had raised sunken wrecks and their ghostly crews from the bottom of the sea and concealed their arrival with a veil of innocent sea mist.

Ambrosius immediately warned Izzy with mind-speak, and she ran to inform Arthur of what was coming. He raised the alarm, trying to alert Owain out in the bay, but it was useless – he and his men were totally unaware of what was coming. George and Ambrosius, conscious of the situation, flew low over *Nicole* and shouted to Owain below what horror was heading their way. Owain got the message, but what could he do? They were powerless to attack such an overwhelming force. No, he must hold fast and simply hope that the blockade would slow their enemy's progress and give Arthur enough time to prepare his army along the beach.

George had an idea forming in his mind. "It's worth a try," Ambrosius replied and commanded his ladies, who were waiting on the beach in reserve, to take to the air. They were to pick up the massive black rocks that populated the beach and head out through the mist, where they were to drop them onto the decks of Creiddylad's ships. George thought that if they were heavy enough to smash through the woodwork, they might just cause enough damage to send them back to their graves at the bottom of the sea. Good idea though it was, they had underestimated the speed of Creiddylad's makeshift navy, and before his dragons could get into position, the ships had rammed headlong into the first line of the blockade. George could hear the horrible sound of splintering wood and agonising cries of men from below. Owain watched in horror as half of his ragtag navy was crushed in front of his eyes.

George, in his enthusiasm to crush the enemy, cried out a line from one of his favourite films, "Let's kick some ass, Ambrosius!" From the sky, the first black rock, as big as a car, came hurtling down towards its target and as it smashed through the deck and hull, a plume of water rose up violently through the gaping hole the rock had left on its journey to the seabed. The rotting ship's superstructure creaked and groaned as if in pain and broke in two before disappearing beneath the surface. George cheered and punched the air with his fist; his plan *was* working! One by one, the dragons dropped their death-dealing lumps of rock onto Creiddylad's ships, breaking their backs and sending them down to their watery graves.

Ambrosius swooped low over what remained of Owain's blockade, and as the cold grey mist melted away, George could see the carnage his dragons' bombing raid had produced. The surface of the sea was littered with floating wreckage, not only of their enemy's ships but sadly, of Arthur's too. The small number of boats that survived Creiddylad's onslaught searched the now calm waters for survivors as well as reclaiming the bodies of their fallen comrades. Despite his young age, George quickly grasped a sharp lesson – yes, they had been the victors of this encounter, but at what cost. He also realised that this was not the end of the war, at best it was a short respite until the next attack. He turned Ambrosius and his ladies homeward and as they touched down on the shores of Rhosneigr they were greeted with cheers of adulation from the army, which was strung out in a line along the full length of the beach in readiness to repel the enemy.

George climbed out of the saddle and marched proudly over to where Arthur and Izzy were standing. He bent down on one knee and said, "We have destroyed all Creiddylad's ships, your Majesty, and sent them to the bottom of the sea."

"Well done, George!" replied Arthur pulling him to his feet, "But as I told you last night, there is really no need for you to bow in front of me."

Izzy flung her arms round George and kissed his cheek. "I'm very proud of you. Ambrosius was right when he said you will surprise us all."

George blushed and pulled away from his sister's embrace, which was a little embarrassing in front of all these knights. He shrugged his shoulders and said, "Oh, it was nothing really. Ambrosius and his ladies did all the hard work, I just guided them."

"Nonsense, George," replied Arthur, "you are a courageous warrior worthy of your sister's praise. It takes true grit to fly into the face of an unknown enemy without fear for your own life."

They were all so preoccupied with proclaiming George a hero, they didn't notice that the sea, breaking gently on the shore, had begun changing colour until it became a sickening blood red. As bubbles frothed on the surface they burst open, spouting a black gas that little by little was creeping up towards them. Ambrosius and his ladies first noticed its evil stench and raised their long necks, hissing loudly at the advancing vapour and flapping their wings in defiance. George sensed Ambrosius's panic and withdrew his sword from its scabbard. Izzy stood frozen to the ground for a second as all eyes turned to the developing chaos. She pulled Caliburn from its resting place, and as it rang out, ordered George to take his dragons and fly out of there.

"But, sis, I want to stay here with you," he answered back.

"Do as you're told for once! We need your eyes in the sky," she snapped.

George returned his sword to its scabbard and ran as fast as his legs would carry him towards Ambrosius, and jumped into the saddle. Within seconds, all the dragons were airborne and hovering over the beach to try and catch sight of what was coming. They couldn't see anything other than the thick black fog that was floating up to the beach, and Arthur's army retreating to the sand dunes. George could see his sister below with Arthur, Tristan, and Daniel all on horseback galloping up and down the beach ordering their men into defensive positions. Myrddin was standing on the highest point looking out to sea.

The sky gradually darkened, blocking out the warm sunlight, and the gentle breeze strengthened into a howling gale, blowing surges of sand into the faces of all those on the ground. Riderless horses took flight in panic, galloping through the encampment as if possessed. Had Arthur underestimated Creiddylad? How could his army hope to fight an enemy when they were blinded by the conditions?

Myrddin peered out over the sea and spotted a lone dragon hovering like a vulture over its prey. *I see you have not lost your mother's cunning, Creiddylad,* he thought. *Well, I may no longer be able to overpower you with magic, my daughter, but maybe I can outwit you with some ingenuity."* He closed his eyes and pointed with the talons of one hand to the heavens. A deafening clap of thunder heralded a tirade of lightning bolts shooting across the bay. He generated rain, but it was just a trickle. Myrddin focused his mind harder, but it wasn't easy for him, his powers were not what they used to be. Still, it seemed the more he concentrated the harder the precipitation became until it was torrential. Finally, the immensity of the heavy rain drenched the sand so it could not be taken up by the wind.

However, it was not over. In all the ensuing panic, no one had noticed the evil wisps of blackness still creeping up the beach and invading every corner of Arthur's camp. It carried on eerily over the sand dunes to the boggy ground beyond, where it separated into hundreds of tiny tornadoes, swirling around until they were finally sucked into the quagmires like water down a plughole. Instantly they re-emerged as black slimy ghostlike figures erupting headfirst from the sodden marshland. Each was armed with the most offensive weapons imaginable. They slithered silently over the dunes, attacking Arthur's army from the rear. Taken completely by surprise and hopelessly outnumbered, they could find no way to kill an enemy that had the body of slime. The only way of staying alive was to stand and parry their blows, but no matter how hard they tried, they could not kill them. There was only one weapon that could dispatch these evil fiends, and that was Caliburn, but there were just too many of them for Izzy to deal with.

Arthur looked on in impotent fury as his men were slaughtered one after another by the incessant assault. Myrddin too was powerless to stop them. Arthur decided there was no other course of action but to retreat.

It was then, when all seemed lost, that Daniel discovered, quite by accident when his slimy adversary backed into a campfire and burst into flames, that they had a weakness after all. He rushed over to Arthur and Izzy and cried, "They are inflammable, we can kill them with fire!"

"What do you mean, Daniel?" Arthur asked.

"Don't fight them with swords, use flaming torches!" Daniel shouted, jigging up and down in an agony of impatience.

"There are too many of them, Dan!" Izzy replied. "It will take far too long to arm every man with a torch. Besides, haven't you noticed it's still raining? But we can improve on your idea." She turned to her father. "Get the men to retreat to the water's edge, and I will call on Ambrosius to set the battlefield ablaze with his fire."

"But we will lose everything, Izzy, our tents, our wagons, our food – everything."

"Better that than our lives, Father," Izzy responded grimly.

"Very well, Izzy, I will get the trumpeters to sound the retreat and head for the seashore. But please wait for my command, I don't want any of my men getting caught up in Ambrosius's fire."

Ambrosius and George had already read Izzy's mind and were flying low over the carnage of the battlefield ready to strike. Myrddin also sensed what was happening and tried to lessen the ferocity of his thunderstorm, but his magic was again not strong enough. Had Creiddylad now taken back control over the worsening situation?

Meanwhile, the trumpeters sounded the retreat and news was relayed amongst those fleeing for their lives to head for the safety of the beach, but alas, many were cut down trying to make their escape. Those that lay injured on the ground were helped to their feet, while those that couldn't walk were helped into carts.

Once Arthur was sure everyone was off the battlefield, Izzy called on Ambrosius to do his work and watched as he swooped low over the battleground, unleashing his fiery breath and incinerating everything in his path. The spine-chilling screams from Creiddylad's deadly army filled the air as one by one they were consumed by the blistering inferno. The thick black smoke stained by the toxic stench of destruction from the burning debris rose up into the sky and hung heavy over Rhosneigr. The plan had worked, but at the cost of losing everything.

The thunderstorm slowly dissipated into the distance from whence it had come; had Creiddylad given up or was she planning another hideous attack?

Ambrosius and George landed on the beach in front of what was left of Arthur's army. George dismounted and walked over to join Izzy, who was standing at her father's side staring in stunned silence at the devastation that lay before them. They had lost half their army. Countless numbers of Bedivere's brave men had perished at the hands of Creiddylad's foul marauders. Many of those that had escaped death were lying injured on the beach, and those that were standing were so exhausted there was no way they could hope to survive another attack.

Izzy took hold of her father's hand, gripping it firmly in hers. She could see the despondent look in his eyes. He looked down at her. "I am so sorry, Izzy, I have let my people down, but most of all, I have let you down. This is not the happy homecoming I had planned for you."

"Nonsense, Father, it's not over yet."

"What do you mean, Izzy? Creiddylad has won, we have no more fight left in our bellies. We can only hope that she has some humanity left in that callous heart of hers to spare your life and the lives of our people."

"No, Father, Creiddylad will not give up until she has destroyed us all and taken Caliburn for herself. If she wants it so badly, then I will give it to her," she said with a challenging stare.

Arthur looked at his daughter with a hint of suspicion. "You are not going to do what I think you are going to do, are you, Izzy?"

"Maybe," she said coyly.

"No, no, no, you are not going to put your life at risk again, I forbid it!" he said sternly.

But Izzy was determined and without another word, grabbed hold of George's hand and ran over to Ambrosius who had already read her mind and knew exactly what was expected of him. George climbed into the saddle and Izzy jumped on Ambrosius's back behind him. As Arthur ran forward in a desperate attempt to stop them, Ambrosius said, "Hold on, little queen!" and took to the air with Izzy holding on for dear life.

"Are you sure you want to do this, sis?" shouted George.

"Trust me, little brother, it's our only option. When you drop me off on *Nicole*, I want you to return to Arthur and tell him to take his army back to the palace. Make it clear to him that he must do this for my plan to succeed." It wasn't essential for Arthur to return to the palace for her plan to work, and Ambrosius knew this, but they both realised he would refuse to leave her unless he thought it was vital.

25

The Final Conflict

Ambrosius circled *Nicole*, and choosing a suitable position, hovered just a few metres over her bow as a mystified Owain looked on. Fortunately her sails had been lowered, giving Izzy enough space to jump clear onto the deck. Owain rushed forward to assist Izzy as she landed on her feet and ran to the cockpit. Ambrosius gained height then turned and headed back to the shore to deliver Izzy's message to her father. Before Owain could open his mouth, Izzy ordered everyone to jump overboard.

"Wait, what are you doing, my lady?" he asked worriedly.

"I haven't got time to explain now, Owain. You and your men must leave *Nicole* this instant!" she replied hurriedly.

"I know you are the king's daughter, my lady, and I must do as I am commanded, but no one is leaving until you tell me what's going on."

"Very well, if I must," she said impatiently. "Creiddylad has all but destroyed our army and my only option is to draw her out as far away from Cuddfan as possible to give my father time to get the survivors and injured back to the safety of the palace."

"And how … do you intend to draw the evil witch out?"

Izzy drew Caliburn halfway out of its scabbard. "With this!" she replied, pulling it out entirely and thrusting it high into the air. It rang out loudly, its clear sound reverberating across the surface of the water. In the distance and out of sight, Creiddylad froze and turned her attention to the source of the sound.

Izzy returned Caliburn to its scabbard. "There, I have done it, I've got her attention. Now please tell your men to get off my yacht!"

Owain reluctantly ordered his men to jump overboard.

"And you too, Owain. Please. I have to do this on my own."

"I'm not going anywhere. I made an oath to your father that I would protect you, and I will do that with my life if necessary."

"Oh, very well," she muttered angrily, "but we will have to be quick, we have wasted too much time already."

Izzy rushed below deck with Owain close on her heels. Once in the saloon she removed her armour and grabbed her lifejacket. She strapped it on and threw Owain the lifejacket belonging to Daniel. "Here," she said, "you will need this."

He looked puzzled but did as he was told for fear of angering her even further. She went to the engine and retrieved the starting handle from where Dan had left it. "While I start the engine, you go up and pull up the anchor," she commanded.

She put the starting handle into the slot and tried to turn the engine over, but Caliburn made it awkward for her in the confined space so she removed her sword belt and placed it to one side. After a few attempts the engine burst into life, and as the boat vibrated in rhythm with its power, she rushed towards the companionway. "Damn it!" she said as she turned back and pulled Caliburn from its scabbard, "I will need you, great sword." She rushed up on deck as it sounded out its war cry.

Izzy placed Caliburn beside the wheel and crept quietly up behind Owain as he knelt on the deck pulling in the heavy chain. He tied off the anchor to the cleat shouting, "All secure!" and attempted to raise himself from his knees but Izzy seized the moment and gave him an almighty push, knocking him off balance and sending him headfirst into the sea. She peered out over the side as Owain vanished from view. The lifejacket inflated automatically, bringing him spluttering back to the surface.

Izzy waved to him. "I'm so sorry, Owain, but you're not part of my plan. This is just between me and my grandmother." She ran back to the cockpit and put the engine into gear, then steered *Nicole* out to sea leaving a very frustrated Owain thrashing about in her wake.

It was now early evening, and the sea's demeanour was worsening, generating an uncomfortable choppy swell that caused *Nicole* to pitch and roll. The wind was also increasing in force, and as the skies closed in, it began to rain. *Is this more of Creiddylad's evil magic?* Izzy wondered.

She could see Creiddylad approach from the starboard side, cloaked in her dragon mantle, and hover over the bow making several unsuccessful attempts to land on the deck. Izzy reduced the engine revs. More than anything she wanted a face to face confrontation with her and if she kept

Nicole's speed up, it would be almost impossible for her to board. As Creiddylad finally gripped the deck with her talons and folded in her wings, she shape-shifted back to her human form. Her face was still heavily scarred, which gave her a terrifying appearance, and this time she didn't try to hide it.

Izzy put the engine into neutral and picked up Caliburn, gripping it tightly as it rang out. She stepped away from the wheel as Creiddylad walked towards her. "That's far enough, grandmother!" she warned her, raising the sword to eye level.

Creiddylad hissed at the sight of it. "You have a lot more cunning than I gave you credit for, Izzy. Maybe you have inherited a bit more of me than from Arthur? Does it not bother you that one day the devil might reach into your soul and reclaim it for himself?"

"I have nothing in common with you!"

Creiddylad stepped a little closer. "Oh Izzy, have you forgotten how you tried to cut down my poor man Meyric?"

"He murdered my friend Huw, he deserved to die. Besides, it was my father who rid us of his evil heart."

She took another step closer. "Did they not teach you at Sunday school that vengeance is the Lord's work?" Creiddylad was trying to make Izzy doubt herself and weaken her resolve.

Izzy lost her temper, shouting, "I am nothing like you!" The sword began to ring out again, reflecting the anger inside her.

Creiddylad took another step forward. "That's it, Izzy, do you feel the evil rising in your blood? Even the great Caliburn senses it. You want to kill me, don't you?"

Izzy realised intuitively what her grandmother was attempting to do to her, so she decided to play along and try to outwit her wicked mind. But she had to tread carefully. Ever since Creiddylad had come aboard, she was continually trying to invade her mind, but something or someone was giving her the strength to deny her entry. She dropped to the deck on her knees. Grabbing Caliburn, she lowered her head and pretended to cry. The rain trickling down her face made her deceit more believable. They were both soaked to the skin and *Nicole* was rolling violently from side to side in the escalating swell making Creiddylad feel sick. She was finding it almost impossible to stand upright having never been a great sailor when on the rare occasion she had joined the Moorefields on one of their sailing trips.

In her impatience to finish their reunion and get off *Nicole*, Creiddylad was happy to believe Izzy was weakening, and in her final bid for Caliburn, moved closer to where she was kneeling. She reached out to her. "Come child … give me the sword … come and join your loving grandmother. I will teach you the ways of my magic and together we will be so powerful." Izzy stayed motionless. "Come on, my dear, I know you want to. We have no need of Arthur. After all, wasn't it he who abandoned you when you were all but a few days old? What kind of father would do that to his only child?"

Of course, Izzy knew there was no way Creiddylad would allow her to live once she had Caliburn in her hands. No, she had to play along with her little game until she had the chance to turn the tables on her. But there was one more thing Izzy desperately needed to know before she made her final move; what had she done with Alison and James? She didn't want to appear overly concerned, so she must keep up the pretence at all costs that she had surrendered to her grandmother's goading. She looked up at her with sorrowful eyes, hating herself for what she was about to say. "And what of the Moorefields … have you dealt with them?"

Creiddylad, happy in the belief she had finally seduced her weak-spirited granddaughter, lowered her guard. "Oh, it was quite easy once I'd given them a helping of my famous hospitality. Let's just say they are … lost at sea," she replied with a snigger.

Izzy shuddered violently and felt an uncontrollable rage surge through her body. She lowered her gaze towards the sword and gripping it tightly, raised herself up in front of her grandmother. She smiled, and slowly lifting her head to stare into her grandmother's heartless eyes, said softly, "Here, my sweet grandmother, come and feel Caliburn's power," and she pointed the blade towards her. Creiddylad grinned in anticipation and looked down at the blade of the prize she so desired. She just couldn't resist the impulse to caress it, and as she slowly stroked the blade with her fingers the sword began to ring, low at first then more and more plangently as Creiddylad finally gripped the blade with both hands. She smiled triumphantly – finally the sword had recognised her as the daughter of Nimue, the keeper of the sword! The prize was hers at last.

Even as Creiddylad made to force the sword from her hands, Izzy realised that if she didn't act immediately, her grandmother would wield it against her. She jerked it back from Creiddylad's grip, slicing through her fingers with its razor-sharp blade, and plunged it deep into her grandmother's heart. Creiddylad staggered and glared at her in horror. "Does its kiss not warm your heart?" Izzy whispered in her ear. Still keeping her gaze firmly on Creiddylad's eyes, she slowly withdrew the blade from her body, then in one swift continuous movement stepped back, raising Caliburn high behind her. Using all her strength she swung it in a great arc to slice cleanly through her neck. For a moment, her head remained in place, staring coldly back at her, then Creiddylad's body crumpled to the deck parting company with her head which bounced and tumbled overboard into the sea.

In the heat of the moment, and barely able to comprehend what she had just done, Izzy failed to notice that *Nicole*, pressed by the strengthening winds, was drifting helplessly into Myrddin's curtain of mist. She pulled herself together and tried to push Creiddylad's remains over the side, but her body was too heavy for her and got ensnared in the boom brake, the rope that prevented the boom from moving freely. "First things first," she muttered to herself and ran back to the wheel, putting the engine into gear and turning *Nicole* back towards Cuddfan. Once she was on course Izzy returned to deal with the body, but still couldn't budge it. The weather was worsening more than ever and she needed to get back to the safety of the harbour with all haste, but there was no way she was going to keep company with her grandmother on the return journey. *Only one thing for it,* she thought, *I will have to use Caliburn to cut her free from the rigging.* She rushed back to the wheel, almost losing her footing as *Nicole* hit a wave, bow on. Grabbing Caliburn, Izzy went back to deal with Creiddylad's remains. She swung Caliburn in a movement that, slicing through the rope with its razor-sharp blade, released Gorawen's body into the water.

Izzy pulled herself up onto the guard rail at the edge of the deck and peered out over the side. Too late she realised her mistake in cutting the rope, and as *Nicole* slammed into another wave, turned to see the boom heading straight for her. As it smashed into the side of her head, her body was propelled into the raging sea. Her lifejacket inflated and brought her back to the surface. With blood pouring from her wound, she watched helplessly as *Nicole* sped away from her into the darkness, leaving her at the mercy of the unfeeling waves. Unable to help herself, she drifted on the tide into the mist, and as she slowly slipped into unconsciousness, released her grip on Caliburn, freeing it to descend to the bottom of the sea beneath her.

26

Sole Survivor part 2

Izzy slowly opened her eyes and stared up at the flickering fluorescent light above her head as it buzzed incessantly like an angry fly caught in a spider's web. Then the rhythmic pulse of the light flashing on and off soothed her back into the safe retreat of darkness and she drifted back into sleep. But her mind, now alerted to her body's senses, went into overdrive and dispatched a shockwave of pain from the side of her head, launching her into full consciousness. Opening her eyes fully and sensing where she was, she sat bolt upright, but the sudden movement sent another spasm of hurt slamming inside her skull. As she reached up to feel the source of her agony, she noticed the needle penetrating the inside of her lower arm, neatly kept in place with sticking plaster and connected by a flexible tube to a bag hanging from a frame beside her bed. Through her flimsy gown, she could see pads attached to her upper body and limbs with a plethora of cables connected to a machine on a trolly close by.

Confused, Izzy ripped the wired pads from her body, triggering the EEG machine into a loud screeching alarm. In blind panic from the noise, she struggled to slide out of bed, but her legs collapsed beneath her and in desperation she grabbed hold of the IV stand to break her fall but pulled it over on herself. It narrowly missed her head and lodged onto the soft edge of the mattress as she crumpled in a heap on the floor. In pain, she let out an uncontrollable agonising scream. Alerted by the alarm and Izzy's cries, the two nurses on duty in the intensive care unit of Bangor Hospital ran into the room, and as one of them put the IV stand back on its casters, the other silenced the EEG alarm and carefully helped Izzy up into the armchair by the side of the bed.

"Just what do you think you were doing, young lady?" the eldest of the two nurses said as she checked the needle going into Izzy's arm. "It's a good job you didn't rip this out." Then she turned to the other nurse.

"Jenny, go and page Doctor Evans while I get Isabella back into bed."

"Yes, Staff," Jenny replied as she left the room.

The staff nurse looked compassionately at Izzy. "You sit there quietly for a moment, my dear, while I make you presentable for the doctor." Izzy gazed into space, trying to come to terms with her predicament. "There we are, that's better," she said, fluffing up the pillows. "Now let's get you back into bed."

As she replaced the covers over her body, Izzy croaked, "Who am I?"

"Don't you remember, my dear?" the nurse replied, folding the sheet back neatly over the thin bedcover. "You're Isabella – here, look." She picked up her left hand to show her what was printed on the tag on her wrist and said, "That's you, my dear."

Izzy focused on the tag and read the name out in her mind *Isabella Aelwen Moorefield*. She looked in complete bewilderment at the nurse. "Is that really me?"

"Why of course it is, my dear," she said as she tidied away the EEG cables and double-checked the IV drip.

"Where are we?" Izzy asked. "How did I get here?"

She was about to answer when a tall young man walked into the room wearing a white coat and a stethoscope hanging out of his waist pocket. The identity label hanging round his neck read 'Dr Matthew Evans'. He looked at Izzy. "Welcome back, Isabella ... you had us all worried for a while," he said softly.

The staff nurse interrupted him and whispered in his ear, "I would like a word with you in my office, Doctor, before you attend to Miss Moorefield."

A few minutes later they both returned, the doctor with a file under his arm. "I understand you have no recollection of who you are or why you are here, Isabella. Staff Nurse Curtis here," pointing to the nurse, "will try to answer some of your concerns once I've given you a thorough examination to make sure you're working correctly after your little sleep."

After much probing and prodding, the nurse covered Izzy up again and followed the doctor out of the room once he had updated the chart at the foot of the bed. Izzy watched through the window of her room and observed the doctor in deep conversation with the staff nurse. Her eyes began to close, but in her determination to get answers she fought back against her body's eagerness to sleep. She grabbed the tumbler from the bedside table, filled it with water and gulped it down in one breath. As she refilled it, the staff nurse returned to her room, pushing a trolley.

"I'm Anita," she said, "and I've been looking after you since you were brought in here. Doctor Evans is so pleased with your recovery, he has booked you in for a final CAT scan in the morning, and if the results prove positive you will be transferred to a general ward in a day or two. For the time being, he has prescribed some medication for the pain." She opened the hinged lid of the cabinet and taking out a bottle, dispensed two tablets into a plastic dish.

Izzy took the pills from her and swallowed them down with the aid of another tumbler of water. Anita locked the cabinet, pushed it aside and updated her chart, then grabbing a chair sat down beside the bed and held Izzy's hand. "It's quite common for patients to lose their memory after suffering a brain trauma such as yours, my dear, so try not to worry too much, it's important at this stage to get you fit and well enough to go home. I'm sure once you're back in your familiar surroundings with family and friends, your memory will eventually return."

Izzy looked at her longingly, wanting more answers. "Now you've told me my name, can you tell me how I got here and why my head is hurting so much?" she said, touching the dressing that covered the wound at the side of her head.

Anita could understand Izzy's concerns. She had worked in an intensive care unit for far too long not to recognise the importance of her patient's mental wellbeing to speed up recovery of their physical health. "Let's try and fill in a few blanks for you. We only know what the paramedic told us when they brought you in. You were plucked from the sea by the coastguard helicopter. You arrived here at Bangor Hospital, unconscious, with a suspected fractured skull, and you've been in a coma ever since. That was two weeks ago. You were identified by the name on the label of your lifejacket. Once the police had confirmed your identity, they found out that you were on holiday with your family aboard your yacht – *Nicole* was her name, I seem to recall. Anyway, they believe your yacht was caught in a violent storm. I remember because I was on duty that night and it was howling a gale when I came into work. Several boats in Menai Strait were wrenched from their moorings and sank. They simply concluded that your yacht must have succumbed to a similar fate."

"Were there any other survivors?" Izzy asked.

"I don't know, my dear. All I know is that the police investigations are ongoing, they are just waiting for you to regain consciousness so they can interview you."

"Well, I'm not going to be a lot of use to them, seeing as I can't even remember my name!" Izzy felt a sudden pain in her lower arm and began to rub it hard with her hand. "What is that?" she yelled.

"Oh, you came in with that, Isabella. Doctor Evans believes it to be an animal bite, but he couldn't decide whether it came from a cat or a dog. Just to be on the safe side, we've started you on a course of rabies injections. But strangely, the wound, tiny as it is, refuses to heal over."

"How odd," Izzy agreed.

"Well, my dear, it's time for you to sleep. You've a busy day ahead of you tomorrow and I've got other patients to look in on." She stood up and jerked the chair away with the back of her legs, leaving Izzy in a state of even more confusion, if that were possible.

It was two days since Izzy had woken from her coma and been moved into a general ward. She was still suffering from amnesia but felt a lot stronger physically, so Dr Evans thought it would improve her recovery to allow her to receive visitors. Her first was a policewoman, who stayed with her for just half an hour. She wrote down copious notes in her little book and although sympathetic, was so abrupt with her barrage of questions that the staff nurse told her she would kick her off the ward if she continued with that unhelpful line of questioning.

Her two school friends, Jenny and Sarah, were constant companions at her bedside and slowly, with their help, patches of her past life began to emerge. But for some reason she just couldn't remember the weeks that led up to her rescue, no matter how hard she tried; it was as though her most recent memories had been totally erased. A steady succession of her parent's colleagues had also been regular visitors, including Jean, who told her she was her father's personal secretary. She was a very close friend of the family and brought in all kinds of treats for her. Although the police had made numerous enquiries into Aunt Gorawen's whereabouts, they had not been able to track her down. Izzy didn't seem to be too concerned as the Aunt Gorawen she remembered was always gallivanting around the globe, dealing with her charity work.

Izzy's enforced stay in hospital didn't go down well with her, and she kept nagging at the doctor to discharge her. Finally, after another dull and boring week, he told her she could go home if she promised to take things easy and continue seeing the psychotherapist – *Miss Mindbender* as Izzy called her. Izzy was happy to agree to this and she was now sitting in the armchair close to her bed, dressed in the new clothes Jean had brought in for her. She couldn't wait to get out of the hospital and was excited at the thought of going back to school. The scar on the side of her head was still evident, but as Doctor Evans had promised, was partly hidden by her flame-red hair, which was beginning to grow back. Despite his best efforts, however, he couldn't do anything for the bite on her arm; although it was not infected in any way, the slight swelling remained.

Izzy stood up as the nurse came in with a middle-aged Asian gentleman wearing wire-framed half-spectacles on the end of his nose; both were carrying bags. "Please don't stand up, Miss Moorefield," he said pleasantly, "I'm the hospital pharmacist and I've just brought in your medication for you to take home with you."

Izzy sat back in the chair. "Can you confirm your name and date of birth for me, please?" he asked, but she looked back at him with an exasperated expression.

"Don't worry, hen," the young trainee nurse said in a warm Edinburgh brogue, "it's just hospital procedure."

"Oh," Izzy replied, "sorry, my brain is still rather sluggish."

After telling him her name and date of birth, he double-checked the prescription details stapled to the plastic bag. "That's fine," he said, removing an assortment of little boxes from the bag. He showed Izzy each container in turn and informed her what the pills were for, when and how often to take them. Izzy nodded and he put them back in the bag.

"Thank you, Miss Moorefield," he said, removing his spectacles and placing them in the top pocket of his jacket. "Have a good day," he added as he walked out of the room.

Izzy looked up at the nurse and they grinned at each other. "I bet you're excited about going home?" Izzy nodded enthusiastically. "Jean phoned to say she's on her way, so not long now."

The nurse swung the large bag she'd been holding up onto the bed, "These are the clothes you had on when they brought you in. They whiffed a bit being soaked in seawater, so one of the nice ladies in the hospital laundry washed and dried them for you."

"That was kind of her," Izzy replied. "Can I take a look? I've heard so much about them I'm curious to see what they look like." She stood up, opened the bag, and slowly removed the life jacket; it still carried faded bloodstains. As she pulled out the rest of the items one by one and spread them out over the bed, she felt a sudden sharp pain in her arm where the swelling was. Her eyelids fluttered uncontrollably and she began to sway away from the bed. The nurse, realising she was about to collapse, grabbed her and swung her round, lowering her gently back into the armchair,

"Are you alright? Should I away and get the doctor?"

Izzy quickly came to her senses. "No, I'm alright. I guess it must have been a bit of a shock for me seeing the bloodstains on my lifejacket." She was fibbing to the nurse – it was seeing the strange clothes that spooked her. Deep in her subconscious something dark had awakened, but for the life of her she couldn't grasp what it was.

"As long as you're sure, hen?" the nurse replied with concern.

"Yes, I'm fine now. Let's have a closer look."

Izzy wasn't surprised at the knickers and bra, but the rest of it was completely alien to her: a pair of woollen hose, a finely embroidered linen shirt, a silk-lined padded jacket, and a pair of beautiful, but salt-stained leather boots.

"Wow!" said the nurse, "this isn't your normal hire stuff. Everyone thought you'd been to a fancy-dress party. My boyfriend is a re-enactor. He charges around Conwy Castle pretending to be a Knight of the Round Table. He gets all his gear off the internet but it isn't nearly this elaborate."

"Was this really what I was wearing when they brought me in?"

"I don't know, I wasn't on duty when they admitted you, but … yes."

Izzy leant over the bed, put her head in her hands and began to cry. "How come I can easily recall things that happened in my distant past but can't remember what happened just a few weeks ago?"

The nurse put her arms round her. "Come on … let's not spoil your big day. I'm sure it will all come back to you in good time. The mind sometimes stops us from remembering the bad things until we're ready to deal with them, and by all accounts, you must have had a terrifying experience out at sea." She plucked a handful of tissues from the box at the side of the bed and wiped the tears from Izzy's eyes. "Here … let me put these things back in the bag for you."

At that moment, Jean entered the room all flustered. "I'm sorry I'm late, Izzy, I couldn't find anywhere to park the car out there!"

Izzy flung her arms around her and hugged her as tight as she could.

Izzy chatted nonstop to Jean on the journey back to her house in Chester. Although the Moorefield family home was in Manchester, she was going to spend the next few months with her and her two grandsons Tom and Alex, whom she was looking after – her daughter had returned to university as a mature student. It would give Izzy's legal advisors time to sort out the will – and then, of course, there was the inquest.

Several weeks passed and autumn was well and truly holding sway. The inquest passed with an open verdict, and Izzy was getting back to normality and attending her old school. Much of this was down to Jean, who treated her as one of the family. Izzy was so grateful for the love she had been shown, especially as she had her hands full looking after Tom and Alex. Her solicitors had completed all the legal red tape, and as a result, a trust fund had been set up for her to ensure a bright financial future. But there were still lots of blanks and unanswered questions that tortured Izzy, especially at night, in the form of vivid nightmares. Sometimes she awoke screaming in the early hours of the morning, disturbing Jean and the boys from their slumbers.

With haunted memories of Christmas now past, and the cold winter months behind her, Izzy welcomed the warmth of spring to melt away the despair she felt at losing her family. Apart from the obvious, the one thing she missed most of all was sailing and she decided to accept an invitation from some old family friends in Deganwy. She travelled down by train, and with her kitbag over her shoulder, walked the short distance from the station to the marina. As she strolled along the narrow pathway by the railway track, she looked out across the estuary and saw Commander

Jeremy Hawkins' power cruiser *Misty* heading out to sea. The last time she had seen it was on the afternoon of the day before they set sail on that fateful voyage.

She arrived at the marina with time to spare so made her way to the office where Tony, a member of staff, was having a crafty smoke outside. He made a great fuss at seeing her again and asked how she was feeling being back in the marina. With a little time to kill waiting for Jackie, Izzy sat on the bench outside the office and gazed out over the marina to the empty space where *Nicole* was once berthed at the end of the main pontoon. She had known it would be upsetting for her to return, but in some ways was hoping it might help fill in the missing gaps in her memory. Tears began to trickle down her cheeks and settle in her lap, staining her clean white shorts.

"Hello, sweet," came a voice from behind. It was the warm northern tones of Jackie Arnold. She turned round and stood up, only to be smothered in affectionate licks from Archie, Jackie's wire-haired border terrier. "How are you, darling?" she added, trying to pull Archie away from Izzy's legs.

Izzy flung her arms around her. "I'm fine, Jackie ... just feeling a little emotional coming back here."

"Of course you are, sweet," she replied warmly as she wiped away the tears from Izzy's cheeks with her hand.

"Don't I get a hug?" said a voice from behind. It was Roger, Jackie's brother-in-law. Izzy turned around to be smothered in his big powerful arms.

"Hi, Roger," she smiled.

"Come on, you two," said Jackie as she picked up Izzy's bag and walked towards the marina entrance, "the gate's been open for an hour already and you know what they say ..."

"Time and tide wait for no man," Izzy and Roger replied in unison.

As soon as they were out in the channel, Roger raised *Mehalah's* sails to take full advantage of the perfect sailing weather. At last, Izzy was on the water again, and that was where she wanted to be most of all. It was where she belonged.

Mehalah was a fast boat, and before long they were rounding Puffin and sailing up the Strait towards Beaumaris. Jackie planned to pick up a mooring at Menai Bridge for the night. Beyond Bangor pier the water was like a lily pond, and once they had reefed in the sails, they motored towards a spare mooring buoy off the two little islands.

As *Mehalah* slowly glided past, Izzy spotted some shadowy figures of herons roosting high in the trees; she felt strangely drawn to them and stood motionless, her gaze transfixed. Roger readied himself to pick up the mooring, and on his signal, Jackie put the engine into reverse, slowing down *Mehalah's* twenty-five tons of forward motion until she gently nudged the buoy, allowing him to grab it with the boathook and haul it up on deck. Once he had fastened the chain to the anchor winch, Jackie cut the engine, and all fell silent.

Peering out of the side of the boat's canopy to ask if everyone wanted bacon butties, Jackie noticed Izzy staring out at the herons. "Don't they look fantastic? Kind of magical place, isn't it?" she said.

Izzy, brought back to earth by Jackie's remark, replied, "Ah, um, yes… sorry, Jackie, I was miles away there. I'd love a bacon butty, thank you, haven't had one of those for ages."

Jackie disappeared below deck to put the grill on as Roger walked back towards the canopy, rubbing his hands together. "Did I hear someone mention bacon butties?"

A voice came from below. "Just putting the bacon under the grill. Tea or coffee?"

As the afternoon became early evening, Jackie announced that she had better take Archie ashore for his usual 'do-da's' before they settled in for the evening. After lowering the dinghy into the water, Jackie asked Izzy if she wanted to come with them.

"Yes, I'd love to," she replied, handing Archie down to her. Jackie started the outboard engine and Izzy climbed down the boarding ladder to sit with Archie, gripping him tightly as they motored off towards the shore. Archie, desperate to relieve himself, broke free from Izzy's grip and leapt out of the boat into the sea with a loud 'splosh'. In fits of laughter they watched him as he frantically paddled ashore, shaking the surplus water from his body as he charged up the muddy beach towards the nearest vertical object. As soon as the dinghy touched the shore, Izzy, thinking what fun it was, jumped out after him, chasing him along the beach. She stopped for a moment, and turning round noticed their deep footprints in the mud behind them. For a split second, she could hear childish laughter and barking, but Archie was at the far end of the beach by now and there were no children to be seen. Just then, a heron swooped low over her head squawking, and landed at the water's edge. She felt a sharp stabbing pain in her left arm and dropped to her knees, clutching it in agony. Archie, on seeing the heron, came bounding towards it barking, and as he dashed past Izzy he sprayed her with mud. At this disturbance the heron took flight and disappeared high up into the trees on the little island.

Izzy's concentration was quickly broken by Jackie's voice in the distance, shouting at them to return to the dinghy. The pain subsided as quickly as it came, and she stood up and turned towards the rocks where Archie was playing 'catch the seagull' and shouted as loud as she could, "Archie! Biscuits!" She knew he would come if the word 'biscuit' was mentioned, and sure enough, as soon as he heard her, his ears pricked up and he ran towards her as fast as his little legs would carry him, leaving a trail of splattered mud behind him. Izzy started to walk back towards Jackie as Archie took an almighty leap in the air knocking her onto her knees in the mud with a loud splat. Izzy laughed, "Oh Archie, you are funny … come on, let's get Jackie!" She jumped to her feet and they ran up the beach together, arriving in a cascade of oozing slime to where Jackie was waiting.

Jackie made a lightning grab at Archie as he tried to run past. "No, you don't, you little bugger!" she said as she dragged him to the water's edge to wash the worst of the mud off his body. Then she took one look at Izzy and added, "You'll need a good wash down too, Izzy Moorefield." They laughed, and as they motored back to *Mehalah*, Izzy turned towards the little island where the heron had taken refuge from Archie's advances and shivered, not from cold, but a strange feeling of connection – and longing.

As they neared *Mehalah*, Roger got ready with the hosepipe to wash Archie, Izzy, and the dinghy down. He took great delight in soaking them both, reminding her of the water pistol battles they had enjoyed with him and her family on the marina pontoons, on long summer evenings after a pleasant sail in Conwy Bay.

Izzy went for a quick shower and changed into dry clothing while Jackie, always the perfect host, prepared and cooked her speciality, roast duck in orange sauce with broccoli, carrots, and roasties. As the girls cleared the table and began washing up, Roger pulled out a selection of DVDs for them to watch. Jackie and Izzy couldn't make up their minds, so Roger picked one for them. "'Excalibur', has anyone seen that? It's about King Arthur, I think," looking at the label on the back. Izzy dropped the plate she was wiping with a crash and stood motionless. They both looked at her as she bent down to pick up the pieces. "I'm sorry, Jackie, I don't know what came over me, my left arm is still giving me jip. The doctor thinks it's the result of an animal bite." Jackie reassured her and told her to sit up in the cockpit while she finished washing up.

Izzy was staring out towards the shore when Jackie appeared from below with a couple of glasses of chilled white wine. "Feeling better, sweet?" she asked affectionately. Izzy nodded and smiled. "Here you are, get this down you," she said, offering her a glass and sitting beside her.

Together they sat enjoying the early evening breeze. It carried the sweet scent of jasmine, probably from a garden belonging to one of the big houses near the shore. It seemed to evoke a memory in Izzy, but like everything else, she couldn't quite put her finger on it. Jackie tried to engage her in small talk.

"How's your diving coming on? Have you done anything since –?" Her voice faltered.

"It's ok to say it – the death of my family, you mean?" Jackie nodded. "No, I must have lost my diving gear on *Nicole* when she went down."

"Oh, I'm so sorry, sweet. I've got a spare set if you ever want to get back to it."

"Thank you, Jackie, that would be fantastic. This trip has made me realise how much I miss the sea, especially around Anglesey. I don't know why, but somehow I feel a part of this island. It's almost as though it doesn't want to let me go. Anyway, I have got rather a lot of money my parents left me so I thought perhaps," she said tentatively, "I should spend some of it and buy my own yacht … just a small one."

"That's a damn fine idea," Jackie replied. "Come on, let's go and make Roger watch a chick flick." They laughed and scuttled down the companionway.

27

Road to Recovery

Izzy spent the next few weeks scouring the internet and dragging Jean around different boatyards, looking for her perfect little yacht. She stipulated that it would have to be of wooden construction, have an inboard diesel engine and enough room for her and maybe a couple of friends to stop onboard for a weekend or more. And of course, it had to be seaworthy as she wanted to sail her straight away: no projects!

She had just got home from school when the telephone rang. It was a Mr Granger who had a traditional (Izzy liked the term 'traditional') long-keel yacht for sale. Izzy had seen the advert and left a message on his answerphone. It had the perfect pedigree: built by Fox's boatyard of Ipswich, and mahogany on oak with three berths. It even had a small navigation table and of course, an inboard diesel engine. *Couldn't be better* she thought. She arranged to go and see it that very weekend in Dickie's boatyard in Bangor, where the hull was being repainted. If Jean couldn't give her a lift, she would travel down by train and maybe stay at Jackie's for the night.

Jean was free after all, and they dropped off at Deganwy to pick up Jackie so she could run her experienced eye over it too. Izzy was full of excitement at the prospect of owning her own boat, and as they drew up outside Dickie's and walked through the main door, she knew her mum and dad would be alongside her all the way. She was met by the agent, who told her the owner had been held up and would be arriving a bit later, but that they were welcome to have a good look over her. He gave her the keys and a ladder to get up onto the boat and they made their way to the yard, where she was standing in a cradle at the side of one of the workshops. Izzy nearly slipped on the ladder in her eagerness to get up into the cockpit. As she undid the padlock holding the hatch in place and pulled it from the slide, Jean commented that it wasn't that big. Jackie walked around the boat a couple of times examining every square centimetre. The new paint job was evident. "Pity they didn't leave painting the hull till you'd seen her first, you can hide a lot of problems with filler and new paint."

Izzy poked her head from over the side of the cockpit, "Our Mr Potter will get to the bottom of her. He surveyed *Nicole* for Mum and Dad when they found her in Oban, and again for the insurance after they'd done all the work. He's king where wooden boats are concerned." Jean asked Izzy the boat's name. "I don't know, it didn't say in the advert," she replied.

Jackie looked round at the stern and read off the name: *Celtic Lady*.

Izzy froze to the spot for a split second and turning to Jackie said without thinking, "I think this boat was made for me!"

It didn't take long for Izzy to decide to buy *Celtic Lady*, and after shaking hands with the owner they agreed on a price subject to the necessary survey by Mr Potter. To celebrate, Izzy treated them to a meal in a local pub. Jackie suggested she should keep hold of her money now she owned her own boat, and a wooden one at that. But Izzy was far too excited to worry about little matters like money.

The following week Izzy got the phone call from Mr Potter to let her know the summarised version of his report. There were only minor issues to sort out and none that would prevent her from sailing her away. She couldn't wait to phone Dickie's and tell them *Celtic Lady* was sold.

Two weeks later, after checking the tides, Izzy and Jackie appeared at the door of Dickie's boatyard, this time to sail *Celtic Lady* back to Deganwy where they were going to have a small celebration to wet the head of Izzy's new baby.

After the little yacht was lowered into the water, Izzy started the engine, and the gentle burble coming from her outlet was an encouraging sign the cooling water was pumping through the system. The guys from the yard crane removed the strops from her hull and Izzy, looking excitedly at Jackie, pushed her into gear. Holding the tiller at the side of her body, they motored gently out of the confines of the harbour into the Strait. The smile on Izzy's face was a picture, so Jackie decided to record the trip for posterity on her video camera. Once done, she grinned at Izzy. "Let's put up the sails and see how she goes, shall we, sweet?"

As they arrived at Deganwy marina, a large party of friends were waiting to take her lines and tie her up to her new berth. Jean was there with her two grandsons and their spaniel Missy, who wasn't sure what to make of life aboard. Jean gave Izzy a bottle of champagne, which, after making a little speech and popping the cork, she sprayed all over the bow of *Celtic Lady*. Everyone cheered, and as Jean opened a couple more bottles, Alex and Tom went round as waiters, filling everyone's plastic cups: all recorded of course, on Jackie's video camera.

Jean didn't see much of Izzy after that, other than school weekdays. Every available weekend she would be at Deganwy doing this and doing that to the boat, getting her ready for her planned single-handed week afloat, sailing around Anglesey. She had taken her out a couple of times, just to get used to the boat's handling characteristics and check out the posh new instruments that had been installed. She was also becoming a proper little shipwright; nothing was too complicated for her to tackle.

On the day she planned to sail, Jean drove her to Deganwy in her car because she had so much stuff to take aboard, and anyway she was keen to see her off on her maiden voyage, so to speak. They unloaded Izzy's bags into a trolley, including the diving gear Jackie had loaned her, and a bunch of roses. They made their way down the gangway to where *Celtic Lady* was moored, and after transferring everything into the boat, Jean gave her a big hug. "Now promise me you'll ring me every morning and evening on your mobile … I won't be able to rest unless I know you're safe."

"I promise," Izzy replied as she stepped into the cockpit and strapped on her lifejacket. She turned on the instruments and started the engine; it burst into life. Once it had warmed up, Izzy released the stern line and asked Jean to release the bow, then with a broad grin on her face, put *Celtic Lady* into gear and steered out into the marina channel. She waved to Jackie and a barking Archie as she passed *Mehalah* on her way out of the marina into the estuary. *Celtic Lady* was no *Nicole* – but she was all hers.

Once she passed the Perch, there was enough wind to raise her sails. Sailing singlehanded meant she had to be very careful not to fall overboard, so after turning *Celtic Lady* into the wind, she clipped herself onto the safety line before raising her mainsail. As she returned to the tiller she unfurled the jib and followed the buoys towards Puffin. As Jackie would say, she was having a cracking sail.

She arrived at Menai Bridge a bit sooner than planned so picked up a spare buoy in the Strait. Things were always a bit more challenging to manage when sailing on your own, and all she could hear in her head was Jackie's words about safety. Having a couple of hours to spare while she waited for the tide to be the right height to safely negotiate the Swellies, she decided she would have a mug of tea and biscuits rather than bacon butties. After all, there was a whole week of sailing to go yet. As she removed her lifejacket, she noticed the scar on her arm was throbbing again. *How odd* she thought. Maybe she had knocked it – very common in the confines of a small yacht to knock oneself without noticing.

She put Old Whistler mark II on the stove and took herself up into the cockpit to wait for it to boil. She was still strangely drawn to this place. Maybe it was because it was the last place she could remember before her mind went into emptiness. Izzy had been in this position in her mind many times, on her own and with the therapist, but could never get any further. It was as though someone had removed those particular files from the cabinet in her head. The high-pitched whistle of the kettle broke her train of thought and she went down below to make a pot of tea, which she brought back up to the cockpit on a tray with a plate of custard creams, her favourites.

After a couple of hours watching the world go by, the tide was right for her to go through the Swellies. Navigating through this short stretch of water could be, for the inexperienced, fraught with dangers lurking beneath the surface. To avoid going aground she must follow a complicated zigzag path using a series of markers as turning points, and although she had made this journey many times before with her mum and dad, she was a little apprehensive doing it on her own. However, she needn't have worried, and after dropping her mooring and motoring towards the bridge, made it through without any problems.

As the weather forecast was so good, Izzy decided to anchor a couple of miles off Rhosneigr beach for the night. The following day she would sail into Holyhead where she planned to do a little shopping. Dropping her anchor into the calm blue waters of the bay and lowering her sails, she settled in for the night. While her evening meal was cooking on the stove, Izzy thought it would be a good time to ring Jean, otherwise she would be fretting all evening. She picked up her mobile and dialled the number. She could tell Jean was waiting for her call because she answered almost immediately. After several minutes of general chit chat, Izzy put the phone down and began serving up her supper.

Later that evening, after filling in the logbook, Izzy went to her case and took out the hospital bag containing the strange clothes she had been wearing when she was rescued. She hadn't had the heart to look at them again since leaving the hospital, but now seemed the right time to face her demons. She undressed down to her underwear and nervously took them out of the bag, one by one, laying them out neatly on the bed; they still had a faint aroma of washing powder from the hospital laundry. She dressed slowly, first in the linen shirt, then the woollen hose. They fitted perfectly, almost as though they had been made for her. She put on the padded jacket and finally the leather boots. Izzy stood up and looked down at herself, caressing the soft fabrics with the palms of her hands. She was unable to explain why she had been wearing such an eccentric costume on *Nicole*, but bizarre as it was, it somehow felt a part of her.

Full of mixed emotions she took the twelve roses she had picked from Jean's garden and went up on deck. There she stood alone at the stern of *Celtic Lady*, cradling the roses in her arms and looking up into the starry heavens. "Hello Mum, Dad, Georgie, Dan, and hello Bella. I haven't forgotten you – just the last weeks we spent together. Will you forgive me?" She pulled the roses out one by one and threw them into the sea below. "These are to say I miss you, wherever you are." Izzy looked down at the yellow buds floating on the water, illuminated by silvery radiance from the moon as they drifted slowly with the tide towards the twinkling lights of Rhosneigr. Tears of heartache gushed uncontrollably from her eyes, trickling down her cheeks and dripping gently like tiny pearls into the sea.

The morning sunrise was rather spectacular, and Izzy took photographs for her new album *Voyages with Celtic Lady*, in which she wanted to keep a record of her first passage. She still couldn't understand why she liked the name so much. Just then the phone rang. It was Jackie, always an early riser, who couldn't wait to hear how her first night on her new boat had gone. *That's the handy thing about mobiles*, she thought, *you're never far away from friends.* As soon as she got off the phone to Jackie, she rang Jean, knowing if she didn't ring her she would be worrying all morning.

At mid-morning, Izzy radioed ahead to the Holyhead harbour master to check the availability of a berth for *Celtic Lady* for one night. Once he confirmed they had a berth, she prepared *Lady*, as she now called her, for another beautiful day of sailing. She turned over the engine, and like a good girl, it started the first time. As it was warming up, she went to the bow to raise the anchor, but it wouldn't budge. She went back to the cockpit and put the engine into forward gear, hoping to dislodge the anchor from the seabed. She returned to the bow and tried again, but it was stuck fast. "Right!" she said to herself, "Only one thing for it, I will have to go down there, I don't want to lose my anchor and chain at this stage." She turned off the engine and went below to get into her diving gear.

Izzy was extremely safety conscious where diving was concerned, and although she wouldn't usually go down without a diving buddy, she had no alternative if she wanted to retrieve her anchor. Before going over the side, she checked there were no other craft in her area and then hoisted a dive flag, so if any other boat did come her way, they would be aware a diver was down and to keep clear.

Once she was ready, Izzy made a quick telephone call to Jackie to put her in the picture and asked her, if she didn't call her back in half an hour, to alert Holyhead coastguard. Jackie was worried, told her to be very careful, and would wait for her return call.

Izzy checked her gear, and standing at the stern of the boat, lowered herself gently into the cold water. She swam over to the bow and grabbing hold of the anchor chain, followed it down to the seabed. Although the water was a little murky, she could just make out what was causing the problem. It was entangled in someone else's anchor chain. She had checked beforehand there were no other boats in the vicinity, but there it was, heading up to the surface in the opposite direction. As she tried to release her anchor from the tangle, she noticed something glinting on the seabed. Intrigued, she swam over to where the shiny object was half-buried in the sand. Gently wafting the silt away with her hand revealed her find. At first, she didn't understand the real significance of her discovery until she grabbed hold of it in her hand and felt power surge into her arm and through her body, unlocking her lost memory in an instant. It was Caliburn.

The pupils of her eyes opened wide, and as she screamed uncontrollably into her mask, bubbles gushed violently from her demand valve, releasing oxygen into the open waters in an effervescent eruption. The frenzied intensity of her emotion shook her whole body into a convulsion. In desperation, she ripped off her mask and mouthpiece, then released her heavy diving gear onto the seafloor, closed her eyes and propelled herself upwards with the sword still in her hand. Her lungs felt as though they were going to explode any minute, and as the sword pierced through the surface, her body followed, punching a hole into the open air with a wash of bubbles. Opening her eyes, she saw the shape of a white hull at the side of her. As she swam towards it she heard voices, and barking. A hand reached down to meet hers over the edge of the boat.

"Come on, Izzy, we've been waiting for you!" As she looked up, Daniel and George's faces peered out over the side, and a flash of red jumped into the water beside her – Bella, overjoyed to see her mistress again. Izzy was back in Cuddfan: she was home.

Is this the end of their adventure – or just the beginning?

About the Author

David was born in 1948 in Swindon, Wiltshire. The eldest of five siblings, he left school at the age of fifteen to begin a five-year engineering apprenticeship at a local company in Dursley, Gloucestershire.

By the early twenties he was married with two daughters, Emma and Sarah. By the time he reached his early forties he had divorced and was facing redundancy. Consequently, he started his own company on the back of his hobby as a 15th century re-enactor making steel armour for other re-enactors and museums. In the late nineties his company, Norton Armouries Limited, grew into a thriving business manufacturing armour and props for many of the Hollywood epics that hit the big screen, such as *Gladiator*, *A Knight's Tale*, *Alexander*, *Timeline* and many more.

After selling his company in 2007 he moved to Bristol to start his own video production company, but the 2008 bank crash forced him to retire, so in 2009 he decided to buy a yacht, *Nicole*, and live aboard her in obscurity in Deganwy Marina, North Wales.

After spending a few months working on the yacht to make her more comfortable to live on, he sailed her to Menai Strait on a swinging mooring and it was here he began writing *Arthur's Seed*. He returned to Deganwy Marina in the late summer of 2010 and began developing his short story into a novel. Over the years he has made several unsuccessful attempts to get it published.

During the first Covid-19 lockdown, frustrated by the process of trying to get publishers interested in his book, David decided he would release the book in serial form as a free bi-weekly video podcast on Facebook. Encouraged by feedback from fans of the series, he created his own website and released the episodes from there. It wasn't long before his growing fanbase was asking 'when the next episode was due', and more importantly, 'where could they buy the book'. Reassured by their enthusiasm for his story and characters he finally decided to self-publish.

His portal to the series www.arthursseed.co.uk will now be host to everything related to *Arthur's Seed* – news of future books from the trilogy, and a blog, plus lots of interesting titbits of information.

Printed by:

Copytech (UK) Limited trading as
Printondemand-worldwide.com
9 Culley Court, Bakewell Road, Orton Southgate,
Peterborough, PE2 6XD